ACKNOWLEDGEMENTS

This final novel took a long while to write as I have been commuting to and from The Wirral where my partner Tom lives.
I wanted to write a closing novel to tie up loose ends in the lives of my police characters for those readers kind enough to have got involved with them.
Thanks again to all my friends and especially to Tom for proof-reading.

CHAPTER 1

The room was overcrowded, hot and stuffy but tastefully decorated for Christmas. Arthur Cunningham felt the familiar ache starting in his gums. His dentist had told him that heat and exercise would aggravate his wisdom tooth problem but he was a very busy, important figure, manager in his bank, a branch of the TSB in Glasgow's Southside and he kept avoiding the issue. Only last week, Kirsty, his dentist, had told him that she was sure that it was an impacted wisdom tooth and she had offered to make him an appointment at the Dental Hospital to have it extracted under local anaesthetic. He had refused the offer.

A sudden, agonising pain shot through his lower gums. It felt as if the whole bottom set of teeth was pulsating. He gasped.

"Arthur. What's up?"

His deputy at the bank, Neil Kerr, was looking anxiously at him. Even his concern rankled with Arthur. The man was too good to be true. Always being praised by customers and staff alike. Married, with a devoted wife and two children who seemed to adore him, he was the antithesis of Arthur who was divorced, with three sons he had not seen for some time.

"Nothing. Only a twinge of toothache."

"Can I get you some painkillers?" said Neil.

"For God's sake, man. Stopping fussing over me like an old woman," snapped Arthur.

FRANCES MACARTHUR

FATAL EXTRACTION

He bypassed the enormous Christmas tree, beautifully and tastefully decorated, no doubt by Neil's wife Anne.

He walked away towards the fire. Anne always had a coal fire glowing in the lounge in spite of having central heating. He felt the heat of the fire caressing his cheeks and winced once again with the surge of pain. It was like....like nothing else on earth, he thought, as it ground through his gums. What was it Rabbie Burns had said? He had called them his 'tortured gums'. He had also called toothache, "the hell o' all diseases." Arthur, no lover of his national poet, after some boring school lessons, for once felt some admiration for the man who could describe his present pain so accurately.

As the pain receded, Arthur fancifully thought of some other tortures, such as having his fingernails pulled out one by one. In spite of himself, he smiled, surprising the young woman who stood near him.

"Arthur, you must have been thinking of something pleasant."

"Hello, Anne. Not really. A good reception, as usual, my dear. Remind me, which of your charities is this in aid of? Animals as usual?"

His sneer was not quite hidden. Arthur was no philanthropist, not even with regard to people and he only attended these charity events because it was expected of him. Animals were in his opinion, smelly and a nuisance. Neil came from a wealthy family and he and his wife supported many causes and were encouraging their two children to do the same. Millie and Oscar were in the room, at the other end, offering raffle tickets to other guests.

"Yes, "Anne said gently. "It's 'Dogs' Trust', this time. We've sort of adopted two dogs and we wanted to raise some money for the cause." Another red-hot stab of pain punctured through Arthur's gums and he gave an involuntary wince but Anne had turned away and this time no one noticed. Quickly making his apologies to Neil, Arthur picked up his coat from the hallstand and left.

In his car, the Monday after New Year, he used his mobile phone to call his dentist, getting an appointment for the next morning as he expected, being a Denplan client. At over £20 a month, he expected preferential treatment as he did with everything he paid for and even with things he didn't.

On Tuesday, he sat in the waiting room, looking out of place in his suit and overcoat. He had always come to this practice in Pollokshaws although he lived in Newton Mearns, as the dentist was the first he had ever felt confident with. A child in the 60s, he could still remember the old bone-shaking drills, the fear of the injections which hurt, the taste of cloves and Kirsty had almost cured him of his fear of dentists when he had come to her in his thirties while living in Shawlands. Maybe it was superstition but he trusted her as he did no other dentist. The downside was having to sit amongst what he thought of as the scum of the earth. The man across from him was wearing a bobble hat…indoors for goodness sake: had he no manners? Bizarrely he was wearing shorts on this cold November day, shorts which allowed his tattoos to be seen in all their glory. Tattoos of winding serpents and devil's horns, of all things, covered his rather spindly legs.

"Naw the noo, Jamie," screeched a young woman at her young son who had been demanding to leave. "Wait till ye've saw the dentist."

Arthur winced but not from toothache this time, in fact the toothache has disappeared when he had left the overheated room yesterday. Only the memory of the pain had made him arrange today's appointment. His wincing now was at the uncouth Glasgow speech. He had 'stotted' balls, 'dreeped 'dykes and 'sooked' lollies with his friends, "doon the back" of their tenement homes but he had moved on from his lowly upbringing and now despised those who apparently had not. Having an English mother who had corrected his grammar and his vocabulary, he had always been 'bilingual', speaking English and Glaswegian in his youth and now had simply sloughed off the uneducated skin he had worn then.

Kirsty, when he saw her, was unsympathetic. Almost at retirement, she had no time for his pretensions, remembering as she did, his earlier fear of her trade.
"You should have had that impacted tooth taken out after I last saw you."
In vain, Arthur requested that she got him a private appointment somewhere.
"The Dental Hospital's the best place for this. The student who does it will have been doing this same procedure for weeks, probably months. Don't be a fearty. With New year coming along, you'll be lucky to hear very soon."

Arthur tried to bluster that he was not scared, just an important man who could pay for his treatment but Kirsty was unimpressed. She rang the hospital and then told him that an appointment would be sent to him as soon as possible. The middle-aged receptionist made a face behind his back when he ignored her smile.

Hogmanay. The evening when Scots celebrate the end of the old year and welcome in the new one. Neil and Anne Kerr, having seen their young children off to bed, welcomed in the new year with friends they had invited. Anne who was a kindly soul had insisted on her husband inviting Arthur Cunningham but she was honest enough to be delighted when he refused the invitation.

Arthur's three sons had similarly managed to get their three daughters to go bed, Tom promising his eldest, Helen, that next year when she was in secondary school she would be allowed to stay up for 'the bells'. The men and their wives sat down for a relaxing evening, one when even Quentin, the minister, could let his hair down and have a few drinks. Oliver and Pat were hosting Hogmanay this year as they had often been out of the country during former Hogmanays because Oliver was in the army.

"Not as comfortable as your manse, Q but Pat and the girls put up a tree this year…a real tree. Just hope the dog doesn't sniff up the pine needles. Oliver laughed and pointed to 'the dog' which belonged now to Tom's girls. It was a fat, elderly cocker spaniel.

"Betsy's 12 now. Remember I bought her right after our honeymoon, Susan? I told you that my father had promised us a dog but that never came about and I decided that I'd have one when I had a house of my own. The girls, when they came along, adopted him as their dog. He keeps up with them but when they go to bed, he, like us, collapses in a tired heap. He won't be sniffing around any tree tonight."

Quentin laughed ruefully. "I'd have loved to have a dog but we have so many visitors because of my job and there would be bound to be some who were either allergic to dog hair or were scared of dogs so I'll have to wait until I retire!"

"And no way I could have one being on the go from country to country," laughed Oliver.

"Pity Mum couldn't come over for the festive season," said Tom. "I feel our girls miss out on grandparents with Susan's and Pat's parents being dead and Abi's folks being in Australia."

"We could have asked Father on Christmas Day," Quentin said and they all laughed.

"Yes, Q, can just see him in a Santa Claus outfit, beaming and handing out presents to all of us!" said Oliver. "Wonder what he's doing tonight."

Arthur was sitting on his own at home. He had gone out to his local hotel but left after one drink as it was full of what he called "noisy revel makers." He was sitting in his lounge and had switched off the TV as it too was all about bonhomie and good cheer. He never watched comedies and remembered his wife, Carol, saying that when he was born they had cut the humour gene along with the umbilical cord. He did not enjoy Scottish music and country dancing either which was the other thing on offer. He had never taken Sky TV thinking that it cost too much. Carol had also suggested that he dress up as Scrooge for Christmas. The book he was reading had not gripped him.

He swirled the amber brandy round his glass then moaned as toothache shot through his gums. He got up and went into the bathroom for some painkillers and having swallowed them, decided to go to bed. He hoped the appointment for the Dental Hospital came soon.

The small, buff-coloured envelope arrived through his letterbox about five weeks later, at the beginning of February with an appointment for February 26 and, having suffered more bouts of excruciating pain in the gym and during a game of indoor tennis, he was not tempted to cancel the appointment.

There being few parking places around Sauchiehall Street, he decided to take the bus and thus it was that he spent a patience-fraying forty minutes going from Waterfoot into town, listening to inane conversations and loud modern music. His temper, like his patience, was in shreds when he got up to get off the bus at Watt Brothers. It was not improved when the driver did not stop there but went on across Sauchiehall Street before coming to a halt at the new bus stop.

CHAPTER 2

"I'm on the bus."
"I wish I had a pound for every time I've heard that," thought Elspeth Hamilton, trying to close her ears to the sounds going on around her on the number 6 bus to Glasgow. It was 11.00 a.m. on a wet Tuesday in late February and she was on her way to meet three of her ex colleagues for lunch at the Glasgow Concert Hall for lunch, after a visit to the Dental Hospital. The journey would take about forty-five minutes. The woman sitting behind her and who had come on after her, was a grey wolf like herself but seemed to have picked up the habit of today's youth for making stupid remarks on her mobile phone. The one-sided conversation was continuing:
"Aye, Betty. It wis late coming but I should be there by aboot twelve at the latest. Here, did you know aboot Max and Mary? They're splitting up…Aye, Mary telt me on Monday when I met her at the chippie. It's no for common knowledge mind, so you never heard it from me."

Tempted to turn round and tell this stupid woman that the entire bus now knew, Elspeth hunched her shoulders in her jacket and tried to ease the tension out of her neck by circling it round both ways gently. Why on earth did people seem to assume that the person on the other end of the phone was deaf? Only last week, she had heard the entire story of another woman's hysterectomy. Then one evening, after listening to a teenager prattle on and on for over half an hour in the seat behind her, on the top deck of the bus home, she had decided that when she got up to get off, if the girl was on her own and there was no one else there, she was going to take the mobile phone from her and hurl it to the back of the bus. Perhaps, fortunately, there had been two other people sitting there!

Today, there was silence from behind her but peace didn't last for long as the boy who had just plonked down beside her had now plugged in his iPod and mistakenly thought that only he could hear the heavy metal band. The thud, thud of the base notes dinned in her ear and she glared at him, to no effect. Diagonally across the passage, a teenage 'hoodie', obviously playing truant from school, had put his feet up on both seats facing him. Elspeth wondered if she had the courage to tell him that other people had to sit on these seats. She decided that she was a coward.

Why were people so selfish these days? Two seats in front, an elderly gentleman had sat on the outside seat and she could hardly believe her eyes when from in front of him a woman who had also been taking up two places, rose to leave and picked her Pekinese dog up from the window seat!

Was she becoming a grumpy old woman, Elspeth wondered as the bus stopped and the woman and two other alighting passengers had to squeeze past two passengers who had decided not to sit down but were standing blocking the doorway, even though there were vacant seats. What had happened to the days when people took other people into consideration, when parents told their children to give up their seats to an older person? Some weeks ago, she herself had risen to give her seat to a heavily pregnant woman while two youngsters remained seated beside their mothers. She could hardly believe her eyes when a young woman had risen to give her seat to an older woman at the local optician's, leaving her two children sitting.

Maybe it was because she was a retired English teacher but she was noticing even more the poor grammar of people she encountered on buses and trains. Just last week, on the way home from London, she had had to listen to two teenage girls peppering every sentence with "like, you know" and "I wis like…". Added to that, one had asked the other where Carlisle was when they stopped there. The friend hadn't known which reminded Elspeth of a friend saying that on a train home from Euston, she had been amused when two young folk rose to get their suitcases at Preston as it was, "only two stops from Glasgow."

Elspeth's husband had pointed out to her on an airport bus in Heathrow, the notice saying, "No bag's over this line".

"Welcome to the home of English," he had muttered in her ear."

She had been at a wedding a few weeks ago where on the menu were 'vegtables' and 'strawberry's' and it had offered 'glutton'-free items."

Two young lads got on at Muirend. They sat, one in front of the other, and proceeded to talk loudly. Why on earth hadn't they sat together and could have spoken more quietly? What made it worse was that just as with the two young girls on the train with 'like', they used 'fucking' all the time. "Ah fucking done it, you know," said one arrogantly.

"Done what?" Elspeth wanted to ask. "It certainly wasn't grow up or take English lessons.

The bus had reached the Victoria Infirmary where a large queue was waiting. The elderly man tried to ignore the fact that there were no seats for all those getting on but one woman who had managed to get past the youths lounging in the passageway, stood her ground beside him and asked him to move into the window seat whereupon he grumpily got up to let her go to the inside then sat down heavily beside her. A man in his forties looked pointedly at the hooded teenager and the youth removed his feet from the seats, without an apology. Two middle-aged women sat down across from each other. The one sitting down beside the hooded figure looked at him in disgust but he just stared back at her insolently, speechlessly challenging her to comment. She said nothing.

The bus moved on.

The middle-aged woman was again on her mobile phone, this time telling her husband to read out the shopping list that she had left beside the fridge. As he named an item, she felt the need to repeat it so the entire bus or those not tuned into iPods, knew what she was going into town for by the time she had finished her call. Then there was a cacophony of sound from the pocket of the youth beside Elspeth and another one-sided conversation began after he had switched off the thumping noise from his iPad.

"To tell you the truth (why did this make her think he was lying?) I won't have time to meet you, Bill. No, Karen wasn't there last night…Am on the bus… aye, going into town…Right, see you tomorrow night."

They had reached the stop across from the bus depot and there followed a long wait for the exchange driver who, when he did arrive, had to get out a couple of times to adjust the wing mirror, then get up again to remove his bulky jacket before putting the bus into gear and moving off. Elspeth looked at her watch. It was nearly 11.40. Almost on cue, the mobile phone came out again and Betty was informed that, contrary to expectation, her friend would not now be on time for their meeting at 12.

"Sorry, Betty. I'll be there when I can. We've just left the bus garage."

'What on earth did people do before the advent of the mobile phone?' wondered Elspeth. They would do what she would have to do if late for her appointment…apologise. At BHS, a steady stream of people got off the bus and no one got on and at Marks and Spencer's, the bus almost emptied. Elspeth looked closely at the woman who brushed past, bumping her young neighbour's elbow. She looked old fashioned in her tweed skirt and poplin coat, not like a mobile phone owner at all. Looking round, Elspeth noticed that only herself, her neighbour and one man whom she judged to be in his fifties right at the back, were still on board. She shifted in her seat, hoping that the young man would move into an empty seat for the rest of her journey but he was so engrossed in his music that he remained where he was. She opened her handbag and took out her diary to check the time of her appointment although she knew full well that it was at 11.50.

They passed George Square and the driver pulled up to let a woman, her young daughter and a toddler, get on at the next stop. The girl ran to the back of the bus, passing all the empty seats. The mother, laden with bags, sighed and followed her. Gone were the days when the mother chose the seat and the child followed! The toddler started to wail and kept on wailing. The mother said repeatedly, "Stop it!", but with no determination in her voice. She told the girl to help but the youngster ignored her mother so the crying continued. It was obviously a temper cry which made Elspeth long to scream at the child.

As the bus turned into Hope Street, Elspeth made sure that her shoulder bag was closed securely. Her stop was outside Watt Brothers. No one wanted the stop before hers so she politely motioned to the young man beside her who stood up to let her pass and she started to make her way down the aisle, nearly slipping on a discarded copy of the Metro newspaper. The bus stopped, Elspeth took her hand off the handrail and was just about to move forward when she was pushed roughly aside and the fifty-something man brushed past her and jumped off the bus, muttering about the stops having been changed without his knowledge. "Really! Manners!" she called after him but she was talking to herself as he had hurried off. What was it that her friend, Pat, had said once to a rude person who hadn't thanked her for holding a door open....Oh yes, "Did you get your money back from th charm school?"

Wishing that she had waited for the number 4 bus as it would have taken her nearer to her destination, Elspeth walked quickly round the corner, sorry that she was too late to look for some cheap perfume which Watt Brothers often sold. Ahead of her, the figure of the middle-aged man was also walking quickly. She passed Deichman shoe shop, remembering the shoes she had bought there for last year's holiday. "Whore's shoes," her husband had teased her, looking at the black, silver and purple, extremely high-heeled ones, nestling in their tissue paper bed. She had only been able to walk in them if she held onto his arm! Maybe on the way to the Concert Hall, or after lunch, she would go into the shop again and look for something elegant but serviceable.

Putting her head down against the wind and rain, jacket hood up, she hurried past Trailfinders. Again, if there was time she might go in and see if flight prices to the Far East had come down at all. She and Ian were celebrating their ruby wedding anniversary next year and had thought of a special faraway trip in spring.

The man had turned in at the Dental Hospital and was waiting at the lifts. As usual they all appeared to be stuck at Floor 6. The man's face wore a scowl. He looked angry rather than nervous. Maybe, he was only going for a consultation. He shook his head sending a fine spray of water in her direction. He was probably used to being in a car and had not come prepared for rain. His fairish hair had gone quite dark with the soaking.

One lift arrived, a tinny voice announcing, "Doors opening." Surely a blind person would hear that, thought Elspeth. It was really another sign of the nanny State where people weren't allowed to be proactive, a bit like not allowing children to play conkers and insisting that everyone sued for accidents even if it was their own fault that they fell down a hole that was patently obvious. Elspeth had a silent giggle to herself. She had slipped down her own back steps a few weeks ago, twisting a knee. Maybe steps should be outlawed!

Perhaps the giggle showed in her face as the man standing next to her now in the lift, looked grumpily at her as if defying anyone to be happy when he was not. He pressed the button for the sixth floor which was where she was going and, naturally, rushed out before her. Swinging through the doors of the waiting room, he surprisingly held them open for her and she thanked him sweetly. At the desk, he was impatient with the woman who could not find his name on her computer and who eventually asked him what he had come for.

"An impacted wisdom tooth. It's to be taken out!" he barked as if she should know that.

"Sorry, Sir. You're on the wrong floor."

The woman directed him to the correct department and he hurried off, muttering to himself.

Elspeth sat down and took out her novel. It was by one of her favourite authors, Alex Gray and was about a murder in the Glasgow Concert Hall, the venue for her lunch shortly.

Arthur Cunningham sat fuming in the department he had been directed to. He'd been there for ten minutes already and he had forgotten to bring his copy of the Times so had to content himself with looking round the waiting room. He was not a people watcher though he always chose the seat facing out towards the room in any restaurant as it annoyed him when his companion's eyes widened with interest at someone or something they could see and he could not. Having secured that seat he paid no attention to other diners.

His annoyance increased at being asked for the name of his next of kin.

"What on earth for? I'm not likely to die, am I?" On being informed that it was standard practice, he grunted out, "Thomas Cunningham." He had been able to give his son's phone number as it was stored in his mobile phone but he had tartly informed the receptionist that he did not know his son's address off by heart.

Now as he sat in one of the rows of parallel seats, he noticed what he called the riff raff of his city. The woman across from him was what he called mutton dressed as lamb. She was middle aged but was wearing leggings which he hated as he could almost see the cellulite which he knew she must have. The younger woman with her was possibly her daughter. They were almost identically dressed but what suited the younger woman did not suit the older one. He would never have let his wife go out dressed like that, he thought, forgetting that his ex-wife would, latterly, anyway, have paid no attention to him. Carol had been quite amenable in the first years of their married life but had grown in confidence as the children arrived, unlike some of his colleagues' wives who became quite submissive as soon as they gave up work to have children.

Arthur had contented himself by laying down the law to his three sons until the eldest one became grown up enough to fight back for himself and his brothers.

"Mr Cunningham?"

A young man in a green overall was standing at the open door, holding a folder.

Arthur rose and went towards him and the young man ushered him out of the waiting room and along a short corridor to a room which contained a dentist's chair, bright lights and another green-suited older man.

He was told to take off his coat which the younger man took from him and he put on the gown which he was given to replace his coat. He brusquely waved away what looked to him like a mob cap or the kind of thing his wife had worn in the shower but he was told politely that it had to be worn for the operation.

"Now Mr Cunningham, we are going to scrub up then Peter here will give you an anaesthetic, a local one which will freeze your gum to let me make an incision and remove the impacted tooth. When I've finished I'll put a few stitches in the gum. I want you to take the rest of the day easy. OK?"

The two men left the room.

Arthur laid his head back on the headrest and tried to calm himself. He had never been in hospital, except to visit his wife after the births of his sons and he was nervous wearing this gown and cap. It made him feel out of control of the situation, something new to him.

He heard a soft footfall behind him and closed his eyes.

"Just relax, Sir. You'll just feel a slight prick in your arm."

Arthur just had time to wonder," Why my arm" when he felt his heart start to race but then a black cloud enveloped him and he didn't feel the floor as he hit it, taking with him the little wash basin and plastic cup.

CHAPTER 3

"Elspeth Hamilton?" queried the young dental student.

Elspeth got up and followed him through a maze of corridors. In a sudden flight of fantasy, she imagined unravelling string to guide her back to reception. She really shouldn't read so much, she thought, smiling to herself.

The young student must have guessed her thoughts.

"I'll take you back when your treatment's over," he said, opening what turned out to be the last set of swing doors and ushering Elspeth into one of the small sectioned-off spaces where another young man, called Sean was waiting for her. The two students worked together every time.

She spent the next hour having her teeth thoroughly cleaned which bewildered her as this had happened the last time she was here and what she had come for was to be fitted with….she called it Fang, a set of teeth designed to fill in the many spaces in her top set. When he had finished, she asked Sean the reason for all this cleaning and he told that this was hospital policy as there was little point in doing expensive work if the patient didn't clean his or her teeth correctly. As if to underline this, he produced a new toothbrush and asked her if she would show him how she cleaned her teeth. Feeling rather idiotic, Elspeth did so and was informed that she was acting as if she was scrubbing a floor when she should in fact be polishing expensive ornaments.

Her next appointment would be in two weeks, she was told. At last, an impression would be taken. The young man escorted her, as promised, to the reception area where she was given her next appointment.

The lift stopped a couple of floors before ground level and, looking out, Elspeth saw what appeared to be two nurses running with a trolley, followed by two men in suits. An emergency by the look of it, she thought but surely that was more fitting for a medical hospital rather than a dental one. She remembered asking her dentist once if he had ever had a dental emergency and he had replied, rather curtly, that there was no such thing as no one died of toothache.

There was a buzz of activity at ground level. Two paramedics ran into the lift and Elspeth could see the blue flashing light of an ambulance parked immediately outside the hospital entrance. As she stepped outside, a police car pulled up sharply behind the ambulance and two young policemen hurried out and ran inside the building.

Elspeth had always despised people who hung around at the scene of an accident so she walked determinedly away. Her father had told her of a trick he used to play whereby he would stare into the sky until quite a crowd amassed beside him also staring skywards. When he heard someone say, "I can see it," he would leave. He told her lots of people loved accidents and would ghoulishly stand around not doing anything worthwhile.

She had time to go into Trailfinders and Deichmans before meeting her friends at the concert hall and, finding out information on flights to Kuala Lumpur in March and buying a pair of elegant, white shoes, made her forget the excitement at the Dental Hospital until later.

The queue for the soup and fresh sandwich deal in the Concert Hall café, snaked almost round to the steps leading to the toilets. It always moved very slowly as the sandwiches were made up on demand but the time passed quite quickly when she was joined by one of her friends. Moira had taught History in the same school and was what the Scots call a 'blether'. She talked non-stop while they waited, telling Elspeth amongst other things, that their other two friends were already seated inside.

Lesley and Fiona had found a table quite near the back of the restaurant. Even Moira was quiet for a while as they ate their lunch and it wasn't till about 2 pm that Elspeth got a chance to tell them where she had been and recall the excitement as she left.

"An ambulance and a police car!" exclaimed Fiona. "I wonder if there will be a story in tomorrow's paper."

"What could have happened in a dental hospital?" queried Lesley.

"I suppose there must be operations carried out there," offered Moira. "Maybe someone died under an anaesthetic."

"Or maybe someone was stabbed or even murdered," Elspeth threw in her tuppence worth. The others laughed.

"Elspeth, you and your murder mysteries!" said Moira. "Why on earth would someone kill someone in a dental hospital?"

They left together, finding it easy to get down the steps outside, as being February, there were not lots of people sitting on them. They stopped at the statue of Donald Dewar before going off in different directions.

Certainly, murder wasn't mentioned in The Daily Mail the next day. Elspeth bought the paper reluctantly, feeling that yesterday's incident might not be mentioned in The Herald but might be found in a small corner of the tabloid. It was on page four, under the heading: "Mystery Death at Dental Hospital", that she read of the death of a man in his fifties. He had apparently been given too much anaesthetic. Police were investigating.

"That's that then," thought Elspeth, certain that she would hear no more about it.

She was wrong.

CHAPTER 4

Police were indeed investigating. It had fallen to two of the police constables in Charles Davenport's section to go to the Dental Hospital on the death of Arthur Cunningham who had been pronounced dead at 1.12pm the previous day.

"He was just lying there, in a green gown with a blue plastic hat on his head," Frank Selby was telling his colleagues, Constable Penny Price and Sergeant Salma Din. "Probably died of fright," said Penny. "I hate going to the dentist let alone the Dental Hospital!"

"Penny, how daft" said Salma. "Dentists have modern equipment these days. They don't hurt you anymore. Once you've had an injection you feel nothing."

"And how many times have you been to the dentist, Salma?" retorted Penny. "Look at your lovely teeth! Not like mine. The dentist told me once that mine were like the Forth Road Bridge. As soon as he'd finished he had to start again. My Dad took me once. He told me there was nothing to be scared about but all he had done was cleaning. When it was my turn I needed about five fillings! Mum never liked the dentist so maybe she passed her fear onto me."

"Here, here, Penny," said Frank. "My worst time was when a tooth broke as he was trying to take it out."

He shuddered.

"Who went with you to the Dental Hospital, Frank?" asked Penny. "Salma and I knew nothing about it till this morning. I was away, remember, for my check up at the Victoria and Salma was in Kilmarnock Road doing traffic cop where the lights had broken down."

"If one more person had shouted, "Just one cornetto," I think I'd have committed murder." Salma grinned.

"I wish that advert could drift off into obscurity or go to the big advert graveyard in the sky."

"Along with that awful one for, "Go Compare," said Frank.

"And that one with the meerkats, "said Penny. "It was funny at first but I want to throw something at the telly when it comes on."

"If you're talking about awful adverts…."

Their DCI had come into the room, unobserved.

"…could you also get rid of the ones for settees, chairs and beds? As soon as one sale stops another one starts!"

"Or the one with the man in woman's shorts, waggling his bottom. It annoys me so much I switch off. What's it for?"

"Money supermarket," laughed Frank, turning to his detective sergeant who had come in with her boss, now also her husband. She was looking very pregnant and would be leaving soon, he thought. In his opinion, she was a bit old to be a mother for the first time and surely should not have stayed on as long as some young expectant mothers did these days.

The three young folk laughed but straightened up at their desks.

"I took Fraser since you were both AWOL," Frank answered what Penny had asked before the advert discussion.

"Where *is* Fraser?" Davenport asked now as the laughter subsided.

"Are you going to send him back to his old department, Sir?" asked Penny, never one for standing on ceremony.

"I feel sorry that just because I'm back full time, he has to go," she added, ruefully.

"Yes, Penny. Sorry but that's exactly what I want him for," said the DCI.

Frank tried to hide a smile. He thought that Fraser was a decent fellow but he also made Frank feel uneducated, not on purpose he knew, but still, it would nice to be just him, Penny and Salma again.

A phone could be heard ringing further up the corridor and, realising that it was probably his phone, Davenport went out hurriedly, followed more slowly by the DS. Penny immediately tackled Frank.

"Don't you like Fraser?"

"Oh, I do really but he's such a clever clogs that I feel stupid when he's around."

"That's not his fault. He never sounds superior," protested Salma.

"I know, I know but I'm not very clever and he is."

"That's your fault, not his. Maybe it's time you went to some night classes and got some culture," suggested Penny.

As this had been suggested to Frank, recently, in a kindly way by his girlfriend, Sue, Frank took the advice good-naturedly.

"What should it be? Opera? Shakespeare? Archaeology?"

"Something Sue is interested in, you twit," said Penny.

"Her church," said Frank, serious for once.

"I'm sure she doesn't expect that from you, Frank," said Salma. "She knows you're a …is it staunch or devout Catholic? I can never remember which is which."

"Devout Catholic," said Frank. "But really, I'm not, am I? I don't go to mass very often."

This was so unlike Frank who until recently had been quite a bigot, that Penny stared at him, her mouth half open. Perhaps fortunately, their boss returned with DS Macdonald following him again.

"That was Mr Fairchild, folks. As we've been allocated the death at the Dental Hospital, he wants us to keep Fraser for the time being, at least until foul play has been ruled out. Salma, please let him know when he comes back from wherever he is. It seems that the death might not have been accidental as was thought at first. Martin Jamieson has found insulin in the bloodstream. Quick to report as usual, Martin, bless him. Arthur Cunningham wasn't carrying anything saying he was diabetic."

"I sent Fraser to the canteen for me, Sir," said the DS, looking a bit sheepish. "I had a sudden notion for a cheese and pickle sandwich."

CHAPTER 5

"I wonder who'll replace Fiona...the DS...Mrs Davenport," said Frank as he and Salma drove to Waterfoot later that day.

The wedding of their superiors had been some months previously and Frank still felt proud of the fact that he had nicknamed them Bonnie Prince Charlie and Flora Macdonald since they had arrived at the station a few years ago.

"I wonder if she'll come back after the birth," was Salma's response. "We might just get someone in as a temporary DS. Talking of which, Frank, have you put in any applications recently?"

"What's the point with clever folk like Fraser going for the same promotion?" Frank said, grumpily.

"You've been in the job longer than he has. That should count for something."

"Trying to get rid of me, are you?"

As usual Frank's bad mood had not lasted but Salma had no time to answer this question as they had arrived at the address they had been given for the murdered man. They had been informed that Arthur Cunningham was divorced and lived alone but his eldest son would be waiting for them. It was an impressive house in one of the newer housing developments in Waterfoot and Salma waited for Frank to make his usual, disparaging remarks about wealthy people. Maybe Frank's class prejudice had gone the way of his racial prejudice and his religious bigotry as he said nothing, simply rang the bell.

A new Mercedes, silver grey in colour, was pulled up outside the front door. Frank commented on this, telling Salma that it was the car he would buy if he won the lottery.

The young man who answered, looked a bit sheepish, Salma thought and his first words gave the reason.

"I'm sorry to be welcoming you into a house I don't know myself," he said. "My father and I haven't been on speaking terms for years and he only moved here recently….a ridiculously large house for a single man butmy father was a pompous ass and a dreadful snob. Luckily the neighbour had a key or we'd have been meeting in the garden."

He laughed.

"I don't know how the hospital got my details though Dad tended to pride himself on being up to date so probably had an iPhone and he might have all our phone numbers in it even though he didn't get in touch."

"Why don't you tell it as it is?" Frank's expression said it all.

Salma preceded him into the house as the man stood back to let them in. It was left to Salma to choose a room which she did; selecting one at the front of the house that she was correct in thinking would be the lounge. They all sat down on the black leather suite, Frank and Salma on the settee. The room looked unused, pristine with its off-white carpet and red accessories, curtains and cushions made from the same pattern and obviously expensive. Salma suspected that the two paintings gracing the walls were not prints.

"My name's Thomas but my friends call me Tom," the young man said," I think my mother got her way with her first son, luckily for me. My brothers, Oliver and Quentin, weren't so fortunate. Don't think Mum had much say in their names. Only sensible thing she ever did was leave the old man. Goodness knows why she ever married him in the first place!"

"Is your mother still alive?" asked Salma. "Maybe it's her we should be talking to."

"Yes, but she lives in Canada now, with her sister who emigrated there some years ago."

"Right," said Frank. "Have you been in touch with the Dental Hospital?"

"Yes. The three of us got together there yesterday. They couldn't tell us much: just that he had apparently died of an overdose of the injection he was given before he was to have a tooth removed."

"There was insulin found in your father's bloodstream. There was nothing on his person to show that he was diabetic. Was he?" asked Salma.

"No idea, Constable," The man looked rueful. "Even had we been on speaking terms, my father was not one to divulge private things like that. Perhaps my mother would know. None of us boys is diabetic and I imagine it's a hereditary thing which would suggest that neither of my parents` is diabetic."

"It's Sergeant," Salma corrected him with smile. "Sergeant Salma Din and this is PC Frank Selby. We should have introduced ourselves right away. I apologise. Would you get in touch with both of your brothers and see if they know, please? I'm presuming that they live here in Scotland or at least in the UK."

"Sorry, Sergeant. I should have made things clearer. We all live in Glasgow but none of us has seen or been in contact with our father for years. I doubt that either of my brothers would know about diabetes."

"Could you contact your Mother…sorry, I'm presuming you still keep in contact with her. Do you?"

"Oh yes, Sergeant. The three of us have visited her in Canada with our families. We each have two fair-haired daughters. Quite confusing when we all get together."

He laughed.

"Then, Sir, would you contact her and ask if your father was diabetic. I don't imagine you will know his doctor so this way might be quicker. Anyway, I'm afraid you will have to break the news of his death to her."

"She'd be a hypocrite if she got upset but I suppose she must have loved him once," the young man responded. "I'll ring her in a few hours. Make sure she's up and about first."

Salma thanked him and gave him the number of the police station and the extension number of their section. She asked him for the key which he handed over, saying that he could probably get a copy from one of his brothers.

"He gave me a copy ...I'm not sure why and I had two copies made for my brothers. Hopefully Q who is methodical, can lay his hands on his copy if we need one. As I said, I got this from the neighbour. I seem to have lost mine."

"I like your car, Sir," Frank said, as they left.

"Not mine...wish it was. Mine's a clapped- out old Renault Megane. The only similarity is the colour."

They left, telling him that they would be back in touch when they had more definite news. It was Frank who commented on the three young men being estranged from their father.

"I know it's quite common for a son or daughter to lose touch with a parent but all three...he must have been a really rotten dad."

"Yes, some people should never be parents," sighed Salma. "It's so unfair when there are people who can't have kids and would make great parents."

It took only fifteen minutes for them to reach the station where they informed the DCI that they were no further forward about whether or not Arthur Cunningham was diabetic.

"The oldest son, Tom Cunningham, will get in touch once he's contacted his mother in Canada," said Salma, going on to explain that none of the man's three sons had been in contact with their father for some years.

Davenport who had a close relationship with his teenage daughter, Pippa, told Fiona this over lunch later.

"How on earth can a father lose touch with *three* sons, Fiona? I can understand perhaps falling out with one child but with all three!"

Fiona looked sombre.

"I had a school friend who hadn't seen her father for years but I found out later that he'd abused her and her sister so neither of them wanted anything to do with him. They were lucky in that their mother believed them and divorced her husband."

She patted her bump.

"This little person will be so loved and wanted, Charles. After seeing you with Pippa, I know you'll be a great dad and I'll try really hard to be a good mum."

"On that topic, will you please think about stopping work, Love? I know you said, and I agreed, that you'd continue working as long as possible but you're getting puffed out just climbing the stairs. The wee person in there must be a Sumo wrestler. Anita wasn't nearly as big as you when she was expecting Pippa."

"I know, baby hippo comes to mind when I look in the mirror," said Fiona, ruefully. "I think you're right. I should perhaps go at the end of next week."

Charles looked so relieved that she punched him lightly in the stomach, asking him if she was such an ogre that he believed that she might not agree with him.

"It's just that you've always said you'd be bored at home until the baby arrived. I know you're not the type to be contented knitting little white things and preparing cordon bleu meals for your hard-working husband."

As Charles was the one who did most of the cooking, Fiona could hardly deny this, so she contented herself with giving him the best hug she could manage these days.

CHAPTER 6

Next day, came the news from Tom Cunningham that his mother had told him that his father had not been diabetic while she was living with him. He had asked his mother for the name of his father's doctor. Again, she could only give the information she had known some years ago.

 Penny, given the job of contacting this doctor, came back with the news that Arthur was still with the same practice though the named doctor had since retired. Penny had made an appointment later that day, to see the head of the practice which was in Newlands. She and Salma were dispatched to interview the doctor. The days of the 'dragon' receptionist had apparently gone and they were greeted by one of a group of young women who immediately rang through to say that the police had arrived and would she show them through. Salma, looking round the busy waiting room, saw the looks of curiosity cast in their direction but forgot that as they were shown through a small maze of corridors to Dr Ahmed's room. His door was open and as he heard their footsteps, he came to welcome them. Although he must have been in his late thirties, he was boyishly handsome and obviously quite intrigued about their visit. "My secretary said you were enquiring about Arthur Cunningham. Javed Ahmed at your service. Is this then the point where I say that all patients' records are confidential?"

He grinned.

Salma smiled and Penny flashed him her cheeky grin back. Salma held up her identity card.

"I'm Sergeant Salma Din and this is Constable Penny Price. We're investigating the sudden death of Arthur Cunningham so you will also know that confidentiality is now able to be broken."

Her smile robbed her words of possible officiousness.

Dr Ahmed sat down behind his large desk and motioned to them to sit down across from him.

"I'm sorry that Mr Cunningham has died. To be honest, I've not had many dealings with him. Quite an abrasive guy, the kind of man who feels everyone owes him something. Made me feel like a lackey rather than his GP. Maybe there was some racism involved but he wanted the senior partner of the practice when the last one retired and that was me. However, I'm being unprofessional. What can I do for you?"

"We need to know mainly if Arthur Cunningham was diabetic," said Salma.

Javed Ahmed swivelled to look at his computer screen. He pressed a few keys.

"High blood pressure, under wraps with eight milligrams of candesartan. Ditto with high cholesterol being kept down by atorvastatin but no diabetes. In fact his blood sugar level at his last fasting test was bang on 5. He created such a fuss about having that test, I remember. You'd have thought I was a vampire after his precious blood! Sorry, being unprofessional again!"

"Anything else worth mentioning?" asked Penny, as always forgetting to stand on protocol and leave the questioning to Salma as her superior officer.

Dr Ahmed looked once more at the screen.

"He came in some years ago, before he was my patient, asking for Viagra. He was warned that there were risks given his blood pressure and cholesterol levels but he must have argued the toss as my predecessor did prescribe Viagra for him."

"Would you give us the date of that prescribing, please," asked Salma.

Dr Ahmed wrote on a yellow post-it note and handed it to her. She glanced down. The date was January 2008.

They thanked the doctor and left the surgery. Back in the car, Penny driving, Salma mused about whether the sex aid medication was for before or after his wife left him.

"I would guess afterwards," was Penny's response. "He sounds like the type of guy who'd want a young woman on his arm after his wife left to show the world that he had what it took to attract a younger woman. Boost his ego. Whereas if his sexual performance had deteriorated when he was with his wife, he probably wouldn't have cared."

"Gosh, Penny, that's cynical for a young thing like you!" replied Salma.

"Well, Serge, based on the men we've met recently, some of them dead: Robert Gentle, the minister, Alan Grant who was killed in Penang. Would either of them have taken their wife's needs into account?"

"Point taken, Penny," laughed Salma.

A phone call once back at the station, to Tom Cunningham, proved that Penny was correct in her assumption. Mrs Cunningham, had left her husband in July 2007.

Penny once again showing little sympathy for the dead man, was heard to declare that he probably met the new woman at the bank Christmas party.

"Probably a young member of staff who didn't like to offend him by rebuffing him"" said Frank.

"You two are pre-empting this case a bit, aren't you?" came a caustic voice from the doorway. How do you know that the man is as bad as you're painting him?"

Penny blushed but Frank stood his ground.

"Sorry, Sir but he can't have been very charming if he alienated three sons and a wife!"

Davenport laughed.

"True, Selby but remember that we have to be impartial in our dealings with all those involved in this case, even the corpse!"

Fiona had joined him in the doorway, a bit of a squash for them both, given her size now. He moved to stand behind her, resting his arm lightly on her shoulder.

"Watch out, Sir," laughed Penny. "I read in the paper yesterday, that women object to a man putting his arm on their shoulder. Apparently, it's a sign of ownership!"

"Well she *is* my woman," Charles said in a mock gruff voice, "and anyway she's got her arm round my waist. What does that mean?"

"That I need support," laughed Fiona. "I've decided folk, to stop work at the end of next week. It's hard to lug this enormous body around all day."

"Are you planning on coming back to work, ma'am?"

For once it was Frank, not Penny, asking the question. Fiona looked at Charles.

"Well," he said. "I'd like her to stay at home but she claims she'll be bored when the baby is asleep."

"I've decided to just wait and see how I feel," Fiona added.

"So, no interviews for your job then, Ma'am!" said Salma, knowing that she could not be accused of self-interest. She had not been long enough in her post of sergeant to try for the nest stage in her career.

"Not yet," her boss said. "Am I being selfish?" They hastened to reassure her. In spite of some teething troubles when Fiona, Charles and Salma had all been new, they now worked well as a team.

"Back to business, Team," were Davenport's next words. "Now that we are pretty sure that Arthur Cunningham's death is murder we'll need to start interviewing…at the Dental Hospital, at his place of business and his social circle and family.

"Doesn't sound as if the family and social circle will take up much time, Sir," said the irrepressible Penny.

"Maybe not, Penny," retorted Frank. "However, maybe he more than alienated someone in that group.

At that point, they were joined by Fraser Hewitt. The young man was looking much happier since hearing the news that he was to remain in the department for a time at least.

Davenport put him up to date with what had just been said, adding, "Good point, Selby. "I suppose we'll have to look into the possibility of his wife or one of his sons avenging a past wrong.

"Well, Sir," said Fraser. "They say that revenge is a dish best served cold."

Frank grimaced. "Is that from Shakespeare, Brainbox?"

Fraser grinned. He seldom rose to Frank's bait. Salma could have told him that that was the best way to treat Frank. She had done the same with his racist remarks and was sure that it was this lack of retaliation that had won him over or made him feel ashamed. She wasn't sure which.

"As is often the case with my vast knowledge, Frank, I have no idea where I got that from."

Penny told them about their findings at the surgery. When she got to the Viagra part, Fraser laughed and told them about his aunt who had met a man on holiday. This man had 'bummed' free meals from her and she, being glad of his company, had let this go. The night before he left he told her that he had brought some Viagra with him and would she tell him if she would have sex with him that night as he did not want to waste one.

"What a cheek!" said Penny. "I hope she sent him away with a flea in his ear."

"She did."

"I wonder if Arthur Cunningham had more success," mused Frank.

CHAPTER 7

The team should have been flies on the wall in a
large house in Newlands, not very far from the
police station on the Friday as they would have a
heard a revealing conversation taking place and
Fraser's comment about revenge, echoed.
The home of Quentin Cunningham was a manse
built in the days when Church ministers' homes
had to have enough bedrooms to sleep any
needy person who came to the door for help. It
was a large, detached, sandstone building with
five bedrooms, perfect for Quentin, his wife and
two daughters.
One daughter, Becky, was sitting on the floor of
the large front lounge as were her cousins:
Tom's daughters, Helen and Sarah and Oliver's
daughters, Laura and Rose. Quentin's youngest
girl, Lizzie, aged three was in bed, having her
afternoon nap. All the children were wearing
school uniform, having been brought here
straight from school at around 4.30 The adults,
Tom and wife Susan, Oliver and wife Pat,
Quentin and Abigail, were scattered round the
room in comfortable seats. This was a room
often used for smaller church meetings so held
these eleven easily.
Laura, at ten was holding forth.
"Helen and I are the only ones of us kids who
ever met Grandfather. Why is that, Dad?"
Oliver was honest as he had always tried to be
with his children.

"Well, Laura, when you were born, Grandma was still living with Grandfather and of course she was with him when Helen was born. They split up when you were only three and Helen was four. Your cousin Sarah was born that year and your sister and other two cousins were born when Grandma was living in Canada and granddad was on his own and we didn't see him anymore."

"He's sent us birthday and Christmas presents, Uncle Olly," said Sarah.

"Yes, cheques," Tom answered his daughter. "Nothing personal."

"Right, kiddos, off upstairs to the playroom," Abigail had risen to her feet, with a warning glance at her brother in law.

"Auntie Abby, can't I stay now that I'm a teenager?" pleaded Helen.

"You're not a teenager until you're thirteen, Helen. You're just eleven. Nice try," said her mother. "We need you to keep an eye on wee Rose and also make sure the rest don't waken Lizzie."

The children trooped out of the door.

"Poor Helen," said her Dad. "I remember when I was her age. Too young to do anything exciting yet old enough to be left in charge! How I wanted rid of you two pesky brothers! Mum was sympathetic but Father was just glad to see the back of us after dinner."

"Yes, Father. I wonder who killed him."

Quentin was pouring drinks as he spoke: whiskies for himself and his brothers, gin for Susan, vodka with orange for Pat and a diet coke for his wife who needed her wits about her with two-year old Lizzie about to waken soon. "Well one of us could have done it! We hated him enough," said Oliver whose occupation as a lieutenant in the army had hardened him somewhat and he tended to call spade a spade' He was on leave right now, fortunately, for the purpose of this discussion but unfortunately as he had been available to commit the murder he had just claimed he could have done.

"Olly! For goodness sake. If you can say that, think how other people will feel," Quentin sounded a bit sanctimonious which was unusual for him. He was a popular minister with his congregation in a nearby Church of Scotland and was not known for being holier than thou. "No Q, he's right. We did all hate him. Remember those beatings! Remember the mental cruelty, promising us a puppy one Christmas and it was a china dog we each got. Need I go on?" asked Tom.

Quentin slumped back in his chair, almost spilling his drink. Abigail came over and sat on the arm of his chair, putting one arm round him.

"Tom's right, Love. Remember how scathing he was when you decided to go in for the ministry and how he refused to come to our wedding because he didn't think I was the right wife for you. Blamed me for your religious beliefs because I had taken you to my church. He wouldn't come to your ordination either…"

"….or to your first book signing, Tom," piped in Susan. "He did come to our wedding but it was probably your Mum who persuaded him."

"No, Mum couldn't get him to do anything he didn't want to do but he thought you were ok because you came from Bearsden and your parents were lawyers. What a disappointment I was to him! No proper job, a penniless writer. My 'scribbling' as he called it last time we met, at your wedding Olly."

"Not now, bro, with two best sellers under your belt."

Oliver sounded proud of his older brother.

Pat spoke up.

"I know you'll laugh but I always think you guys were a throwback to former days. The oldest son who'd inherit the title, didn't work, the second son went into the army and the third into the church!"

"Patricia! Have you been reading Georgette Heyer again?" her husband teased her as laughter rang round the room and lessened the tension that had crept in when the children left.

"Seriously, Gang," said Tom. "Father must have made many enemies over the years and don't they say that revenge is a dish best served cold. Perhaps the killer was someone from way back, even from the days before us."

"He certainly didn't have any real friends. Mum had loads. I remember how glad I was that she stood up to Father about seeing them and how sorry she was to leave them when she went to Canada to stay with Aunt Nan," added Oliver.

"Did you ever get the impression that your Father hit your Mum as he hit you three?" asked Pat.

"I don't think he did. She was an obedient wife but she never seemed cowed. He tended to hit us when she wasn't there."

Why on earth didn't you tell her?" questioned Abigail.

"Well, I don't know, just thought it was something that happened to kids, I suppose," said Tom. "I was twelve before I stood up to him, told him I'd report him to my teacher at school if he hit one of us again. I'd just seen him take his belt to Q who was only eight and something kind of snapped in me."

"Well, let's think back to who might have hated him enough to kill him, years later."

Susan threw her husband a sympathetic look. He was so gentle with their two daughters as she was sure Oliver and Quentin were with theirs. They were such happy little girls!

"He had an older sister, Nell her name was," said Quentin. "She married a joiner and they emigrated to Australia almost right away. He never kept in touch. It was Mum who told me about her and the cousin we have over there. We've all gone to Canada a few times to visit Mum but I plan to go to Australia when the girls are older. I told you two guys about them. Did you ever get any more information on Aunt Nell or her family?"

"Nothing," chorused his brothers.

They had both been keen on doing a family tree but the initial enthusiasm had worn off.

"I remember years ago, Pat, that Mum told me that Anne Kerr who kept in touch with her, had written about trouble at the bank. I think Father sacked someone, one of the tellers, for pilfering the petty cash," Oliver chipped in.

"It wasn't as if the person was robbing the safe!" said Tom. "Anyway, I think we should tell the police what we know."

"I hope no one finds out…" began Tom.

At that moment the door opened and Helen came in to say that Lizzie was awake and hungry. Abigail told her to call the others down and she would make sandwiches for everyone before they all set off for their own homes.

As their brood of happy children clumped down the stairs, Oliver and Quentin told Tom that they agreed with him

CHAPTER 8

"Sir, how did Arthur Cunningham get to the
Dental Hospital?"
Frank posed the question to Davenport on
Monday as soon as they were all seated in the
Incident Room.
Charles Davenport looked preoccupied and
Frank had to repeat his question.
"Sorry, Selby. What did you say? Bit tired this
morning. We had a disturbed night. Fiona....DS
Davenport...was in quite a lot of pain. I rang the
NHS helpline but although I was told not to
worry...apparently cramp is quite normal at this
stage in pregnancy... we didn't get back to sleep
till just before it was time to get up. I've left her
sleeping."
Explanation over, he smiled at the young folk
seated in front of him, pulling at his ear lobe as
he did when thinking. The white board beside
him and facing his audience had one name on it:

ARTHUR CUNNINGHAM.

Below the name was written:

Insulin in bloodstream

"I said, 'How did Arthur Cunningham get to the
Dental Hospital, Sir?"
"Could have driven. We'll have to check for any
cars left in nearby car parks or in parking
spaces..."

"…unless he has more than one car, Sir, that's not likely as his Mercedes was parked in his driveway when Sergeant Din and I went there yesterday. I thought it was his eldest son's car but it wasn't."

"A man with that size of house *might* have another car, Sir," said Penny.

"True, Penny. Who would know a thing like that? Let's get over to his house and do our usual check for address book, bank statements, work address. All we found on his person was his credit cards and driving licence with his address on it and his mobile phone. We could ask a neighbour about the car."

"Who do you want to go there, Sir?"

Penny as usual could not wait for her boss to give instructions.

"I'll go, Miss Impatience and take yourself and Fraser. Frank, would you and Salma get in touch with the Dental Hospital. Get Cunningham's dentist's name and address and get over to the practice. Speak to anyone there who knew him at all. Try to get an idea of his personality from people such as the dentists and receptionist. Meet back here after lunch."

The three-strong police team drove over to Newton Mearns. Living there, as he did, Davenport had known what to expect from the address.

"He either inherited wealth or had an important, well paid job," he said as they walked up the long path, a path free of weeds, between areas of grass which unlike his own were not covered with leaves or debris from the heavy winter winds. "Must have a gardener too."

"Maybe he's a keen gardener, Sir," ventured Fraser.

"Perhaps but someone who likes gardening would have bushes and signs of flower beds. There are just regimented trees with concrete slabs between the grassy sections."

"I wonder if he moved here after his wife left him," mused Fraser.

"No, he only moved here quite recently, his son told Sergeant Din," Penny reported.

She took the key she had got from her colleague and opened the impressive door.

"Penny, you and Fraser check upstairs. You both know the kind of things we are looking for. I'll check downstairs."

As he finished speaking, his mobile phone rang. The two constables, halfway up the stairs, stopped when they heard the panic in his voice. "I'll come right away."

"That was the Southern General. Fiona's been taken there. Can't stop to explain. Get on with the search then go back to the station. Get a taxi. I'll ring there when I can."

A search of one of the large front bedrooms revealed that Arthur Cunningham watched TV and drank when in bed. It didn't take Sherlock Holmes to work that one out, Fraser told Penny when he came back downstairs.

"A copy of The Radio Times on the floor beside an empty whisky glass and a bottle of Chevas Regal. This was in his bedside cabinet."

He produced a copy of a novel with a lurid cover, depicting a half-dressed woman.

"His wardrobe was pretty empty but next door was what I imagine was his dressing room with two other wardrobes stuffed full of clothes. Two dinner suits, a dress kilt, trousers, lots of pairs. Shirts, some cardigans and in drawers, packets of unopened shirts and copious pairs of underpants and socks…no vests."

"Ok. Well, I've got his address book from his study, a folder with his last twelve bank statements…a very tidy man, Mr Cunningham…must have shredded old stuff…a diary for last year but not a current one and this…"

Penny held up a locked box.

On their way out, Fraser went next door to get his hat while Penny rang for a taxi to take them back to the station.

Back at the station, they met Salma in the hallway. She looked panic-stricken. She grabbed Penny's arm.

"Penny. I've been looking out for the boss coming back. I saw the taxi. Where is the DCI? He's been summoned by Mr Knox to come immediately."

"He's been called to the hospital. Something to do with the DS. Ring up to Knox's secretary and explain that."

Salma scurried off to the room she shared with the other young ones. Penny and Fraser followed her in.

They heard Salma explain the situation. They saw her face tighten. She hung up.

"He must see someone now about the new case. It'll have to be me."

Salma almost ran out of the room. They heard her feet going down the corridor then coming back.

"Where's my comb? I need my hat."

"You look as smart as ever, Salma," said Frank.

"Here's your hat. Now go."

CHAPTER 9

It did not help Salma as she was going up in the lift to remember that her DCI had always said he felt as if he was going up to see God. They had all heard him joke with Fiona about Grant Knox and his lack of people skills. Now she would be facing him for the first time. She had never even seen him in the distance, for goodness sake, whereas they had all met and talked to Solomon Fairchild, his deputy, the man who seemed to know all about each and every one of them.

The lift stopped and Salma got out. The hallway was carpeted and the atmosphere hushed. There was none of the hustle and bustle associated with police stations. She turned left, the only way she could go as on her right there was only a blank wall. She was glad that the carpet silenced her footsteps and made her feel almost invisible. She thought of Harry Potter's invisibility cloak and the fact that he could go anywhere in it, unseen. She grinned, just as a man came out of the second room in the corridor.

"Sergeant Din, I presume? I'm glad you find police work something to grin about."

He looked like a bulldog in human form, Salma thought. He seemed to have no neck. The small, piggy eyes in a florid face did nothing to calm her suddenly racing heart.

"Yes, Sir. I mean, no Sir. I mean yes, I'm Sergeant Din and no, I don't find my work something to grin about."

"Stop mithering about, woman and come in to my office."

Nobody had told her that Knox was English and she could only guess at what 'mithering' meant. He turned and led the way, not stopping to usher her in. He sat down heavily at his desk, not inviting her to sit. He picked up a thin folder from the immaculately tidy desk, selected a sheet of A4 paper and waved it at her.

"This murder at the Dental Hospital, some days ago, is an arrest imminent?"

"No, Sir. We only knew for sure yesterday that it was a case of murder. We met one of the dead man's sons two days ago but we had to wait till he contacted his mother in Canada to get the name of the GP Mr Cunningham attended. Then we had to interview the GP and only then did we know that we had a murder on our hands."

Salma lifted her chin higher. She resented the criticism of her boss which was implicit in this man's stupid question about an arrest. She suspected what he would ask next and she was correct.

"Where is Davenport, anyway? Where is DS Macdonald?"

"DS Davenport, Sir."

"What? Oh yes, they got married, didn't they! One ought to have been moved to another station, in my opinion. Never mind. Where are they?"

The DS was taken into hospital suddenly, Sir and the DCI went there"

"What's wrong with her? Couldn't he have waited till visiting time?"

"She's expecting her first child, Sir. I imagine DCI Davenport was very worried when he heard the news."

Salma's voice was raised. She hated injustice, having been subjected to a lot in her younger days and for a moment she forgot to whom she was speaking. Luckily for her, there was a knock on the door which opened, revealing a man very different to Knox.

"Grant…oh sorry, I didn't know you were busy. Hello, Sergeant Din. Sorry to hear about Davenport's wife. Have you had any news from him?"

"No, Mr Fairchild. Mr Knox called me up here just after we heard about the DS."

"You can go, now, Sergeant but tell Davenport to keep me posted about the case. It's crucial that you get quick results before the trail goes cold. What did you want, Solomon?"

"I'll escort Sergeant Din to the lift, Grant and come back. Nothing that can't wait."

Fairchild's considerate manner dispelled the feeling of dismissal Salma had just experienced. When the door had closed and they were on their way to the lift, he said, with a twinkle in his eye, "Good friend of yours that Constable Price. Charged into my room, a few minutes ago, breathing fire like a mini dragon and saying that you'd been called up to Mr Knox and she wanted me to help you out."

'Only Penny could do something like that and get away with it,' said Salma. 'She would probably have treated Mr Knox to a lecture on politeness and consideration for others.'

Fairchild laughed.

"She's an angel, Mr Fairchild. I was terrified in there."

"Ok, Sergeant. Down to…well if Knox is seen as God this must be heaven so…you must be going down to hell."

Salma laughed.

"Tell your fellow conspirators that Mr Knox is going to be away from Friday for three weeks so they can relax a bit."

Salma's descent in the lift was calmer than the ascent.

"Solomon Fairchild knows *everything*, Penny. He knows Knox is called God. He knew that the DCI had gone to hospital to see the DS. Any news by the way?"

"No, nothing yet," piped up Frank.

"Oh, Penny, thank you, thank you for getting Mr Fairchild to intervene. Believe it or not, I was about to lose my temper and probably my job. He was being so uncaring about the DS going into hospital. He probably didn't even know she was pregnant."

"Whereas Fairchild probably knew how and when the baby was conceived," laughed Frank, "and the name that's been chosen!"

"Knox asked if an arrest was imminent! Can you believe that? Oh, he's going to be away for a few weeks so we won't feel him looking over our shoulders for a while."

The phone rang.

Salma picked up the receiver. She listened and said only, "Thank you, Sir. She's in our prayers."

Her eyes were wet as she lifted her head to face them.

"That was the DCI. The DS is having a Caesarian operation. She went into premature labour then couldn't give birth naturally and the baby was getting distressed. He'll keep in touch."

"The best thing we can do now is try to get on with the case," said Frank, somberly, realising that his female colleagues needed distracted from the worrying news. "Salma, you're the Big Chief now. What should we do?"

As he had hoped, this took Salma's mind away from worrying about Fiona. She assigned Penny to look at the bank statements, Frank to read through the address book and said that she would ring Tom Cunningham to see if he had any objection to them trying to open the locked box which would be the property of him and his brothers now.

Fraser returned from the canteen bearing a tray with three mugs on it.

"Sorry, Boss, they didn't have any brandy for you. Will tea do?" he laughed. "You look unscathed, that means unhurt, Frank.....only joking," he added as Frank's face showed irritation at being given this definition.

Frank laughed good naturedly. He was never moody for long and understood that he deserved this kind of comment from Fraser whom he was always accusing of being bookish and clever.

"Fraser, would you ring Tom Cunningham for me. Tell him we took some items from his father's house. He'll have to sign them out to us and I need his permission to open a locked box we found there.

By going-home time there was still no sign of Davenport and no further news.

CHAPTER 10

Charles restlessly paced the floor in the waiting room at the hospital. Nobody had been to see him since the news that Fiona was to be operated on and that was…he looked at his watch for the umpteenth time…over an hour ago. His wife was over forty and this was her first pregnancy. So many things could go wrong. He couldn't remember any names of them now except placenta previa which meant that the placenta came away before the baby was delivered but surely that couldn't happen during a controlled Caesarian operation.

He looked at the magazines strewn across the table and picked up one called 'Heat' but it was full of stories about so-called celebrities and had photographs of pregnant 'stars' which just reminded him of Fiona. He threw it back onto the table and sat down wondering if he should venture out of the waiting room.

What would he and Fiona do if their child should be born mentally or physically deformed? He pushed his mind away from this thought and made himself think about his current case.

About half an hour later, a nurse found him, slumped down in his chair, half asleep. She tapped him gently on the shoulder and he shot up, startled.

"Mr Davenport. You can see your wife now."

"How is she? Is she ok? What about the baby?"

"The surgeon is with her now and wants to speak to you both together."

As he followed the young nurse along the maze of corridors, Charles went over her words. They sounded alarming. Why should a surgeon need to speak to both of them? Was Fiona dying? Was the baby dead?

The nurse reached swing doors and held them open for him. He walked in briskly. Whatever the news, he must be strong for his wife.

Fiona lay back against the pillows. Her face, usually so rosy and animated, was pale and tense. She put out a hand to grasp his.

The surgeon, a middle-aged man, stocky and dark-haired, looked exhausted and his expression heralded bad news.

"Mr Davenport, my name is Beattie, Ian Beattie. I performed a Caesarian operation on your wife. Mrs Davenport, you came through it well as did one of your babies...."

"....one of the...there was only one," Fiona said, weakly.

"Often one baby hides behind the other in the womb so the second heartbeat isn't detected. Your baby girl is fine but the wee boy has congenital defects. There will have to be tests done before I can tell you exactly what is wrong with him. I'm sorry. I'll send in someone who can help you at this time."

He hurried out of the room.

Charles bent to kiss Fiona gently on her forehead. She squeezed his hand even more tightly.

The door opened again and a young woman entered the room. She was wearing a clerical collar but her clothes were casual.

"Mr and Mrs Davenport, I'm sorry if you think I'm intruding at this sad time. My name is Jennifer Lawson and I'm one of the chaplains based in the hospital. Mr Beattie is concerned that your baby son might not live and he sent me to find out if you want him baptised. I know this isn't something you've had time to think about, let alone discuss so I'll leave you just now and come back in about half an hour unless there's anything else you want from me."

Fiona was crying softly so Charles thanked the chaplain and she went out, leaving them alone as promised.

They sat in silence for a few minutes, then Charles said, "I'd like our son to have a name and be blessed by God even though I am an agnostic, my love. What do you want?"

"Me too, Charles. Will he be Kenneth Charles, as we planned?"

"Yes, Love."

Charles was unable to stop his tears falling now. They held hands and cried together.

When Jennifer Lawson returned, they were calm and determined.

"We want both our babies christened together, please," said Fiona. "When will it happen?"

"Just give me time to set things up. I'll get one of the nurses to bring along your daughter so that you can hold her for the first time, then I'll bring along your wee son."

"To hold for perhaps the last time," thought Charles, sadly.

The minister left and, shortly afterwards, a nurse brought along their new daughter, warmly wrapped in a white shawl. She handed the baby to Fiona and Charles glanced down at them both.

"This wee one is going to have all the normal things done," he said, taking his phone out of his pocket and putting it into photographing mode. He took some pictures.

"Charles, what about Pippa? I know she's just young but don't you think she'd want to see and hold her brother and be there for their christenings?"

Charles's eyes were moist once again. He sat on the bed, hugged Fiona and their daughter and spoke very quietly:

"You are some woman, Fiona Davenport, thinking of Pippa at a time like this. I don't know if she's old enough to take this in her stride but I do remember being left behind when my mother and father visited my grandfather who'd just had a stroke. He died and I felt really left out and wished I had been there. I know there were only protecting me but kids are tougher than we often give them credit for, so yes, I think we'd better have her contacted and brought here. I'll ring the station and ask Penny to go to her school and bring her here, unless you think I should ask my sister to do it."

"I think Penny is the better choice, Charles. She's nearer to Pippa in age and so kind and thoughtful...not that Linda isn't."

Charles got off the bed, bending down first to kiss his daughter and Fiona.

"I'll have to tell the team what's happened, Love."

"Of course. Charles. This wee one. Is her name to be Kathleen Fiona, as we planned?"

"Why not?"

"Do you want something from your side of the family instead. I don't think I want any more children after what's happened. It was probably my age that caused the …problem."

"Don't blame yourself, Fiona. It took both of us to get you pregnant and no, I don't need a family name. Kathleen Fiona she is."

Charles rang the station from the corridor which was just as well as his voice broke while he explained to Salma what had happened and asked her to send Penny to the school to collect Pippa, telling her to ask Penny to simply say that there was to be a christening at the hospital and he would explain the whole thing to her himself when she arrived.

"It wasn't fair to ask Penny to take on that job. I just hope she can field the questions Pippa is bound to ask," he told his wife.

At that moment the chaplain arrived with a wheelchair, to take them to the wee hospital chapel. They explained that they wanted to wait till their older daughter got there and asked her opinion about a youngster Pippa's age being put in this position.

"I think you're very wise. Your daughter is old enough to cope and yet young enough to bounce back quite quickly. Her imagination might paint worse pictures than reality will do and she might feel left out which isn't a good start for an only child…I take it there aren't other kids as you haven't mentioned them...being faced with sharing her parents anyway."

"Oh, Pippa's excited about it; she's not shown any jealousy…so far. She's my stepdaughter," explained Fiona.

"I know but if your wee boy survives and needs lots of attention, even more than any new born baby would need, she might feel some jealousy then, especially if she'd been left out now."

The chaplain left, saying that she would call back for them in an hour which would give time for Pippa to get there and have things explained to her.

CHAPTER 11

Penny went up the front steps of the secondary school. It had been her school when she was secondary school age but she had never climbed these stairs which were only for staff and visitors so she felt nervous. Also, she was unsure of how she should tackle this situation which was new to her. She pushed open the swing doors and walked in. The office window was on her right. She tapped on the glass panel which opened immediately. The young woman was obviously expecting Penny.

"Hello, Constable. Pippa Davenport is with the head teacher. That's her door across there." She pointed across the hallway.

"Just knock and go in. She's expecting you."

Penny did as she had been told and a voice called her in as she opened the door. A woman was rising from her seat and Penny remembered her from a previous case. As then, the head teacher was calm and in command of the situation.

"Constable Price, isn't it?   Christine Martin, head teacher. You might remember me from a few years ago. I was head teacher of the school where David Stirling was murdered. Pippa's all ready for you. She knows that her Dad wants her at the hospital to meet her new sister."

She turned to the seat where Pippa was sitting, looking excited.

"Up you get, Pippa. Constable Price is a busy woman."

Taking her lead from the head teacher, Penny was brisk and business -like. All the way to the hospital, she parried Pippa's questions, saying, when asked, that she had no details of the baby and that Pippa's Dad would give her all the information and was she not a lucky girl to be missing school. Pippa, like Penny was a chatterbox and she talked away ten to the dozen, telling Penny about the room that had been decorated for the new baby.

"I wouldn't mind a baby brother but a sister would be so much better. I could tell her all about the Chalet School when she's old enough. I'm more interested in Agatha Christie books myself now that I'm older," she confided to Penny as they drew up outside the hospital.

The Southern General, now called the Queen Elizabeth University Hospital, was an imposing sight but the maternity unit was not as new as the rest and Penny had been there before so she could lead her young charge in the correct direction.

It was obvious to Penny that her boss was under great stress but Pippa, excited about the baby, did not seem to notice and chattered away excitedly as her dad led her away. Charles sent Penny a meaningful look over his shoulder, saying that he would get back to them later.

"If Salma's allowed to take charge, I know you'll all give her your support. Same if it's someone new, seconded till I get back."

"Someone new?" I hope it's not my boss, Roger. He's so lethargic and he's got no imagination at all."

Fraser sounded horrified at this prospect when Penny reported what their DCI had said.

Perhaps up in 'heaven' his view was shared. Salma, summoned upstairs again, was called into Solomon Fairchild's room much to her relief. Seated at his desk with a cup of tea in one hand and a chocolate digestive biscuit in the other, she was informed that due to staff absences, he had persuaded Knox to hand over supervision of the current case to himself.

"I'll come down every morning for staff meetings and check that every possible avenue is being covered but apart from that I'll be leaving things in your more than capable hands, Sergeant Din. I think this responsibility will look good on your CV."

The only person Salma told about this latter part of the conversation was Penny who was, as was to be expected, delighted for her friend and colleague.

"Salma…that's great. We'll help you all we can. I know how keen you are to move up the ranks. Me, I haven't got an ambitious bone in my body, prefer no responsibility but just love my work." Salma was quiet.

"Salma Din! Are you scared of being in charge? Surely you can see what a compliment Mr Fairchild is paying you?"

Salma seemed to come out of a reverie. Penny would have been amazed to know that into her friend's head had come the thought, "Was the GP, Javed Ahmed, married?"

Frank and Fraser were also delighted to know that Salma was to be their new boss for the time being. Neither of them knew Solomon Fairchild well but had heard favourable remarks from those with whom he had come in contact.

"Just watch out, Fraser old son. He has the gift of second sight. Seems to know what we 're all doing before we do!"

They all laughed. Then Salma, looking serious, asked Frank if reading through Arthur Cunningham's address book had been helpful. He had also been asked, in Penny's absence, to study the bank statements.

"Well, I'm surprised he bothered with an address book. There was his doctor's practice, the address of his dental practice, his bank address, what I'm assuming is his ex-wife's address in Canada...if she reassumed her maiden name and it's Paterson and only a few more names...an M Blackwell, a G Hawken and a J Lambert."

"What about the bank statements, Frank?" asked Penny. "Any more help from them?"

"Hey Penny Farthing, Salma's my boss now, not you!" Frank laughed.

Penny blushed.

Salma laughed.

"Frank, she takes over from the DCI at times. Why would it be any different with me?"

"Ok but please, Boss, just don't pull your ear and say, "Right team!"

"And don't encourage Frank with any hints of romance," added Fraser who had heard ad infinitum from Frank about his matchmaking success with the DS and DCI.

Salma felt her cheeks heat up and was glad of her darker skin but even so, Penny noticed her stiffen slightly and this body language made her resolve to question her friend later on when they were alone.

"Bank statements, Selby." Salma pretended to be officious.

"Sorry, Serge. The statements only go as far back at last January. I think he must have been the kind of man who shredded things like that after a year. Plenty of direct debits for the usual things, council tax, electricity and gas, that sort of thing in his current account statements. Surprised he hadn't gone paperless! Only one deposit account. It's got a very healthy amount in it. Oh, direct debit to an ISA account…£200 every month."

"Why is it that in crime novels, the police always seem to find records of a mysterious amount being paid out every month," moaned Penny.

"That leads them straight to a blackmailer who in turn has recently died under suspicious circumstances and they go right from there to arresting the blackmailer's son for the murder!"

They all laughed then Fraser, looking serious again, asked Penny what had happened when she took Pippa Davenport to the hospital.

"Well you know I was told not to mention the little we knew; just that she had a baby sister or brother and her Dad and Fiona wanted her with them. The head teacher, Mrs Martin, had been informed...."

"...yes, I rang her when you were on the way, Penny," said Salma.

"Thanks. Well, she set the tone for me by saying that Mr Davenport wanted Pippa to meet the new baby so we just chatted in the car about the baby's room and about the wedding."

"We don't know much more except that there were two babies born and one is ill," said Fraser.

"The DCI said he'd get back to us later," Penny told them and with that they had to be satisfied. Salma went up to the room which would be hers for the immediate future and which had been the DS's room and Penny followed.

When her friend looked quizzically at her, Penny shut the door and asked her why she had reacted when Fraser had joked about romance.

"Oh, Pen. It's just that my brother has started getting serious about finding me a husband. He thinks, especially now that I have my brother and sister to look after, that there should be a man's influence in the house."

Penny was indignant but Salma said that it was to be expected and that her aunt and uncle had sided with him.

"Don't worry, Penny. I'm not giving in without a fight. Now off you go and let me get settled in here. Oh, would you ask Fraser to ring the Dental Hospital and get the name of Arthur Cunningham's dentist and the address. Frank and I were to go but it got forgotten about in all the upset over the boss not being here."

CHAPTER 12

Tom Cunningham came to the station later in the day. As the eldest brother, he had assumed responsibility for the funeral. Being an author, he could choose his work schedule unlike his brothers, though he and Olly often teased Q about his only working on a Sunday. Q probably worked harder than most people with a nine to five job, as he was on countless committees and had a large parish to visit. His congregation was dwindling and he often bemoaned the fact that funerals far outweighed baptisms and weddings but it was still quite large compared with other parishes such as Pollokshaws and Shawlands. Penny met Tom and ushered him into an interview room which he looked round, commenting on the tables and chairs as looking more comfortable than he had expected.

"Glad there's no tape recorder," he laughed.

"We'll save that for when you're accused of murdering your dad!" laughed Penny then sobered, realising that at such an early date, Tom could not be ruled out as the guilty person. Tom must have thought the same as he stopped smiling. Without the ready smile, his face was quite stern and Penny could see that the young man had, like most people, two sides to his character.

They both sat down and Tom handed Penny a small bunch of keys, reiterating that he was happy for the police to open any unlocked drawers or boxes. These keys had been on his father's person when he died and Tom had been given them when called to identify the body. Penny had, on Salma's instructions, brought the locked box they had found in Arthur's study, saying that the sons had the right to know what was in it. She put it on the table in front of them. The smallest key turned in the lock.

The box, though very small, was full. Penny wrote down each item as she took it from the box.

"One newspaper cutting. It's the bottom half page from the birth and death section of a paper. A packet of golf tees, from Harrods.

She lifted a small object from the box.

"It looks like an engagement ring, quite modern I would say as it's quite wide, not like the wee thin rings folk my Mum's age and older had but it's too small to belong to a man."

Penny peered inside the ring but could see nothing inscribed.

"Could this be your Mum's ring, Mr Cunningham?" she asked.

"Please call me Tom, not Mr Cunningham. That's my father's name. I've no idea but I think, as you say, it's a bit modern for Mum's era. I could ring her and ask if she kept her ring, if you want. But, wouldn't she have given him back the wedding ring too?"

"Well, I'd have thought if she didn't want to wear them, she'd have sold them," said Penny, blunt and to the point as usual. Tom agreed with her. He said he would contact his mother just to be sure.

Penny thanked him, saying that she would be grateful if he did that and rang her the next day at the station. She asked about his brothers and what they did for a living and he chatted for a while about his nieces and his brothers with whom he was obviously close. She asked about the likelihood of his father having two cars but Tom could not help her there.

Feeling that she had all the background information she was going to get, Penny rose from her seat, signalling that the meeting was over. Tom got to his feet, looking a bit bemused. "Those things, apart from the golf tees, were nostalgic things for my father to keep. Not a bit like him."

Penny, remembering the scant bank statements, felt the same and said this to the others when she joined them. Salma came down from the DS's room. She felt odd there but she knew that it made sense in case she had to interview anyone and she had to be seen to be in charge. Frank had added that she would also have access to Davenport's coffee machine next door and could treat them to decent coffee every day. Salma had laughed and agreed but insisted that they still call her Salma as she was still very much one of them.

"Well, for an unsentimental, almost hard man, Arthur Cunningham kept some sentimental items in this wee box," Penny said, holding it up. She showed them every item. Fraser, inspecting the newspaper page with the birth entries, volunteered that he thought it had come from a local paper, not The Herald anyway as that was the paper he read every day and the print was different.

"It's quite old, not like yesterday's paper. Some years old, I would say."

Solomon Fairchild entering the room at that point, smiled at them benignly. He knew that Davenport valued his team highly which was his reason for delegating leadership to Salma. Even Frank, whom Fairchild with his finger on the pulse of the large station, knew to have been less than an asset to this department before Davenport's arrival, was shaping up to be a likely candidate for promotion.

"Hello, Sir," Salma said and she and the others got to their feet.

"It's OK folks. Sit down again. I just came to tell you that DCI Davenport has been granted a week's leave. He'll be back next Monday, all being well. His two babies…"

"...two babies, Sir?" said Penny in surprise. "We thought we'd heard wrongly."

"Yes there were twins. They've been baptised in the hospital and the baby boy has a condition called myotubular myopathy. Apparently, Fiona has a gene which has a 50% chance of affecting a baby. It's not very hopeful I'm afraid. He asked me to tell you this. He knows you'll all be concerned but at the moment he doesn't want any phone calls."

Fairchild squared his shoulders then he smiled. "Come on then, Team."

Frank turned a laugh into a cough.

"It's OK Selby, I won't rub my ear. Just thought calling you Team might put you at ease."

Frank went a bit pink: the others laughed.

"What do you have so far? Sergeant Din, give me a summary please. Pretend I know nothing and start at the very beginning. The rest of you chip in if The Big Boss forgets anything."

Penny, Frank and Fraser sat down, pulling their seats into a half circle. Fairchild perched on a desk. Salma remained standing, facing them all.

"Well, Sir. A man called Arthur Cunningham died at the Dental Hospital on Tuesday 26th of February. Martin Jamieson reported that there was insulin found in the bloodstream and we found out the next day...."

".... His sons didn't know if their dad was diabetic so we'd to wait till Mr Cunningham's ex-wife was contacted in Canada..."

Penny's voice tailed off.

"Sorry I got carried away...."

"It's OK, Constable Price. If I want any details, I'll ask but Sergeant Din is, I think just trying to give me the gist of things,"

Solomon managed to keep the laughter out of his voice.

"The wife said that he wasn't diabetic when she was with him and gave us the name of his doctor. The Doctor, Javed Ahmed, was able to tell us that Mr Cunningham was not diabetic. That was when DCI Davenport was given the death as a murder to be investigated," Salma continued.

"Sum up his family for me, Sergeant."

"He has three sons, all living in Glasgow, Sir. Thomas, Quentin and Oliver Cunningham, none of them close to their father. The oldest son, Thomas, gave us permission to open a locked box we found at the dead man's home and we've looked through bank statements and an address book."

Salma looked at the others.

"Anything I've missed?"

"No, Salma but…I mean Sergeant," said Fraser

"Please, Sir I asked the others to keep calling me Salma. I'm only acting chief here for a wee while, hopefully. Is that OK?"

"Of course it is. I'll use all your first names too if that's OK, Carry on Fraser, lad."

Fraser, looking a bit pink in the face, continued.

"I got his dentist's name from the Dental Hospital, Sir, but I haven't been there yet, I'm afraid."

"Anything else of interest from his GP, Salma?"

"Just that he'd asked for and been given Viagra and we checked the dates and that was after his divorce."

"Anything of interest from the bank statements and address book?"

"Just that he hadn't many friends and he obviously burned or shredded statements after a year. There were no large amounts being paid out regularly," said Penny. "Or paid in."

"What about the locked box?"

"I opened it in front of his son, Thomas, this afternoon," said Penny. "There was an engagement ring with no inscription. Thomas Cunningham offered to phone his mother in Canada and ask if she still had her ring. Because of the time difference, he'll ring us tomorrow. There was a newspaper cutting…oh and golf tees from Harrods, Sir."

"Anything else, Team?"

Solomon Fairchild looked round them all.

"We're pretty sure we've found Arthur Cunningham's car," said Salma.

"What about the newspaper cutting? "

"It was from the Hatches and Dispatches page of a paper, Sir, "said Fraser. "It's not from The Herald and from the addresses mentioned, I would say it came from a local paper but not The Extra. Maybe from East Ren or Ayrshire."

"Date?"

"No, Sir, the article was in the bottom half of the page."

"Well, Salma. What do you recommend is done now?" asked Fairchild.

"Well, Sir, I think we have to ask his dentist what he was like, find out where he worked. The dentist might know. Folk tend to talk to their dentist about all sorts of things. Should we try to work out which bus he took into town if the stranded car is indeed his? Interview the passengers, see if he was followed to the dental hospital…."

Salma tailed off.

"Yes. You have so little to go on to get an idea of what this man was like." said Fairchild.

"Sir, we do know that he wasn't' liked by his sons," said Penny.

"But they hadn't had anything to do with him for ages, Pen," said Frank. "He might have changed."

"We'll have to study the births and two deaths in the paper, Sir," continued Salma

"Ok, Team, "I'll leave you to get on with things. Check the ring. See if you can find out where it was bought. Try to find out as much as you can about the dead man. Yes, interview bus passengers on the off chance that the man was followed to the Dental Hospital….

"… but would someone just happen to have insulin on them," Penny butted in.

Fairchild laughed.

"It does sound unlikely, Penny, but maybe diabetics *do* carry insulin all the time. That's something worth checking up on. Who would have access to insulin?"

Fairchild got up to leave.

"I'll keep you up to date with any news I get from the Queen Elizabeth Hospital."

CHAPTER 13

All the team were on time on Tuesday morning. Salma asked at the desk if Mr Fairchild had left any message about DCI Davenport but there was nothing. She went sombrely up to the DS's room and, deciding to cheer the rest up, went across to Davenport's room and made them all coffee. When she entered the room where they were all sitting, Fraser and Frank looked as despondent as she felt. She made them laugh by pulling on her ear lobe and saying, "Come on, slackers. Drink this and then get to work." Fraser told them that on the way home the previous evening, he had stopped off at the dentist whose name he had been given at the Dental Hospital.

"It's a very up to date place in Pollokshaws...well maybe it's Shawlands. I'm never too sure where the boundaries are and Pollokshaws East Station, right next door to the dentist, is, I think, in Shawlands whereas Shawlands Station is in Pollokshaws! It was a terrible place to park, under the railway bridge. I had to clean my car to get rid of all the pigeon droppings!"

"What news did you get there?" asked Penny, impatient as ever. "Did the pigeons bring any messages?"

She laughed.

Salma, looking at her friend, wondered why Penny wasn't as glum as the others

"Well, I spoke to his dentist, Kirsty, and she said he wasn't a nice guy. He thought that money talked and expected special treatment though Kirsty is a National Health dentist in what's mainly a private practice. She said he'd been really scared of dentists till he came to her for an emergency extraction some years ago. He didn't want to change dentist for that reason. He'd been having trouble with a wisdom tooth for some time but wouldn't have anything done till it got a lot worse and she persuaded him to have it removed at the dental hospital as it was impacted."

"What's that?" asked Frank.

"I think it's when the tooth doesn't come through the gum: kind of grows sideways," replied Fraser. "At the dental hospital, they slit the gum. Erin's Mum had one done but hers started bleeding after the numbness wore off and she had to go back and have the stitches taken out and the blood sucked out and the hole re-stitched. "

He laughed.

"Apparently there was a haematoma, a blood sack, Frank, and no, I don't know all about it, I've just got a good memory. The student who had done her tooth had been doing this for weeks and he had two haematomas on the same day. Erin's Mum thought she was dying. She thought he said haemophilia and she forgot that only men could have that."

"Very interesting, Hewitt," said Salma, dryly, "but back to the point. Could she tell you anything else about Arthur Cunningham, apart from him being afraid of dentists and thinking that money should talk?"

"Well, he did tell her about his marriage break up. Blamed his wife for not being interesting anymore! She said he hinted that he could get any woman he wanted but she didn't encourage him to expand on that."

"I wonder if the ring was meant for wife number two and if so did she turn him down or who called off the wedding?" wondered Penny out loud. "I can't see him buying a ring without making sure first!"

"Could there have been a wedding and another woman left him?" said Frank.

"Then he'd also have kept the wedding ring, surely," said Salma and surely he'd have informed his sons…"

"…and his ex-wife," added Frank.

"Was he divorced from his first wife? Remember we're not sure of this. We found a Carol Paterson's address in the address book, remember and thought that she'd changed back to her maiden name?" said Frank,

Salma wrote in her notebook, "Remember to ask the sons if parents were divorced."

"Maybe he didn't tell his sons about a new woman, He sounds the type of man who would do what he wanted. He wasn't close to his sons and probably thought there was no reason to tell his ex-wife," volunteered Frank.

"Why would he keep the ring?" asked Penny.

"Maybe in case he found a replacement!" said Fraser, cynically.

"Surely he wouldn't cold-bloodedly not have an inscription in case he needed it for another woman!"

Penny sounded indignant but could not hide the sparkle in her eye. Salma decided to ask her why she was so happy today, especially having been called into work at a weekend and with the worry about their bosses and their new baby.

"I thought to ask the receptionist about him too and she just made a face and said she was glad that all their patients weren't as rude as he was," said Fraser.

"Well," said Salma. "We'll have to try some jewellers' shops to see if we can find out where he got the ring, in the hope that perhaps he took the woman with him. I don't think many men buy the ring as a surprise nowadays and Arthur Cunningham wasn't the type of man to go in for surprises, I don't think...."

"...no but I don't think he's the type of man who would consider that his lady friend might want a choice!" said, Penny.

"Right, Frank. You and Fraser get off to the Argyll Arcade. It's the most likely place for a Glasgow man to buy a ring. Take the ring, of course and even if it isn't one of their rings, they might recognise something about it and they have special magnifying glasses to inspect it with."

Frank and Fraser went off and Salma turned to her friend.

"Penny. Is something happening that I don't know about? You seem a bit happy for someone in the middle of a murder enquiry with possibly no Saturdays off!"

"Well, I rang Gordon to cancel our day together on Saturday, well our afternoon only as he was working in the morning, and he was unusually annoyed. He said he had something special he wanted to ask me. Oh, Salma, I think he's going to propose. When we were down near Tarbert a few weeks ago, he came up behind me on one of the beautiful beaches and I felt something in the air but nothing happened. We were going to go back there on Saturday."

"I take it from the sparkle in your eyes that you'll say, yes," Salma said, grinning.

"You bet."

"So what now?"

"Well, we're going to go on Sunday instead. Can I have at least Sunday afternoon off?"

"Well, the boss usually gives us the afternoon off. Doesn't he say all work and no play doesn't make for a happy team? I'll stick to that if he isn't back."

"Penny hugged her friend.

"Right, well, I want you to find out which bus or train Arthur Cunningham would have taken. I think we can assume that it is his only car in his driveway. There's been no report of an abandoned car in the area. When you find out the likely time of the bus, draft an article for the papers asking anyone on that bus to come forward...you know the format. Keep your mind off Gordon and Sunday will come quicker."

Salma pickled up the tray with the empty coffee cups and left the room. She was going to ring Dr Ahmed and ask if people on insulin were likely to carry it around with them or keep it at home.

CHAPTER 14

Penny had just drafted an announcement for the next day's papers when the phone rang. Fraser answered it. She heard him say, "Thanks for telling us that, Mr Cunningham...sorry, Tom...if you get any other bits of information, please let us know."

"I guess that was Tom Cunningham," said Penny. "He asked me not to call him Mr Cunningham."

"Yes, he said that was his father's name and as he is a writer and doesn't have staff, he's managed to be called Tom most of his life. Penny, what did you call your father?"

"Daddy when I was wee, then Dad. Why?"

"Me too and I'm sure I've heard you say, Mum and Dad, Frank. It's just another example of how estranged Tom was from his father that he always calls him Father. Very Victorian."

"Yes or very respectful towards him which he isn't! What did Tom Cunningham want?"

"He said that his father's neighbour, apparently a friendly old guy, spoke to him over the hedge last night when he was over at the house and said he'd given Arthur a lift on the day he went to the Dental Hospital. He was about to pass him at the bus stop but stopped and asked where he was going. Arthur had just read the bus timetable at the bus stop and said he'd just missed the 4A. Mr Gideon, the neighbour, offered to run him down to Clarkston where he could get the 6 bus and Arthur accepted though it gave him a longer walk at the other end, the 6 bus going up near the Royal Theatre whereas the 4 goes along the street parallel to Sauchiehall Street where the Dental Hospital is. Oh, Tom also said that his mother still had her wedding and engagement rings. She told him that his father asked for them back and she refused to give them to him. He was so unpleasant when she left that she came away with less than she should have, just to get it over with, she told Tom. He was angry with himself that he and his brothers hadn't taken much interest, just being glad that their mother was escaping from what they were sure must have been an unhappy marriage."

Fraser hit the heel of his hand against his forehead.

"Sorry, Boss. I forgot to ask if his parents were divorced."

"Don't worry. We can soon ask them."

Penny went back to her newspaper article and amended it to ask for anyone travelling on the 6 bus into town on the relevant day to come forward. She had just finished when Salma appeared to tell them that she had rung the surgery, but had been told that that Dr Ahmed was extremely busy. She would have to wait until next day to contact him.

The phone rang again. Frank answered it this time.

"Hi, Mr...sorry,..Tom. What can I do for you? No don't be silly, you're not being a pest...what? Fine. Oh, Tom were your parents divorced or just separated?"

He listened then rang off.

"Apparently when the three sons met a few evenings ago, someone remembered that their mother had mentioned pilfering of petty cash in the bank. A friend of hers had written to her about it. Tom said that Q, his name for Quentin, brought it up and he, Tom, wondered if the police were called in and he..."

"...or the person lost their job and bore a grudge," finished off Penny, never one to stand on ceremony and famous for finishing off other people's conversations.

"I suppose the bank would have kept a record of that," mused Salma. "Fraser, get on to that but first check with Tom Cunningham that it was the same bank as the one his father was manager of when he died. Frank, were they divorced?"

"He doesn't think so."

Fraser picked up the phone. Penny helped Salma carry the dirty coffee cups up the corridor to the little toilet there, where they washed the cups and replaced them in Davenport's room. Penny contacted Quentin Cunningham, the minister, who agreed to be at home that afternoon. The other two sons were also free.

Fraser put down the phone and told them that Arthur Cunningham was manager of the same bank he had been in when the boys were still at home. It was not a large branch but Arthur had failed to move on after his wife left him.

"Tom thought that his mother had been an asset in his father's early career, being the daughter of an official high up in the same bank but that after she left him he became persona non-grata in banking circles. So I'll get along there this afternoon. Ok Boss?"

Salma grinned.

"Yes please, Fraser. Get off to the bank this afternoon after you and Frank have checked out the jewellers. I'll speak to the GP tomorrow. Might be better to talk face to face with him. I can now hold the fort here and get names of bus passengers who contact us, hopefully. Frank, later, I think you and Penny should make a start on interviewing the other two sons. I think we should speak to them and the daughters-in-law, try to build up a picture of the murdered man."

"OK Boss. The sons are all available this afternoon," said Penny,

CHAPTER 15

Frank had driven himself and Fraser into town and they had parked in North Street carpark and walked from there through to Argyll Street and the arcade which housed many jewellers' shops. Frank had grumbled that it was like looking for a needle in a haystack but Fraser, sensibly, had reminded his colleague that a lot of police work was slog and that sometime it yielded results. Before going into town, they had decided to take one side of the arcade each, each unknown to the other, thinking that a by- product of the visit could be to find out prices of engagement rings for their respective girlfriends. Frank had photographed the ring kept by Arthur Cunningham, for Fraser and himself, keeping the real item in his inside pocket should they need it. Frank, typically, had seen it as casing the joints: Fraser as reconnoitering.

It was a slow process. Some of the more well-known shops kept a record of all items sold, whereas others only did this for expensive pieces.

It was Frank who got lucky as in his fifth shop, the young assistant pointed him in the direction of an older woman, saying rather nastily that he should talk to *Miss*.,.she emphasised this word…Kelly, as she got misty-eyed over every engagement ring sold and had been here since the 1990s.

Miss Kelly was busy so Frank had the chance to study some trays of engagement rings. He had started saving about a year ago and he reckoned that he had enough for one a ring on one of the cheaper trays. His girlfriend, Sue, wasn't a snob where jewellery was concerned or a snob at all really, so he was sure that she would be happy with one of the rings he saw there. It was his parents, mainly his dad he was concerned about. His dad was proudly Catholic in spite of seldom going to church and although he seemed to like Sue, Frank was not sure how he would react to his son marrying, not just a Protestant but a practising Protestant whom he knew would want to be married in her own church.

He noticed that Miss Kelly had finished with her customer and he walked over to the counter. He explained his mission and handed over the photograph of the ring.

"One of our cheapest engagement rings. We sold a lot of these to young couples some years back. That particular ring isn't sold now."

"This one would have been sold to an older man, quite a well-off guy," mused Frank out loud.

"I'd have thought that an older man with money would have paid for something more valuable for his fiancée," said Miss Kelly.

"Well," said Frank, "The man in question wasn't a particularly likeable man. He'd already been married and had three sons. Maybe he didn't want to spend a lot second time around."

"Or maybe the new woman was holding out for a ring before…granting him any favours," Miss Kelly ventured, going a bit pink in the cheeks. She coughed.

Feeling that once again he was getting nowhere, Frank thanked her for her trouble and was just leaving when she called him back.
"There was one man I remember because he was so horrible. Usually couples are so happy but he was definitely not pleased to be buying this ring. The woman was a lot younger than he was…just a young girl I remember but quite determined all the same. She saw a ring she liked but he refused to pay for that one, insisting that if she 'had' to have a ring she could choose one from the tray he had pointed out. It was one of our cheapest rings, like that one in your photograph. I think it was one of those cases I mentioned where the girl was refusing her favours till the man proved his intentions of marrying her."
Frank took the ring out of his pocket and handed it to her. She inspected it closely then took out her eyeglass and inspected it again.
"I couldn't swear to it but it looks like one of ours from years ago."
Frank asked her if she could describe the couple but all she could remember was that the man had quite greasy dark hair and was quite fat whereas the girl was fresh faced and dark-haired.
"It was ages ago, maybe five, six years ago."

Once again Frank thanked her and left the shop, almost bumping into Fraser.

"I think I might have found the right shop, Fraser but all it tells us is that it was an engagement ring for a younger woman and the man, if it was Arthur Cunningham, was reluctant to spend much on the ring. The assistant felt that the woman was refusing to have sex with him until the ring was on her finger. Refusing her favours was the way the old biddy put it," laughed Frank. "So if he had his way with her after buying the ring, he could have cast her off…sorry, I'm sounding like a Kirsty Austen heroine…when he tired of her."

"Having probably never intended to marry her in the first place….and who's Kirsty Thingummy?"

"She wrote "Pride and Prejudice. Ask Sue about it. It's a favourite book, for women especially. Why would Arthur end up keeping the ring?"

"If he's the mean old sod, the assistant thought he was, he probably kept it in case he had to con another young woman," said Frank, grimacing. "Let's get back to the station. Don't think we'll strike it any luckier than I did and you've to get to the bank before it closes."

"And you've to go with Penny to see the other two sons."

Back at the station, Frank reported to Salma who, like him, seemed to think that they had found out the reason for the ring in the box. Frank went back down the corridor where he found Fraser telling Penny their news. The three left the station together, Penny and Frank for their meetings with the three sons and Fraser to go to the bank. Not long after they had gone, Salma had a call from Dr Ahmed, annoyed that his receptionist had told Salma to wait till the next day and asking her to come along as soon as suited her.

CHAPTER 16

Charles and Fiona stood in silence. Charles held his new baby daughter in one arm, the other was round Fiona's waist, as they stood and looked down at their little son in his incubator. Fiona held one of Kenneth's tiny fingers gently. Against all odds, the little lad had survived his first few days but now they had to leave him there and go home. Mindful of what the chaplain had said, Pippa had been told everything. Charles had then explained that for the next few days it would be a great help if she stayed with one of her school friends as this would free him from the school run and this, plus some time off work, would mean that he could support Fiona with their new daughter and visits to and from the hospital, At the weekend, he told Pippa, she would be a great help to both of them and her new baby sister.

Pippa had nodded wisely and then rung up Kerry who lived in Shawlands, to ask if she could stay for a few days. Charles would take her there with a small suitcase and explain the situation to Kerry's mother.

"Come on, Love, he said now to his wife and after one last gentle squeeze of Kenneth's finger, Fiona stood back and let Charles touch his son, gently. They had taken the joint decision to both return home though the hospital had facilities for a parent to stay. Fiona had Kathleen Fiona to care for and they knew that their little son would be well looked after.

It was a sad homecoming. The little spare bedroom had been decorated for one healthy baby, in shades of lemon and white. Charles had had time to read about his son's condition and knew that, should he come home, he would need his own room to keep him as free as possible from infections. This would mean adding an extension to this house or a move to a larger one. They were fortunate to have the money from their sale of Fiona's flat in Shawlands but it would be a difficult decision to make as either choice would mean disruption at a time when they could do without more stress. Fiona fed Kathleen and the little girl fell asleep almost immediately. Charles had made them a cup of tea and they sat together at the kitchen table while they drank it.

"Well," said Fiona, ruefully, "I guess one decision's been made for us. I won't be going back to work in the foreseeable future."

"My gut reaction, Love, is for both of us to leave if Kenneth comes home. Oh I don't mean I would give up working, just that I would leave my present post. We could move to a larger house, perhaps in the country but within driving distance of a hospital. I could get a transfer to somewhere where the job is less demanding of my time and energy."

"What about Pippa's schooling, Charles?" asked Fiona." Would she not hate to move school? She's just got settled in."

"Easier for her to move after first year, than later but we'd have to discuss it with her, of course, though she can't dictate what we choose to do and we're all having to make decisions we'd rather not make."

"And if Kenneth doesn't...make it? What then?"

"Well we'll have a bigger house than we need but that wouldn't be a disaster.

Being practical, Love, it's better to buy and sell a house in spring or summer so why don't we wait until, say, May and if he's still with us then we move. What do you say to that?"

"That's a good idea, Charles. It would maybe be better to be away from our old lives, start completely afresh but neither of us could face any upheaval right now."

Fiona stood up and coming round the little table, gave Charles a hug which he returned gladly.

Meanwhile, Pippa was at school, surrounded by her friends who were agog to know why she had been taken out of class the previous day. Kerry had told Hazel at the end of the day. Pippa was solemn. Her usual cheery face looked anxious. "My new wee brother has a serious illness, called myotubular myn...myopathy...I think I've got that right. He might die soon and even if he lives, he'll be an invalid though Dad said he'd heard of a new treatment that's being tried on Labrador puppies!" she added excitedly.

As the bell rang at that juncture for the last period of the day, they had to rush to their respective classrooms, Pippa and Kerry to History and Hazel and her friend to English. As her father was at the school gate to usher Pippa into the car, no one got another chance to ask questions.

Questions were what Pippa flung at her Dad on the way home to Newton Mearns. She hadn't concentrated very much in lessons that day and the teachers who had been told of the situation had been lenient with her lack of concentration so she had thought a lot and had a lot to ask.

"Is Kenneth still in hospital?"

"Will Kathleen sleep in your room or in her own room?"

"Can I help bath her?"

"Woah, Pet…give me a chance to answer! Kenneth is still in hospital. Fiona could have stayed with him as there are beds for mums and dads but she started to breastfeed Kathleen…"

"…. Yes, Fiona told me she wanted to breastfeed the baby when we thought that there was only one baby. She said it helped the baby to not get germs…sorry Dad, go on."

"You are so like Penny Price, Pippa. She keeps butting in," laughed Charles, realising as he did so that he hadn't laughed for some time. "Kathleen is going into her own room right from the start. We'll have to try hard not to mollycoddle or spoil her because of Kenneth's illness and yes, you can…may… help to bath her, at the weekend when you come home. Now when we get home, get your night things and change of school shirt and underwear to take to Kerry's."

"Why did you change 'can' to 'may', Dad?" Mr Snedden told us to say, 'May I', not 'Can I', but I don't think he told us why."

"I'm sure he would tell you: you were probably dreaming. If you say, "Can I?" it means, "Am I able to" so if you say, "Can I help to bath Susan, you are meaning, are you able to do it and of course you are…it's not a hard job."

"So if I say, "May I?" am I asking if I am allowed to do it?"

"That's right, Pet."

Charles stopped at the local shops, having realised that they were running out of milk and bread. They had been so concerned about leaving Kenneth and about having everything Kathleen needed, that they had forgotten about themselves.

Ten minutes later, he pulled into the driveway and Pippa quickly unfastened her seat belt and was inside the house before Charles could warn her to be careful about what she said to Fiona. He need not have worried.

"Hi Fiona. It's great that you're back home. Where's Kathleen? Can I go and see her or rather *may* I go and see her before Dad takes me to Kerry's"

On being told that she could but not to wake her if she was asleep, Pippa was up the stair like a streak of lightning. She was so normal that even Fiona was noticeably relaxed when Charles met her in the hallway. The discussion about their future could wait.

CHAPTER 17

It was a busy afternoon for the team. Fraser went to the bank where the dead man had been manager. He was ushered into a room where he was offered tea of coffee by the assistant manager, Neil Kerr. After thanking the smiling young woman who brought the tea and assuring her that he could pour out by himself, the man sat down across the desk from Fraser.

"I was expecting this visit, Constable," he said. "How can I help you?"

"We'd like to find out all we can about Arthur Cunningham and also a wee bit about the person who was sacked because of pilfering some time ago," replied Fraser.

Neil Kerr looked embarrassed.

"It's not good to speak ill of the dead, I believe but Mr. Cunningham…I had to call him this all the time except if we met socially.

He smiled.

"He said when I first arrived here, "You will call me Mr. Cunningham at work but if we go for a drink you can say, 'What can I get you, Arthur?'. Yes, Constable, those were his very words."

Fraser had looked skeptical on hearing this exchange. It had sounded almost Victorian.

"I'm getting a picture of him already, Sir. I guess he was difficult to work for."

"He was indeed. He got very angry when mistakes were made and of course nervous staff make more mistakes. There were lots of tears shed among female staff."

"Was the pilfering episode a mistake or a real theft?"

Neil Kerr looked uncomfortable.

"It was soon after I arrived here, a few years ago. Jenny Flynn was about twenty-three and had just recently been appointed as a teller. I found her efficient and willing but around Mr. Cunningham she was a nervous wreck. It seemed to me as if he enjoyed getting her uptight. Then things changed and he started kind of flirting with her though not in a nice way. He would say nice things but sarcastically. I once heard him tell her that he wished she would apply to her work as well as she applied her make up. Do you know he then actually pinched her bottom and I was expecting her to file a complaint about sexual harassment but she never did. Maybe too scared to, the way bullied kids are scared to report the bully."

"Do you think they ever became an item...lovers?" asked Fraser.

Kerr spluttered.

"Gosh, I wouldn't think so. I would have said she would hate him rather than love him."

"But perhaps the bully bullied her into a relationship of sorts," continued Fraser.

Kerr thought for a minute.

"It was odd that he didn't get the police in over the theft, so maybe they were or had been an item. I wonder. Maybe Jean Anderson would know. They weren't exactly friends but they sometimes took their lunch break together. Will I call Jean in, Constable? You're lucky. This is Jean's last week with us. She's getting married to another teller here and the bank still won't let married couples work in the same bank."

Fraser said he would like to talk with Jean and Neil Kerr left, arriving back shortly with a small fair-haired woman, in her early thirties, Fraser estimated.

"I've told Jean you'd like a word about Jenny. I'll leave the two of you alone while I take Jean's place at the counter."

He smiled at them and left.

"He's so nice," volunteered Jean. "You wouldn't catch Mr. Cunningham doing that. Sorry, I know he's dead but I can't pretend to have liked him."

She tossed back her shoulder-length hair and looked at Fraser as if daring him to criticise her.

He laughed.

"Honest people make my job a lot easier, Miss Anderson. Now perhaps you can tell me honestly if there was anything going on between Mr. Cunningham and Jenny."

"I asked Jenny if there was, I asked her a number of times but she always denied it. Yet he flirted with her. God it was horrible to see him do that. Like a predator playing with his prey, I always thought. She would give nervous giggles and flush up."

"How did she come to be accused of stealing from the bank, Miss Anderson?"

"Well that was odd too. She'd kind of started standing up for herself, almost fighting back. I thought of it as the worm turning. I was pleased. Then one day, it was late night Thursday, and we'd finished cashing up and were getting our coats on. Mr. Cunningham came storming out of his office waving a piece of paper and saying that something didn't add up. He made us all wait. I remember that Mr. Kerr tried to take the paper from him but he wouldn't let him have it. He said that there was a fifty pounds' discrepancy in Jenny's figures. She went so white I thought she was going to faint. He grabbed her handbag, unzipped it and took out her purse. There was a red fifty-pound note in it. I remember thinking I'd never had one of those in my purse in my life but Sir, Jenny would never have stolen anything and surely if she had been able to steal, she'd have had the common sense to take the money in small notes or hide the money somewhere!"

"What happened then?" asked Fraser.

"Mr. Cunningham told her to leave and never come back!"

"So he didn't get the police?"

"No. I remember thinking it wasn't like him."

"Did Jenny not fight her corner?"

"No, she kind of looked, I don't know, shocked but not shocked. I thought later that she looked almost a mixture of relieved and horrified. I thought maybe she was grateful to him for not getting the police then I wondered if she just thought that there was no point in trying to fight against him. She ran out, Sir, and I never saw her again."

Fraser thanked Jean Anderson and asked her to tell her boss that he would like to see him again. Minutes later Neil Kerr came back into the office and Fraser asked him to give his side of the £50 incident.

Kerr looked uncomfortable.

"I didn't think that Jean was a thief but the money *was* found in her bag and she didn't deny it. I might have argued her case but it seemed as if Mr. Cunningham had been more than generous, letting her go without getting the police in."

"Was that the kind of thing you expected from him?"

"Well….no…but if I'd pulled him up on it, it would have meant Jean being accused of theft and I didn't want that."

"So if he'd set her up, he won?"

Kerr looked miserable.

"Yes I suppose so, if you put it like that."

"Did you ever see Jenny again?" Frank asked.

"No, I didn't. I don't suppose she'd want to see any of us after what happened."

"So Jenny Flynn could have been the woman Cunningham was buying the ring for. Bought the cheapest one he could find, told her not to wear it to work and probably suggested that other staff might be jealous. Broke the affair off when he got bored, took back the ring and got rid of her in case she told others about it."

Penny's eyes sparkled as they often did when she was coming out with a scenario she had concocted.

Penny had gone with Frank to visit Quentin Cunningham at his manse in Giffnock. The first thing he said as he ushered them into his study, lined with books and with a desk covered in papers, was, "Please call me Q. I loathe my name. Really should have it changed by deed poll. I'd like to ask my congregation to call me by my first name but I hate it so much, I just let them call me Mr. Cunningham which in turn makes me think of my father so I can't win. Sorry, I'm babbling. Please sit down."

Penny and Frank sat down on two strategically placed chairs in front of the minister's huge, oak desk. He lifted one lot of papers and threw them into the nearby waste bin.

"Bang goes one attempt at a sermon," he laughed. "I'm supposed to be talking about God the Father on Sunday but it's the one thing I find hard to do, talk about God being like a kindly father. I never had that type of father and I always think of the child who when asked why God was like her father, said, 'Is it because he's not here?' Sorry, rambling again. Guess I'm nervous, " he said, with disarming honesty.

"Please don't be, Sir, sorry, Q," said Penny. "We just want to get a picture of your father and try to find out why anyone would want to kill him."
Q laughed.
"Well, you can start with us three boys, except that we wouldn't have taken it that far. Just didn't want him in our lives. 'Thou shalt not kill', is my motto and I think you'll find out that I'm quite Buddhist about not killing anyTHING not just anyONE. I can even claim never to have killed a wasp as my children will tell you with disgust....."
".... which is what a friend of mine was like," laughed his wife coming into the room in time to catch her husband's remark.
"She told the kids in her class at school when a wasp came in the classroom window and panicked them all, that a wasp wouldn't sting unless it felt it was being attacked so they should sit quietly instead of flapping at it. She said that she swore the dratted insect heard her as it made a beeline, oops, excuse the dreadful pun, folks, for her and landed on her hand. A wee fellow as the front said, "Miss, it's on your hand. She said that she knew that and was she making a fuss? Then it stung her! The same kid said, "That stung you, didn't it? "
"Yes," she replied, "and am I making a fuss?" She said her hand was throbbing with pain and luckily the bell rang and she stayed smiling till they left. then swore and rushed off to the nurse! Oh, I'm Abigail, Abi. Sorry for interrupting."

Penny and Frank laughed, then Frank said that he was sorry but it was necessary to ask them both where they had been at the time of Arthur Cunningham's murder, reminding them of the time and date.

"I was visiting one of my parishioners, I'm sure, as that's one of my days for visiting. I've got a book I mark off when I've done a visit. I'll go and get it."

He left the room and his wife sat down.

"Mrs. Cunningham, where were you at that time?"

"Abigail, please, I hate Mrs. Cunningham 'cos that's what the congregation call me and I'm either Quentin's wife or Becky's mum, most of the time. Where was I? Probably looking after my youngest daughter, Lizzie who's just three. Round about mid-day on a Wednesday, you said, I'd have taken her to pick up her sister Becky at school. She refuses to have school dinners so I have her here from about 12.30 till 1.20 when I take her back to school. Q tries to get back for lunch then too but sometimes he's delayed with work, either a committee meeting or a visit. Here he comes. He'll be able to tell you exactly where he was that Tuesday. I can't remember if he got home that day for lunch."

Flourishing a notebook, he said, as he came in, "I was with Mrs. Adam. She can't see too well as she has macular degeneration, diagnosed before they found that injections could help at times. Her husband died last year and her son lives down South and only gets up to see her every two months to stock her larder and fridge. She's a lovely old soul: never complains. Sorry, you didn't need to know all that. I remember looking at the clock there and realising that if she wanted me to make a cuppa and share it with her, I'd miss family lunch but she didn't and I got in just after Abby and the girls."

Penny had been scribbling this down and Frank thanked them then asked how they had got on with the dead man. Q, looking a bit sheepish, said that they seldom saw him and Abigail added that her father-in-law had almost severed connections when Q went into the church and then was even more distant when they had married as he blamed her for him "getting religion", as he put it. He'd sent money for Becky at birthdays and Christmas but hadn't started that with their younger daughter, Lizzie, though they had contacted him. He had come to neither christening.

"And he simply posted a cheque, never wrote them birthday or Christmas cards," said Q, rather bitterly.

His wife got up and went to stand beside him, putting her hand, on his shoulder. He smiled up at her.

Penny and Frank got up to leave. Just as they reached the door, Frank remembered to ask if the funeral arrangements had been made and was told that Tom was seeing to that, being the eldest son and also the one with most free time though Oliver who was on leave might be assisting him.

"All I know, Constable, is that I am not officiating. It would be hypocritical and also very hard to find good things to say about him!"

Penny, impulsive as ever, asked what kind of father Arthur had been when the boys were growing up.

"I'd have welcomed the absentee father of the child I mentioned earlier but he had few friends so he was too much there. He delighted in punishing us for every trivial little misdemeanor but I was luckier than the other two as when they began to grow up, they protected me from him."

"What about your mother?" asked Frank. "Did he abuse her too?"

"I've thought about that but I'm sure he didn't. She was quiet but never seemed scared of him and she went out a lot. She had lots of friends and relations. He kept our beatings till when she was out and we never told her. We were discussing this the other day and we just thought that this was part of family life, till we were older and saw other fathers with their children.

She did leave him eventually, goodness knows what she ever saw in him in the first place but she waited until we were grown up. She hated leaving her grandkids but she got the chance of a home with her sister, in Canada. She's been back a few times and we've been over there a couple of times too."

Penny thanked him for his honesty. They stood up then noticed a family photograph on a table near the door. Penny asked, a bit hesitantly, if they could borrow the photograph to copy.

"It's ok Constable. I know you'll have to check our alibis. You don't need to be embarrassed to ask," said Quentin. He removed the large photograph from its frame and the two constables left.

"I know I've said this before, Penny, but how lucky we both were with our families. I assumed until I was in my teens that every child came from the same kind of background as I did."

"Yes, me too, Frank. My Dad died when I was quite young but I was spoiled with affection from both Mum and Dad."

It didn't take them long to drive to Oliver's house, a modest bungalow in Giffnock. It was Oliver who came to the door and welcomed them in, showing them into what was quite a bare room with only a TV and lounge suite. It was obviously a family room in spite of the almost bare walls which only held one picture, as there were toys and books lying around.

"PC Penny Price and PC Frank Selby, " said Penny, shaking his hand, then going across the room to the settee and glancing at the picture as she went.

"That's your family, Mr. Cunningham?" she asked though she was sure she was right.

"Yes," replied Oliver. "Me, my wife, Pat and our daughters, Laura and Rose. Laura is the eldest. She's 10 and Rose is 8. Excuse the bareness of the room but Pat and I travel wherever my army job takes me and so far there's always been a decent school for the girls so they've come too. I rent a place as I only get home every three years."

They all sat down, Penny on the settee, Frank and Oliver on the matching armchairs.

"So your wife, Pat, doesn't work then?" asked Penny.

"She tries to get temporary jobs wherever we go. I sometimes feel guilty that she gave up her profession. She was a GP in Stirling when I met her. I keep trying to get her to start writing. She's an avid reader and Tom would give her advice, I'm sure."

"Why? Does your brother,Tom, write?" asked Frank, with interest.

"Yes, he does. He's had two books published recently, crime novels. You may have heard of him. He writes under the name of Thomas Hazelton."

"I'm not much of a reader, Sir but of one my colleagues will be interested," replied Frank.

Frank sounded genuinely interested and Penny also made a mental note to ask Tom Cunningham for a signed copy of one of his books. She had been thinking recently of presents to give to her colleagues when she left to get married and this would be a good one for Fraser.

"He's written, "Death Doesn't Smile" and "Death Doesn't Care," said Oliver.

Penny intervened at this point. They still had Tom Cunningham to see again to get his whereabouts on Wednesday last and time was marching on.

"Mr.Cunningham...."

"...Oliver please."

"Oliver, sorry to have to ask this but would you tell us where you were last Tuesday around midday, please."

"Pat and I were out for lunch at 'The White Cart' in Busby. We go there for drinks most Saturday nights when we can get a babysitter for the girls and we decided to have a quiet lunch there. I'm afraid we didn't do anything that would have drawn anyone's attention to us. If I'd known I'd need an alibi for Father's murder, I could have started a fight."

He laughed then apologised.

"Sorry, it's not funny...."

"...what's not funny?" asked a pleasant voice and into the room came a slim, attractive woman in her thirties.

"Me saying I wish I'd started a fight last Wednesday when we were out for lunch, to give me an alibi," said her husband getting up and going to meet her.

"This is Pat, my wife. Sorry I didn't catch your names though you did tell me them."

"PC Penny Price and PC Frank Selby, Sir," said Frank.

"We didn't like Arthur. He came to our wedding because I was a doctor and he went to Tom's because Susan's parents were lawyers but he didn't go to Q's wedding because Abby hadn't gone to university...."

"...and she'd introduced Q to the church scene," added Oliver.

"He was an out and out snob, showed no interest in his grandchildren and after my Mum-in law- left him, we gave up seeing him at all so we weren't interested in him enough to want to get rid of him," finished Pat.

"I hope you don't me asking, Sir but we've noticed that you all call your dad, Father," said Penny.

"Yes, when we weren't calling him Sir. We had to call him Sir if we were taken into his study for a punishment."

"Yes, your younger brother told us about the, 'beatings', he called them," said Penny.

"Q was lucky. By the time he was old enough to have that punishment, Tom had realised that beating your child was not the norm and he told Father he would report him at school."

Frank asked for a recent photograph of the two of them, saying that he would go to The White Cart and see if anyone could verify that they had been there.

On their way to Shawlands to visit Tom Cunningham, Penny voiced what she had been thinking of during their chat to Oliver and Pat, namely that Pat, having been a GP, might have had access to insulin. That and the fact that they seemed to have no witnesses to their lunch in Busby, surely made them possible suspects. Frank, who was driving, had agreed that it was possible but also pointed out that though the couple had maybe had the chance to commit the murder, there was not, as yet, any reason for them to have done so.

Tom came to the door with unkempt hair, looking a bit distracted. He invited them in, explaining that he had been in his study, writing.

"Maybe a bit insensitive to be writing right now but, well it is a murder mystery," he laughed. Seated in the aforesaid study, across a desk that was littered with paper, empty mugs and biscuit wrappers, Tom asked if they had any news for him.

"Well we think that your father might have had a love interest," said Frank.

"A sex interest, you mean," said Tom cynically. "I doubt that my Father ever truly loved anyone except himself."

"That was probably where the ring came from, the one in the wee box," said Penny. "Can you throw any light on that or on the person he fired from the bank," added Frank.

I vaguely remember Mum and him arguing about someone in the bank but I was quite young at the time and I don't remember what it was about. When I was older and thought back to it, I imagined that he'd been having an affair as we all suspected that when we got older. You see, Mum was a strong person. That was probably why he dominated us when she wasn't around and ignored us when she was. Olly and I thought when we were older that he probably chose other women who were submissive."

Penny was scribbling away so it was Frank who broke in: "Sorry,Tom but we're having to ask everyone this question. Where were you on the day of your father's murder, around midday?"

"I knew you'd be asking me this and I was alone, in my study, here, writing. No one to give me an alibi, I'm afraid. Susan was in town, shopping but she was meeting friends for lunch somewhere, so she'll have an alibi."

"Yes but Susan was in town and so not that far from the dental hospital," said Frank as they drove back to the station.

Salma arrived at Dr.Ahmed's surgery..The receptionist apologised when she went to the desk, saying that the Dr had had an emergency house visit to make but had asked that the sergeant be shown into his room and offered refreshments.

Salma thanked the young woman and asked for a coffee. She sat in the room sipping her drink and wondering what the emergency call - out had been. There was a photograph on the desk of a young girl aged about ten or eleven. Daughter? Sister? She imagined Dr Ahmed to be in his middle to late thirties, so it was unlikely to be a sister and if it was a daughter why wasn't there a picture of his wife? She gave a wry grin as, being honest with herself, she had hoped that he was unmarried. It had been a short leap in her dreams to think that he might, just might, have been as interested in her as she was in him. Surely the chemistry she had experienced when in his presence could not have been one-sided!

Salma had had very little experience of men because of her religion and because of her work and the fact that now that she had no parents and was busy caring for her siblings. Her brother having come back to Glasgow to live, had constantly reminded her that it was his place to choose a husband for her and she had opposed this, strongly, reminding him of his carefree life before meeting his Muslim wife some years ago. So far, she had succeeded in telling him that she was a career woman but now she wondered if her ambition to become a DS in the future might be dismissed if a certain handsome doctor with an infectious grin became part of her life.

Mentally she scolded herself for being silly. If it wasn't his daughter in the photograph and he was not married, then he probably had a partner or fiancée.

At this point in her thought, she heard voices outside the door and the doctor came in followed by the receptionist who took the empty cup and left the room. Dr Ahmed smiled at her and apologised for keeping her waiting.

"It was a young patient who is now on the way to the QE hospital maternity unit. She wasn't due to have the baby for another two months but this one is definitely on the way."

His eyes clouded over and the smile wavered.

"I get a bit paranoid over babies and deliveries as my wife died giving birth to my daughter." He picked up the photograph.

"That's her, Serena. She's nine going on nineteen."

He gave his delightful grin.

"Now Sergeant Din, what can I help you with this time?"

Salma grinned back.

"I have a sister, Farah who's the same age and she acts much older than her brother who's twelve. My Mum would be going white with worry but she died quite recently so it's me who'll be aging prematurely!"

"I don't see one white hair in that beautiful black hair of yours," was the reply.

Salma blushed, grateful for her dark skin.

"That's kind of you, Dr. Ahmed."

"True, not kind," he smiled. "Now I suppose we'd both better get back to our jobs. What can I do for you?"

"It's quite a simple thing, really. Would a diabetic person carry insulin around with them?"

"Is that important?"

"Well, yes. If someone was carrying insulin because that was a natural thing, then the murder of Arthur Cunningham could have been unpremeditated but if diabetics don't carry their insulin then someone planned the murder."

"I'm not going to help much, Sergeant Din as diabetics often do carry their insulin pens, if for example they are going out for lunch or dinner but not if they are going to be at home for the next injection. Some diabetic patients don't inject, they just take tablets, Metformin usually."

"So we're not much further forward then. The murder could have been either premeditated or unpremeditated, "said Salma, glumly.

She got to her feet, thanking the doctor for his help. She would have been pleased to have heard Javed Ahmed's musings after the door closed.

"She could have found that out using Google or she could have sent one of her constables. Hm. Wonder if she'd come out with me if I asked her."

The team congregated in the Incident Room late in the afternoon. They already knew about Fraser's findings about Jenny Flynn and Penny's idea that she could have been engaged to Arthur Cunningham and now Penny and Frank told the others that Quentin Cunningham and his wife seemed to have water tight alibis for the day of the murder.

"He was quite bitter about his father, seldom saw him and told us of the punishments given by him to his three sons. Oddly though, he didn't think his father abused their mother," finished Penny

"Oliver and his wife can only alibi each other," said Frank. "Unless someone at the pub or restaurant they were at recognises them from the photo you will no doubt want me to take there, Boss."

Salma laughed and it was Penny's turn to wonder why her friend looked so happy.

"Got it in one, Frank. Could you do that on your way home tonight?"

"It's not on my way home but for you, anything," said Frank in a mock subservient voice.

"What about Tom Cunningham? Did you manage to see him as well?" asked Fraser.

"Yes. He hasn't got an alibi, was at home writing and although his wife, Susan has friends to vouch for her at lunchtime, she was in town so not too far from the dental hospital," said Penny. "I hope it's not another Orient Express case and they were all six involved," laughed Fraser and on that note, he and Frank left for home.

Penny waited while Salma put on her jacket and then asked her why she looked so happy.

Salma looking a bit shamefaced said that she had been to visit Dr. Ahmed.

"He's so nice, Penny."

"Salma Din, do you fancy him?" demanded Penny.

"I think I do, Penny and although he's got a young daughter, he hasn't got a wife as she died giving birth to the daughter. But, how on earth am I going to get to know him? Any ideas?"

Penny promised to give the problem her best attention and, laughing, they went out together.

CHAPTER 18

"Elspeth, you were at the Dental Hospital when that man died suddenly, weren't you?"
Elspeth's husband, Peter, had had to shout this at her, over the sound of their new washing machine. They had been having a bad time with this new machine. The first time they had tried the drying facility, one of the reasons they had bought it, having moved to a flat with no washing green, it had turned out clothes almost too hot to touch and Peter's favourite shirt now had what Elspeth feared would be permanent creases. The second time she had put well-washed dark red pillowcases in with two of her husband's shirts and dye had come out all over the shirts. Concentrating this time, she had not heard him call though to her.
"Elspeth, have you gone deaf, dear?"
Peter was in the kitchen now and repeated his question.
"Yes. Remember that I looked in The Daily Mail the next day and it said that there had been a mysterious death, probably due to someone having been given too much anaesthetic. I didn't think that could happen in a tooth operation. We read later that the man was thought to have been killed…"
"…shut up, woman and listen for once."
Peter's indulgent grin robbed his words of any nastiness. He waved that day's Herald at her.

"The police are asking for anyone travelling on the 6 bus into town that January day to come forward. Did you get the 4 or the 6 that day?"

"The 6. Is there a 'phone number to ring?"

"Yes. Here it is... 649 2315...you've to ask for a Sergeant Din or anyone in her section of the police station. Obviously, the police suspect foul play."

Thus it was that Elspeth was sitting in the waiting room of a large Glasgow police station, later that day, waiting rather nervously to speak to a police officer. She looked round the rather bare room. There were no magazines on the small table but then maybe it was usually criminals waiting in this room and they didn't cater for them in the way that doctors and dentists catered for their patients. Elspeth who had a rather fertile imagination, pictured herself sitting across a metal table from two police officers, speaking into a tape recorder. Her hands started to get clammy and her throat dry and she remonstrated with herself for being an idiot. She was not guilty of anything except being on a bus!

The door opened and a pretty Asian woman came in.

"Mrs Hamilton?"

"Yes," replied Elspeth.

"Please come with me and would you like a tea of coffee while we talk?"

"Tea, please," said Elspeth gratefully.

She was taken downstairs into a rather sparsely furnished room. There was indeed a tape recorder on a ledge but the policewoman did not switch it on and there was no one else present. Another pretty policewoman brought her a cup of tea and two digestive biscuits and left the room. The first policewoman sat down and motioned to Elspeth to sit across the table from her.

"My name is Salma Din, Sergeant Salma Din and at the moment I am in charge of the investigation into the death of an Arthur Cunningham. Sorry to bring you in here but all the nicer rooms upstairs are occupied with other passengers on the bus that day."

Elspeth tried to recall who had been downstairs on the bus, remembering only that some of them had annoyed her.

"We are wondering if you noticed anyone getting off at the nearest stop to the Dental Hospital," asked Salma.

"Well, I did. I was going to the Dental Hospital myself," replied Elspeth. "A boorish man got off the bus with me, He'd hogged an outside seat near the front and was annoyed when a woman asked him to move to let her sit down. Nearly knocked me over in fact. He was going to the Dental Hospital too. We went up in the same lift."

"Did anyone else get off the bus with you, apart from him?"

"I don't think so," said Elspeth.

"Did anyone go up in the lift with you?"

"Yes, it was quite full. People who worked there, some of them, as they didn't have on outside clothes, a young man and a woman. I think that was all. They all got off before me and that man. We got off on floor 6. He'd gone to the wrong floor as it turned out. I think he was directed to Floor 2 and I saw activity there on the way down after my treatment, as the lift doors opened at that floor and that silly voice said, 'Doors opening Floor 2.' "

Salma thanked her for her time and said she had been very helpful.

"Was he, that man, the one who died?" asked Elspeth.

"I think it's possible."

Salma showed her upstairs and thanked her again.

"It was really exciting, Peter. I think a man I met on the bus was the man who died or was killed. He was a boor, nearly knocked me down while I was getting off the bus."

"Well, he must have annoyed somebody a lot more than you,if he was murdered!" was her husband's dry comment.

The team met in the Incident Room, having each interviewed people who had been on the bus. Apart from Salma, none of their interviewees had got off the bus at the stop nearest to the Dental Hospital.

"My guy seemed to have been too engrossed in his music. He knew he'd been on the bus at the time mentioned but he couldn't even remember how many people were downstairs on the bus with him. He had his earphones round his neck as we spoke," said Fraser.

"The woman I spoke to had to bring her two kids with her," said Frank, disgustedly. "They were with her on the bus that day and if they were as awful then as they were just now, she wouldn't have noticed if someone had been murdered on the blasted bus!"

"The man I spoke to was upstairs. He remembers that the bus passed Watt Brothers because he took the chance to look at the anoraks in the window but he didn't notice who got off near there. He said the top deck was empty apart from himself," was Penny's contribution.

Salma told them about her woman who had probably got off the bus with Arthur Cunningham.

"She described him as a boor which fits him," she commented, "and she doesn't think anyone else got off the bus. She went up in the lift with him at the Dental Hospital and he got off at the same floor as she did, only to find that he'd gone to the wrong floor. Everyone else got off before them so if the murderer was on that lift, he or she must have known where Arthur Cunningham should have been going and simply got off at the right floor and waited his or her chance or…"

"…or the murderer was already in the hospital and knew in advance that Arthur was coming," chipped in Penny.

"Maybe worked there," added Fraser.

"Or maybe it was completely unpremeditated. Someone saw him there, followed him either from the wrong floor or when he got out at the right one," said Salma.

"How would his sons know he had an appointment at the Dental Hospital?" asked Fraser.

"Better check the lists of people who had appointments there that day on the off chance that one of the family was there and..."

Penny stopped.

"Yes, Pen, just happened to have insulin on them," laughed Frank.

At this point Salma decided she should go upstairs to tell Solomon Fairchild what they had found out so far and ask if he had any advice for them. The rest of them, she said, could type up their interviews.

CHAPTER 19

"Well you lot, your easy life has just come to an end!"

The rich tones of Charles Davenport interrupted Salma's briefing session mid -morning.

Penny, Fraser and Frank jumped to their feet and turned round, Penny as usual speaking first:

"Sir, you're back...great ...but Salma's been great too…how are the babies…how is the DS? You weren't supposed to be coming back till Monday."

Davenport grinned. He felt that he had not done that for some time. He'd asked Fairchild for leave and had spent those days going back and forward to the maternity hospital with Fiona, to see his son.

"Penny, you're just like my daughter. Slow down. Firstly Yes, I'm back. Kenny's not being allowed home for a while yet, so Fiona has sent me back till then. I don't want to talk about it yet."

He coughed and changed the subject.

"Yes, I know Salma's been great. Mr Fairchild has kept me informed. Next, Kathleen is fine, even puts up with me changing her nappy and lastly Fiona is doing OK though she does get a bit tearful which is understandable with post-natal blues and worry over Kenny."

He went past them and patted Salma on the back.

"Well done young-un. I've heard how well you've been doing. This spell will look good on your CV."

Salma thanked him. Penny noticed that she looked less enthusiastic than she had thought her friend would be and wondered if a certain Asian doctor was responsible for Salma being less interested in promotion than before.

"Thanks, Sir. Would you like to take over or do you want me to finish summing up? I was just going over what we knew so far and was about to allocate our jobs for today."

Davenport, in answer, sat down next to Fraser. "Just one thing to add, Boss then you go on. I need to be brought up to speed and for today you can give me a job too. Fraser, Mr Fairchild said to tell you that you're to stay with us till the end of this case, Son. OK?"

"Gosh, yes, Sir," Fraser beamed.

Salma summed up what they had suspected, namely that Arthur Cunningham had had a woman for whom he had grudgingly bought a ring but had obviously taken it back or had it thrown back at him." The latter was Penny's suggestion, Sir," said Salma, to laughs from the others.

She continued, saying that Arthur had been killed by a lethal injection of insulin and that people with diabetes sometimes carried insulin with them so the murder could have been either unpremeditated or planned.

As they all knew now, his three sons had no love for him but did not seem to have any reason to murder him. His ex –wife, not divorced, was happily living in Canada. He had had a young woman sacked from the bank for petty theft but had not involved the police so she had no reason for hating him.

Alibis for the day of the murder were summed up. Quentin Cunningham had been visiting an elderly, almost blind parishioner. His wife Abigail had picked her elder daughter up from school and had lunch at home with her two daughters and later her husband. Oliver Cunningham had been having lunch at The White Cart with his wife, Pat and that was about three quarters of an hour from town. Tom Cunningham had been at home, writing and his wife, Susan had been in town meeting friends for lunch and shopping.

"None of the alibis seems to be unshakeable, Sir," Salma told Davenport. "The elderly lady probably would agree with what her minister says, might not be aware of days of the week. Oliver and Pat didn't meet anyone they knew. Tom was alone and his wife could have slipped into the Dental Hospital as she was meeting her friends in town for lunch. I think the only one with a solid alibi is Quentin's wife, unless she left the kids with someone but she wouldn't have had time to get back to get the older one to school.

"She could have got a neighbour to look after them and take the older one to school, "Fraser pointed out.

"I hope this isn't going to be a …what was the film about heaps of people on a train who all stabbed someone to death, the one you mentioned, Brainbox?" said Frank.

"That was "Murder on the Orient Express" one of Pippa's favourite Agatha Christie plots, "said Davenport. "It's not just brainboxes who know that, Selby."

Frank blushed.

"So, I think, Frank, that you should, as you offered before, go to The White Cart and see if by any chance the manageress remembers Oliver and Pat being there."

"Sorry, Salma I meant to take a photograph last night but it went clean out of my head," said Frank.

Davenport put up his hand.

"Please, Boss may I go with Frank. I know Anne, the manageress and I want a word with Frank too, so can kill two birds with one stone."

He noticed Frank looking alarmed.

"Nothing to worry about, Son."

"That's fine, Sir," said Salma. She continued, telling Penny that she could try the neighbours of Quentin and Abigail, see if anyone had been asked to babysit the two girls and perhaps ask the mothers at the school gate at lunchtime if they had seen her.

"Mothers often chat and get to know each other."

"Fraser, you get on well with old ladies, so you go to see…."

Salma glanced down at her notes.

"...Mrs Adam. You'll have to get her address from Quentin Cunningham but he'll be expecting that, I imagine."

"I'll get the names of Susan Cunningham's friends and check times with them. Not much we can do about Tom's lack of alibi but I think if he had murdered his father, he'd have made sure that he had one."

She looked at the others.

"Have I missed anything, team?"

Davenport grinned again.

"Catching my phrase, Sergeant?"

Salma once again was grateful for her darker skin as she blushed, knowing that this salutation had started out as a joke.

Penny rescued her by asking what they could do about the woman sacked from the bank,

"Yes. We can get her last known address from the bank or from Jean Anderson who was her closest friend at the bank. Whoever gets back to the station first could ring the bank. Thanks, Penny. Anything else?"

There being nothing else, they dispersed to their various tasks, Davenport only stopping to once again thank Salma for her sterling work in leading the case. He suggested that she continue being in charge till Monday by which time he would have caught up with the case and she thanked him for his confidence in her.

CHAPTER 20

In spite of Davenport's assurance that there was nothing wrong, Frank was silent on the first part of the drive up to The White Cart in Busby. Then, as if he had just realised that he had been lacking in interest, he asked his Boss how his two new babies were.

Davenport told him of the pleasure that the wee girl, Kathleen, was giving them all, Pippa especially who had taken charge of bath time every evening that weekend. Then face darkening, he went on to tell Frank that Kenneth was still too fragile to come home and that when he did it would have to be to his own room, one kitted out with an oxygen tent and other hospital paraphernalia.

"We've decided to take Kathleen in with us though Pippa offered to share her bedroom. She has to get her full quota of sleep, being a growing girl herself and anyway, Fiona wouldn't have slept well, leaving things to Pippa. If...when...Kenny comes home we might have to move to a bigger house."

Charles had discussed his probable leaving the station with Solomon Fairchild earlier in the day but was not going to give Frank this information ahead of the others hearing about it. Instead he turned the conversation to Frank, asking him if he had applied for promotion recently.

Frank said that he had not.

"Why not, Son?"

"Well, I've not been too successful before, have I Sir?"

"True but you've improved greatly over the last year. You're punctual, tidy and if I'm not mistaken young Penny has finally persuaded you that racism, sexism and all the other isms are wrong, "Davenport laughed.

Frank blushed.

"Well, Sir, it was mainly Penny but I've come to like Salma and my girlfriend is Protestant and I like her, obviously, so I've come to see that it's not only white, Catholic males who are acceptable."

"Right, Son, I'll help you fill out an application form for the post of sergeant, once we get back."

At this point, they had reached The White Cart and Frank pulled off the main road and into the car park. It being only just after 11am, there were plenty of car spaces and he chose one nearest the door as the windscreen was showing little drops of rain which could be the forerunner of heavier rain to come when they were leaving.

"What are you having, Sir. Tea or coffee?"

Frank in the early days had been criticised by his boss for drinking alcohol on duty.

"Coffee for me."

Davenport handed Frank a ten-pound note and Frank went across to the bar where he ordered two coffees and, showing his warrant card, asked if it would be possible to speak to Anne, the manageress whom he had ascertained by phone call before they left the station, would be on duty.

About five minutes later, Anne arrived, a slim dark-haired woman in her thirties. She acknowledged Davenport whom she had met previously when he and Fiona had lunched there. He asked her to sit down which she did.

"Were you here on January 21st, Anne? "asked Charles. "It was a Tuesday. Can you cast your mind back to the folk having lunch then?"

Anne was silent for a minute then she nodded.

"Did you see a couple talking?"

Frank handed over the photograph they had got from Oliver and his wife.

"Maybe this will jog your memory."

"I know them a bit. I've spoken to them once or twice. Sorry, I've remembered that I wasn't there that day but there are the regular Tuesday lunchers, two small groups of men who work locally, I think. Maybe they could help you."

Davenport thanked her. She was about to move away then turned back.

"Has your wife had her baby yet?"

"Yes, twins, last week. Unfortunately, the wee boy isn't well enough to come home yet but the wee girl is home with us."

Leaving it at that, he turned to Frank and Anne left them to finish their drinks.

"So, it could have been the Cunninghams, Sir," said Frank.

"Yes but not conclusively. We could ask if they shared a joke, I suppose."

"He did say he wished he'd started a fight here, Sir," remembered Frank.

At that moment Anne came across to say that one of the men who came in on Wednesdays was sitting in a corner through at the back. Frank went over to the man who was sipping a pint of beer and reading a newspaper. He showed him the photograph and asked him if he had seen this couple having drinks a week ago last Tuesday.

"Sorry, mate. Don't pay much attention to other folk. I don't recognise them but…"

"Yes?"

"I do remember laughter coming from somewhere. I looked over as it's not often you hear folk talking these days, let alone laughing. They've usually all got their noses in iPads or mobile phones. I told my mates there were a couple of lovers in the corner. Cynical really. Why shouldn't a married couple share a joke?

"Anything else?" asked Frank.

"Just that they weren't youngsters or oldies. Sorry. I was with my mates and the corner is a bit dark as you can see…where Anne, the manageress is sitting with a guy."

He was obviously not a perceptive man as he had not noticed that Frank had been with Anne and the 'guy'.

Frank re-joined his boss and told him what had been said.

Davenport thanked Anne and they finished their drinks and went out to the car. As they pulled up at the station, Davenport reminded Frank to get an application form, on the internet.

"Maybe you'll be thinking of marrying your young woman, quite soon and the extra money will come in handy!" he joked.

It was quiet in their part of the large station. Bob, as usual on charge at the desk, told them that the others had all left.

"Get your report on today's visit typed up, Frank. I'll get up the corridor and give Fiona a ring. Bring that application form. When the others get back we'll meet up in the Incident room and see if we're any further forward.

Salma was next to arrive. Both of Susan Cunningham's lunch friends had been out but the husband of one who was at home with a heavy cold and the mother of the other, had promised to get them to phone Salma at the station.

Next came, Fraser. He had visited Mrs Adam, an alert little lady, in spite of her poor eyesight and eighty-seven years. Salma asked them all, Davenport, Frank and Fraser, to keep anything they had to say till Penny was back. Maybe by that time, Salma would have had her phone calls.

"Fiona took wee Kathleen to visit the hospital this morning. There's no change in Kenny, I'm afraid."

Fiona had been very tearful on the phone, blaming herself for her son's condition as she had done so often in the last week. They had been told that myotubular myopathy was due to a faulty gene in the mother, a gene that was 50% likely to cause a baby's defects. Davenport once again had tried to comfort her, saying again that it was not her fault, she had done nothing to give herself that gene. Of course, Fiona knew that but in her bleak moments, common sense deserted her.

When Penny had not arrived back by 12.30, Davenport declared his intention of going home for a short time. The other three went to the canteen where Penny joined then about half an hour later, No one had been at home in one of the houses nearest to the manse and there was no car outside and the elderly man on the other side had been so garrulous that Penny had heard all his complaints about the youngsters of today and the police failure to catch the ones who persistently knocked on his door and ran away and it had been almost half an hour before she had managed to ask about the minister's wife and his children. She had known her questioning would prove fruitless as the old man could not see into the road or into the manse garden because of the heavy shrubbery in his garden and she was right, though the man did seem to like the family who in his opinion, knew how to bring up their children.

When Penny had finished telling the others this part of her investigation, they had all, Penny included, finished their lunch so they made their way back to their part of the station, just beating their boss into the Incident Room.

Salma had told Davenport that she had promised the team the afternoon off the next day and he now confirmed this, telling them that he'd use the afternoon to catch up a bit. Thanks to computers, he could take all their notes home.

Penny slipped up the corridor and, blushing, asked if it would be possible for her to have the whole of Sunday off.

"You see, Sir, I think that Gordon was about to ask me to marry him last week and didn't and he's taking me back to the same place tomorrow and was so upset when I told him I might have to work. He's not usually like that Sir as he's often called out at weekends and…."

Penny looked up from staring at the floor, to see her boss grinning.

"It's ok Miss Price. I was young once too, hard to believe I know. Yes, you can have the whole day off tomorrow and if he doesn't propose you can put in some overtime later on…only joking," he added seeing her embarrassment.

CHAPTER 21

Gordon picked Penny up at her flat in Shawlands at 9 o'clock. He had not told her where they were going but she had a good idea that they would be going back to the Mull of Kintyre. Gordon had holidayed there for many years as a child and had enjoyed taking Penny, on Saturday, two weeks ago, to picturesque Tarbert and then on to Machrihanish beach. He had always stayed there with relatives, his Dad's cousin and her husband and two sons.

True enough, he headed for the Erskine Bridge and, thinking that she should not let him know that she had guessed his intentions, she asked, innocently, where they were going.

"We never made it to Campbelltown the last time, Pen and there's a fabulous place there which has won an award for its collection of whiskies for two years running. It also has a brilliant macaroni cheese on the menu and I know that's a favourite of yours."

Resisting the temptation to tease him by saying that surely they could get that particular dish much nearer to home, Penny contented herself by saying that she had liked the area and was happy to be going back. She added, helpfully.

"Can we go back to that fabulous beach, the one with the surfers on it? You should have brought Rory and Joe. They'd have loved a run there."

"They'd just be in the way today. We might stay for an evening meal…make a day of it."

Penny mentally hugged herself and kept quiet until they were approaching the junction which led to Helensburgh or Loch Lomond where she asked which route Gordon was taking, though she thought she knew what his answer would be.

She was correct.

"The Loch Lomond way as usual. Now that the road is wider, it's quicker and more scenic. Do you want to stop for coffee somewhere? Lomond Shores like last time or wait till Inverary?"

"Let's wait till Inverary, this time."

They drove through Arrochar and up The Rest and Be Thankful. Gordon drove carefully, mindful of the possibility of fallen scree.

"I didn't tell you last time, Penny, of the time I had to go along that old, Roman Road…can you see if over there, down to your left? I had to wait in a long queue for a convoy car to lead us along it. This road we're on now was blocked by fallen rocks as it often is."

They drove on to Inverary where they stopped at a toilet then set off again.

It was about twelve thirty when they approached Tarbert but Gordon was anxious to drive on to Campbeltown for lunch. Penny, usually hungry, had lost her appetite and was nervously wondering if she had been wrong to say to Salma that she expected Gordon to propose to her today. They carried on.

However, when the plate of macaroni and chips arrived after they were seated in Ardshiel, in Campbeltown she suddenly felt hungry and it was Gordon who did not finish his lunch.

"Let's not have coffee, Pen, save that for later eh?"

"Ok, Gordon. Where next?"

"I thought you wanted to go back to Machrihanish Beach?"

"I do."

"Right, let's go then."

Gordon parked in a layby and reached over to the back seat for his quilted jacket, advising Penny to do the same as, being March, the exposed beach would be very chilly.

"Like last time, Pen and you only had a cardigan on. Remember?"

Penny smiled and got out of the car to put her jacket on. They walked hand in hand down to the vast, deserted beach, being buffeted by the wind. There were no wind surfers yet, only one lone walker with a large dog walking far in the distance.

Gordon spun Penny round to face him.

"Penny, I'm not good with words as you should know by now, so I'll just come to the point. I'm going to be moving to Prestwick, to a new practice, as joint manager, in April. Will you marry me and come with me?"

He reached into his jacket pocket and pulled out a small box and, kneeling on the damp sand, he opened the box and offered Penny a solitaire ring.

"Get up you clot, you'll get your knees soaked and of course I'll marry you!"

Gordon chuckled and put the ring on the appropriate finger. It fitted perfectly as he had hoped it would, having surreptitiously sneaked away a ring she wore on the same finger of her right hand at times.

"Typical Penny. Calls her future husband a clot. Are you sure you don't mind moving to Prestwick?"

Penny looked worried

"Obviously I don't mind moving house but what about my job? It would be a long commute every day."

"Surely you can get a move to either Ayr or even Prestwick. You could travel until something right turned up. I have to start work in April but might have to travel until we find a house we like. I thought we could get married in summer. What do you think? Look, let's have that coffee now, in Tarbert, and discuss everything."

Penny sat in the car looking at her lovely engagement ring. She was so lost in thought. that Gordon was parking at the harbour in Tarbert before she knew it.

They chose a small café which looked out onto the harbour and because it was February the place was deserted. They ordered two lattes and Gordon persuaded Penny not to eat anything as he had plans for their evening meal.

"I think this place will be popular with kids so we probably won't have it peaceful for very long."

"Gordon, you know how, old fashioned I've been about our not sleeping together…"

"...yes, though I've been the one to put a stop to going the whole way, on occasion, Miss Prim," laughed her now fiancée. He stopped laughing when he saw the serious look on Penny's face. He leaned over the table and took her hand. "We'll get married first, Pen. I won't try to persuade you to change your mind now that we're engaged."

Penny's eyes filled with tears. She squeezed his hand then suddenly sat up straight.

"Gordon...I haven't got a ring to give to you!"

"Silly woman! How could you know that I was going to propose to you today and anyway I'd rather have a wedding ring than an engagement one. We can choose those rings together."

Ever honest, Penny blushed before telling him that she had half suspected his proposal.

"I felt you were going to ask me last time we were on that beach. Were you?"

"Yes, I suddenly wanted to but I wanted to do it properly with the ring and I hadn't bought it yet."

"What if I'd turned you down, Mr Black?" Penny giggled at the thought.

"Plenty of other women just desperate to change places with you!"

She punched his arm from across the table as the door opened to let in four chattering teenage girls. They were followed by three boys.

"Maybe better to have background noise while we discuss our personal affairs," said Gordon a bit ruefully.

They discussed his new job. A friend, whom he had made at university on the vet course, had inherited an animal clinic from his uncle. It was a good-going concern and the older vet who had worked with his uncle wanted to retire so Sam had asked Gordon to be his partner.

"I've never asked if you want kids, Pen. Do you? It's just that Prestwick would be a nicer place to raise them than Glasgow."

"Of course I want a family! I'm an only child who'd have loved to be part of a large family. What about you?"

"Not too large! I'd like two, maybe three...though I'd like us to have a few years just by ourselves."

"Me too."

Penny's eyes sparkled then she looked serious. "The only fly in the ointment is having to leave my job. I love the folk I work with."

"Yes but your DS probably won't come back. I know she was thinking about it but she's an elderly first time mum and the unexpected double birth will have taken it out of her, not to mention the upset of having a sick baby and Frank will surely get promotion one of these days. Would you not have tried for promotion yourself...maybe still will, so that leaves Salma and your boss and Salma and you can visit each other. She could stay some weekends."

Penny had cheered up as he spoke.

"You're right, Gordon. Not about me. I don't want promotion but about Frank and Salma and DS Macdonald...oops DS Davenport. The only snag will be finding a boss as understanding as Mr Davenport."

"Right that's settled. I think I know the answer to my next question. Do you want a church wedding?"

"Oh, yes though if you don't...."

"...being a horrible atheist!"

"Agnostic please. That's not so definite," said Penny, seriously.

"OK, as an agnostic, I don't need a religious ceremony but if it's important to you then it is to me too! Your local church isn't very picturesque, especially now that they've pulled down the multi storey next to it. Do you want us to look for a nicer venue?"

"No. I don't!" said Penny vehemently. "It's not what it looks like, it's the fact that it's *my* church! We can save the photo-taking till the reception and choose somewhere *picturesque* for that!"

"That's more like the woman I know and love," laughed Gordon. "I thought you'd morphed into a simpering, acquiescent fiancée. Where would my lady and mistress want to have the reception?"

"Nowhere too expensive. I'd rather put our money into a deposit for a house. I have some savings but if we keep our wedding small, I'd like to pay for it ourselves. Mum has Jack to consider now and I'm not his daughter, no matter how well we get on."

"Agreed. Any ideas?"

They sat for another hour, having ordered a second coffee. It was now 5.00.

Penny wanted a 'house with stairs' and a garden, having been brought up in a tenement flat and now sharing another flat with a friend. They agreed on a maximum of thirty people at the wedding. Only close relatives, mainly friends. No separate evening group, all thirty to be asked to the whole event. They reasoned that their parents could not complain if they were not funding the wedding.

"My bridesmaid will be Salma of course," said Penny. She giggled. "Have you not got a handsome, Asian friend who could be your best man?"

"You know I haven't, silly. I'll ask Sam, the guy I'll be working with. Any flower girls or page boys?"

"Definitely not!" exclaimed Penny. I don't want any kids at my…our wedding. Do you?" she added, belatedly.

"Me neither. They end up dancing or trying to with their grannies and grandpas and hogging the limelight," laughed Gordon.

The last part of their conversation had taken place in the car. It was now nearly 6 o'clock and pitch dark.

"Right Pen. I'm going to take you for a classy meal in The Stonefield Castle Hotel which is just up the road from here. When I was a young boy here on holiday it was always the 'posh place to eat' and we never went. I took the chance of booking it yesterday."

"I'm not dressed up enough for that!" exclaimed Penny.

"Don't worry. These days you can get by in anything and you look smart in those black trousers and pink blouse. Just take off the sweater. I brought a tie but I won't put it on…so I'll be casual too. We can or rather you can, have few drinks in the bar first. Being with a policeperson, I'd better not drink anything alcoholic. Might get myself breathalysed!"

They had marvellous meal in a restaurant lined with windows which would have given them views out over the loch and decided to honeymoon there rather than go abroad.

It was too late for Penny to ring Salma when she got home but she could not resist texting her, hoping that her mobile phone was either switched off or in another room and she would get the news first thing in the morning.

CHAPTER 22

Salma enveloped Penny in a bear hug as soon as the latter stepped into the station the next day. Bob, at the desk, smiled and metaphorically pinned his ears back, to be rewarded with a good bit of juicy gossip for the canteen later in the day.

"Penny! You were right. Congratulations!

"It's the man you're supposed to congratulate but who cares!"

Penny showed off her new ring and almost floated on up the corridor, Salma following more decorously. Frank was not yet in but Fraser had a ring finger held up in front of him and responded with suitable pleasure for his colleague. It was left to Frank about ten minutes later to add humour to the occasion.

"Penny Black! What 'price' that for a name! Does the poor man know what he's letting himself in for? He'll never get to finish a sentence now!"

"I knew I was rare, Frank Selby and soon I'll have a name to prove that," countered Penny, grinning. "Gordon's got a great new job as joint manager of a Prestwick vet clinic and we're going to be married in June...do you know we'd made all the other plans yesterday without thinking of a date! Gordon starts work in April and we'll look for a house down there...."

"...what about your job here, Pen?" asked Salma, a bit anxiously.

Penny's grin faded.

"That's the only snag and for me, a big one but Gordon pointed out, Salma, that you could come and stay some weekends, Frank will probably get promotion…and you, too Fraser," she added hurriedly though she had not known him for as long as the others, he being her replacement after a bad accident had put her out of commission for some months

"Gordon said that he didn't think that DS Macdonald…Davenport…would return here after what's happened, especially if one of her babies is seriously ill."

"Gordon says…Gordon says…gosh Miss Price, you've become very subservient since he put that ring on your finger. Mind you, I hope he's right about my promotion...and yours' too, clever clogs Hewitt."

Fraser aimed a mock punch at Frank, then looked a sheepish.

"I don't think I'll be here but not because of promotion. Erin and I were talking at the weekend about the future and I think I'm going to retrain as a teacher…of English, same as her. I love literature, as you've all found out to your cost and hearing her talk of her classes, I think I'd enjoy that job more than this, especially if I was sent back to my last department. If I'm accepted at teacher training college, I would start in September probably."

"You're mad, Man," said Frank. "You're a dead cert for promotion and soon and think of all those awful weans!"

He shuddered and they all laughed.

"Talking of jobs, "said Salma. "We'd better get down to ours or we'll all be looking for new careers!"

"Just one more thing, Salma, before we start," said Penny. "I want you to be my bridesmaid. Would you be Ok with that...I mean it wouldn't be against your religion, would it?"

Salma's eyes filled.

"Oh, Penny I'd be thrilled."

"And you're both invited to the wedding of course," Penny turned to the two men.

There was a discreet cough from the doorway and they turned, dismayed, to see Solomon Fairchild standing there.

"Wedding? I knew there must be some very important gossip to stop you all from getting to work!"

Penny, her cheeks burning, took the blame though she could see that Fairchild's eyes were belying the severity in his voice.

"It's my fault, Sir. I'm sorry, it's my wedding...well, I'm not sorry it's my wedding but..."

Everyone burst out laughing then Salma took charge, inviting her boss to come up to her new temporary room to discuss the case and what they were about to do.

"You lot know what we'd planned for today. Get working," she said seriously.

In DS Macdonald's room up the corridor, it was Fairchild's turn to be serious.

"Sorry to spoil your happy day but Charles Davenport rang me at home last night. They had both babies christened, with Pippa there."

"Penny thought that was why they'd called for Pippa, Sir"

"He doesn't want to have to explain his son's condition to all of you and asked me to pass it on. I'll tell you, you tell the others then don't discuss it unless of course he brings it up. This myotubular myopathy is a very serious condition. I'd never heard of it till recently but saw a programme on TV a few weeks ago where they were treating Labrador puppies who had it. Some new drug was working extremely well on the dogs and they were running about happily. Not that that will help Charles's new son as they will probably have to test for a lot longer before trying out a new drug on a human baby."

"What chance of survival has the wee boy got, Sir? Do you know?"

"Charles said that in years gone by such a baby was left to the side to die but of course nowadays that couldn't happen. He's been on the internet and found out that the oldest survivor was about 13. They had both babies christened, as I said. The boy is Kenneth Charles and the girl is Kathleen Fiona. Charles had told Fiona that he was going to tell you all but he reneged on that as he was too upset. At the moment Kenneth is holding his own: that's all they can say."

Fairchild squared his shoulders.

"Right Sergeant Din...to business. What, if anything, have you found out since we last spoke?"

"Well, Sir, we found out that Mr Cunningham was on the 6 bus, not the 4A from Eaglesham. A neighbour who saw that he'd just missed that one, gave him a lift to Clarkston and he caught the 6. Penny drafted a notice for the Evening Times and the Herald asking passengers on the 6 bus going from Clarkston into Glasgow at about 10.30 to come forward. His appointment was for 12.00 midday.

We've interviewed the ones who came forward and one remembered Arthur Cunningham, In fact she was at the Dental Hospital too and remembered that he went to the wrong level, Level 6 and was directed back down to Level 2, she thought it was.

Frank and Fraser went to the Argyll Arcade to visit jewellers there and we think that Arthur Cunningham bought the ring, one of their cheapest, for a young, dark-haired woman.

Fraser went to the bank to ask about the person who was accused of petty pilfering some years ago. Her name was Jenny Flynn. I went to see Dr Ahmed, Mr Cunningham's GP, to ask about the likelihood of someone carrying insulin around with them. Some do and some don't. Penny and Frank interviewed Arthur Cunningham's other two sons as we've only ever had dealings with Tom the eldest one. He told us that he didn't have anything to do with his father and it turns out that the other two didn't either. They've given us more of an idea about the dead man and DCI Davenport always told us that it was important to get to know the corpse. They saw Tom again too and asked every man where he and his wife were at the time of the murder. They all have alibis except Tom."

We've checked most of the alibis and they seem to stand.

Solomon Fairchild patted her on the shoulder. An avuncular man, he could get away with this sort of gesture which in another man might be seen as condescension or sexism. He could see that Salma was upset by the news he had just given her and wanted her to know that she had his sympathy and also his blessing for what the team was about to do.

Together they went back to the main staff room and he left her there to tell the others about the baby and also get them motivated in carrying out their tasks.

He was justified in his selection of Salma as leader of the team as, after telling them about baby Kenneth, Salma told them that the best thing they could do for their boss was get this murder investigation well on its way to being solved before he came in again.

"I suspect that he knows we've been told about his baby boy and is giving it time to sink in before he comes in this morning."

It was a sombre but determined group who went along to the Incident Room.

CHAPTER 23

Salma was standing out at the front beside the white board on which Davenport had written:
 ARTHUR CUNNINGHAM.
INSULIN IN BLOODSTREAM
She had added some names while the others were chatting and now looked a bit undecided. Penny, noticing her friend's puzzled expression said," Salma I think you should just carry on as if the boss hadn't come back. I mean I'm sure he'd have rung in if he didn't plan to come in today but there might have been an emergency with wee Kenneth or…

"…No, Constable Price, no emergency, just one DCI reporting in late. Sorry team. Will you let me off this one time, please?"
His humble tones brought grins to four faces.
"Please, Sir, I know you said I could be in charge for a few more days but I'd prefer if you took over."
Salma's tone was pleading.
"Thanks. I take it I'm forgiven. Right Salma, so you'd be happier if I stood out here and you could join the others. Yes?"
Salma said nothing, just grinned at him and moved quickly to sit between Penny and Frank. Davenport perched himself on the desk beside the white board.
"Right, Frank. You fill them in about what we learned at the White Cart."

"One man who usually goes in on a Wednesday at lunchtime was there yesterday. He said that a couple in a corner were laughing a lot so I guess we need to speak to both Oliver and Pat Cunningham and without mentioning the laughter, ask if they remember what they were talking about."

Davenport wrote. "laughter" underneath the two appropriate names.

A phone started ringing up the corridor. Salma jumped up then sat back down again. On being told that she had better answer it, as for the time being no one apart from them and Solomon Fairchild knew that he was back in harness, she got back up and left the room. She was back in a couple of minutes to tell them that one of Susan Cunningham's friends had rung in, her mother having told her of the police visit and Salma had asked her to come into the station. The woman had a free afternoon and had agreed to come in at 2pm.

"I just hope the other woman's husband remembers to tell her to contact me. He was so sorry for himself. Why is it that men, like my dad and brother, feel that they're dying if they have a cold yet are really stoical when something big happens to them?"

"Gordon's the same," laughed Penny. "He calls a bad cold, man 'flu."

"May I, as a fallible male, interrupt this interesting conversation, ladies and ask Fraser to tell us about his visit to the elderly lady whom Quentin Cunningham said he was visiting?"

Penny and Salma looked sheepish and quietened down. Fraser told them that Mrs Adam had opened the door of her ground floor flat in Cathcart without putting the chain on and on being told that he was a policeman, had stood aside, holding onto her zimmer frame to let him precede her into her lounge. She had asked him to sit on the settee and she had taken the seat on his left, telling him that she had advanced macular degeneration so there was no point in asking to see his warrant card.

"I put it into her hand anyway, Sir," Fraser explained, "and told her to at least check that I had a card even though she couldn't read what it said. I also told her never to open the door without putting the chain across but she just laughed and said that she'd lived to 87 without meeting a criminal and she preferred to trust folk."

"She'd probably put up a fight if a burglar did get in, "said Frank, with admiration in his voice. "Like my Gran. I wouldn't like to get on *her* wrong side."

"Ok so what did she say when you asked about her minister's visit?" enquired Davenport.

"I asked if she had many visitors. I thought I'd edge round to asking about the minister but she said I was a policeman, not a social worker so would I get to the point! I bet she was a teacher in her younger days, Sir. I felt as if I should sit up straight and say, "Yes Miss!", but I simply asked her if her minister had visited her last Tuesday."

"I bet she asked why you wanted to know?" said Penny.

"Too right, "replied Fraser.
" 'Why do you ask, young man?' she said. I told her that Reverent Cunningham's father had been murdered on that Wednesday and that he'd said he'd been visiting her late morning. She said indeed he had been with her and that her care assistant had arrived shortly afterwards to prepare her lunch so the visit had been cut short. I asked if she had any idea what time he left and she said that she knew exactly as Margaret, the care assistant was always on time and she came at 12.30 so Mr Cunningham must have left at about 12.45 as he stayed with her till the food was brought through."
"Macaroni cheese, it was, young man and he said it was one of his favourites."
"She went on to say that I could ask him what the old lady had had for lunch and that would prove he was there, unless I thought she could have been "in cahoots" with him and had agreed to alibi him."
Davenport wrote, "macaroni cheese" under the name of Quentin Cunningham.
At this point, above the laughter, Davenport who was nearest to the door, heard the phone ringing once again in what had been his wife's room and he told Salma to answer it again.
She returned to say that the other friend of Susan Cunningham could come in around 3.15 as she had to pick her grandson up at school at 2.45. She would have to bring him with her

"I said that was fine. Someone would entertain him while she spoke to one of us. She was more curious than the first woman but I said I would explain once she was here."

Davenport wrote, "two friends" under Susan Cunningham's name.

Penny was the last to tell about her morning. She had interviewed two neighbours. One had been elderly and he had said that he couldn't see much of either the next door garden or the road because he had leylandi bushes right round his house.

"He looked quite fearsome, Sir but he told me that he had always kept the bushes a reasonable height until his arthritis had stopped him doing the cutting down and that he kept meaning to get in a gardener before the neighbours on either side complained."

Penny had thanked him and gone to the house three houses down on the other side of the manse, as there had been no one in the two nearer houses. A harassed au pair girl from Poland who luckily spoke good English, had told Penny that Abigail had sometimes collected her 'charge' for her but not that day as on Tuesdays she met up with another au pair girl at the school gates and they took the children for an ice cream or cake at the local café.

So I went to the school, Sir. Hoped to be in time to speak to some mothers. I saw Abigail Cunningham with… Lizzie, I presume, so I waited in the car and luckily her older daughter, Becky, I think she's called, ran out among the first children to leave after the bell rang. She pointed her mother out to the teacher in charge and was given permission to go to her. Abigail hurried off with both of them so I got out and spoke to a woman Abigail had been talking to. She said that Abigail nearly always came to the school and that only occasionally, the minister came to collect his daughter.

I asked about last Tuesday and she said she was almost certain that she had spoken to Abigail as Abigail had asked if she would bring her son to a children's event at church the following Saturday. They were running a Beetle Drive for church funds. It was great fun, she said. When I asked if she could be sure it was Tuesday that she had spoken to Abigail and not Thursday or Wednesday, she said it was either Tuesday or Wednesday. I was going away, Sir, when she ran after me and told me it definitely was Tuesday as she was in a hurry to pick up her son as he had a piano lesson at 5 o'clock on Tuesdays. By the way, Sir, I rang the Dental Hospital before I left, to see if there was a Thomas Hazelton on their books for that Tuesday and there wasn't. I thought maybe Tom used his penname…silly of me but worth a try."

Penny ran out of breath and stopped.

"Good thinking, Penny," said Davenport.

Salma had left during Penny's report as she would be interviewing the two friends of Susan Cunningham and wanted to prepare for the interview and had already heard most of Penny's report.

That afternoon at 2pm when Salma reached the front desk there was a woman sitting on the bench seat. She stood as Salma approached and introduced herself as Helen Peacock. Salma shook hands before leading the woman up the corridor to the privacy of the DS's room. She was not a suspect so an interview room would be too austere. Seated across from Susan's friend, Salma first ascertained that she was speaking to a Miss Peacock who was a friend of Susan Cunningham.

"I am."

"I need you to tell me if you met with Susan Cunningham, last Wednesday around lunchtime, "Salma came straight to the point. "Her father-in–law, as you might know from the press, was murdered on that day and we need to rule out any possible suspect…"

"…Susan a murderer, sorry a murderess…I don't think so. She wouldn't even swat a fly."

Salma wished she had a £1 for every time that had been said in the course of police interviews. A number of times the insect lover had proved to indeed be the murderer, she had been informed on training courses.

"Would you just give me some information about your meeting, Miss Peacock,"

"Well the three of us met in Marks and Spencer's tearoom in Sauchiehall Street."

"At what time?"

"Well it was supposed to be at 12. I was there in time but Susan and Terry were both a bit late. Came in together in fact at around 12.10. I'd just looked in my diary to check that I had the time right. The number of times one of us has got the date or time wrong is unbelievable," she laughed.

"But we're good friends... have been since schooldays...so we forgive and forget."

"When did you leave?"

"I left first at about 1.30. I had a dentist appointment in Shawlands at 2.20 so I don't know when the others left though I remember Terry saying that she was going on somewhere else."

"What about Susan Cunningham. Did she say where she was going afterwards?"

"No she didn't or if she did I've forgotten."

Salma thanked her, asking her to wait till her interview had been typed up so that she could sign it. She went down to her own desk to type up the interview and shortly afterwards Helen Peacock left.

Salma repeated the procedure with Terry Arnott. Terry had met Susan on the ground floor of Marks and Spencer's and they had gone up in the lift together.

"I was glad that I met Susan as I thought we were meeting at 12.30 and was going to browse round the store first," she laughed. "You'd be surprised at the number of times one of us gets the time...or even the date wrong."

"Did Susan say why she was late, "asked Salma.

"No she didn't but I assumed she'd been held up at home or by traffic. She wasn't very late, just 10 minutes. Her husband works from home. He's a writer," she added. "Susan often gets involved in letting him talk things through with her. He can't bear it if she isn't around when he needs to sound something off her! I thank my lucky starts that Michael, my husband is out of my hair for five days a week!"

"Thanks, Mrs Arnott. I take it that none of you works? You're too young to be retired," Salma asked.

"Susan did work after school. She was a receptionist in Victoria Infirmary. Then she met Tom who was a male nurse there till he gave up to write. Susan carried on working to support him but now that he's had two books published, Susan has become a full time Mum and personal assistant to Tom."

"Helen was an assistant head teacher in a secondary school in Bridgeton. Her school closed and she decided she'd had enough. Her parents had left her a bungalow and quite enough to live on," so she decided it was 'time to smell the roses' as she put it. We used to meet in the evenings and made fewer mistakes with times and dates then," she laughed.

"Which of the three of you left the tearoom first?"

"Helen did. She had a dentist appointment. I left Susan in the tearoom. I had to get home. A Dyson was being delivered between 2 and 6 pm. Naturally after I broke my neck getting there for 2pm, the dratted thing didn't arrive till minutes before 6."

"Did Susan by any chance say where she was going?"

"No, not to me anyway."

Terry left and again Salma typed up the short interview.

CHAPTER 24

The team convened in The Incident Room. The white board was now covered with information and it was to this board that Davenport drew his team's attention.

"Here is the cast list: unknown female for whom Arthur Cunningham bought an engagement ring. Ring subsequently found among his possessions: Carol Cunningham stroke Paterson, the deceased's wife, now living in Canada: Thomas Cunningham, deceased's eldest son, a writer: Susan Cunningham above's wife, unemployed: Oliver Cunningham, the second son, home on leave from the army: Pat Cunningham, above's wife, unemployed: Quentin Cunningham, youngest son, a minister: Abigail Cunningham, above's wife, unemployed."

Davenport had pointed to each name as he read it out. He sat down on the edge of a table and looked round at his colleagues.

"Have I missed anyone from my list of dramatis personae?"

"Your what, Sir?" asked Penny, sounding puzzled. Frank's brow was also furrowed. Fraser looked as if he was about to speak then thought better of it. Salma just waited patiently for her boss to explain.

"That's what you call the people in a play, Penny. It's a metaphor seeing the possible killers as the characters in a murder play."

"Metaphor!" said Frank in disgust. "I never could find them in the English class. Similes were ok. They were easy to find with 'like' or 'as'. Why on earth we had to know these things I never could understand as if you ever mentioned one in a critical review, the teacher used to write, "So what?' in the margin,"

"Yeah, like all the stuff about scansion, iambic whatsits! If you wrote that something was an example of that the teacher also wrote, "So what?" said Salma.

"The bit I couldn't get, "said Fraser, joining in, "was why we had to learn large chunks of plays and poems then were told off for quoting them in essays. Erin was asked by one of her pupils why they weren't asked to learn things like her mum had to and in fun she told them they could learn Macbeth's, "Is this a dagger?" speech for the following day. She couldn't believe it when she came into the room to find them all muttering the speech. She said she spent nearly the whole period listening to each one reciting! On the subject of figures of speech, she loves it when one of her kids finds an exaggeration and calls it a 'hyperbowl' instead of hyperbole, "he added laughing.

Salma, grinning, told of the time her teacher, trying to explain a rhetorical question, had asked a boy at the front, "Do you think I'm stupid, James?"

"The rest of the kids were all holding their breath waiting to see if he would answer her."

"Well," said Davenport, dryly," do you think we have all day to waste on your anecdotes? Yes, Selby that's a rhetorical question."

Franks reddened and the others looked sheepish. It was almost as if they had relaxed now that their boss was back to shoulder the responsibility.

"Sorry, Sir," said Salma. "What about the woman sacked from the bank? Or the girl he was engaged to?"

Davenport wrote "sacked female" on the board, then invited them all to say who they thought most likely to be the murderer, if indeed any one of them was.

"It could of course be someone from his past, maybe recent past or someone he had cheated financially or by sneaking off with the person's wife."

"Or, Sir, as revenge is a dish best served cold," Frank looked smug as he used Fraser's' words from a few days ago," it could be someone he hurt or cheated some time ago."

Davenport agreed. He looked despondent, obviously thinking of how many unknown people could be responsible for the death of this quite unlovely man.

Penny, unable to resist a final comment, said that she hoped like Frank that it wasn't going to be a Murder on the Orient Express scenario with umpteen people plunging needles into the dead man.

That caused a laugh and Davenport's shoulders relaxed.

"Ok…comments please on the list of possible suspects."

Penny spoke first.

"It should be easy, Sir, to rule out Oliver and Pat Cunningham. I mean if they do tell us that they were laughing and can describe any of the men from the two groups present in The White Cart, that day…"

"…and we can rule out Abigail as another young mum said she was outside the school." said Salma.

"…and we can rule out Quentin Cunningham because that old lady said he was there over lunchtime and although she can't see, she would have known him by his voice, "added Fraser, interrupting Salma. "And I rang him this morning to check what the old lady had for lunch and he said it was macaroni cheese and he remembered because it was one of his favourite meals."

"Well done, Fraser," said Davenport.

"So, Sir, that leaves Tom and Susan. Tom had the best chance as he works from home. We haven't asked if he rang anyone or if anyone saw him over lunchtime and his wife was near the Dental Hospital at the appropriate time," Frank put in his twopence worth.

"Susan's friends both mentioned that Susan came in late for a 12 o'clock meet up. She arrived with one who was also late, at 12.10. She was once receptionist in a hospital where Tom was a male nurse but I don't imagine either of them got a supply of insulin in case they wanted to murder Arthur Cunningham years later. I'd personally rule out Susan. Although M&S tearoom is very near the Dental Hospital, it's cutting it a bit fine to presumably get out of a uniform, catch the lifts which are I've heard slow in coming and get to M&S without being at all flustered which surely her friend who met her on the ground floor would have noticed."

"Yes, Sir and wouldn't she have tried to change the time of meeting if she knew she was going to commit a murder and be late," added Penny.

"Well, Selby, your job this morning is to see if anyone noticed Susan Cunningham after her friends left her. Did she stay on or did she leave just after them? We have a photograph of all six members of the Cunningham family…thanks Penny for thinking of getting them. Get individual photos from that. Show the photographs round the dental hospital floor that Arthur Cunningham was on. Maybe also show it on the floor he went to by mistake according to our witness, Floor 6, just in case someone waiting there recognised him and killed him in a sudden, unpremeditated act."

Charles had spent a long time last night reading over his team's notes so was confident that he had the floor number correct. "Penny, get round to Tom Cunningham's flat and see if he made any phone calls at the crucial time or anything else that might give him an alibi. You might ask him if he's arranged the funeral yet. Mr Fairchild told me that he'd given permission for the funeral to go ahead. He rang Tom Cunningham himself." Penny got up with alacrity.

"Oh and ask about the reading of the will, all supposing that there *is* one. Do we know the name of Arthur Cunningham's lawyer?"

"No, Sir but I was going to ring the three people mentioned in Mr Cunningham's address book this morning. Maybe the lawyer is one of them," said Salma.

Penny returned in about an hour to tell her boss and Fraser who were sitting in The Incident Room, that Tom had just that morning finalised the funeral arrangements. He said that Quentin would be scandalised that his father wanted a humanist funeral but that he,Tom was not at all surprised, given that his father had not come to his grandchildren's christenings or to Quentin's wedding, being disgusted that one of his sons had 'gone into' the church.

"My Mum went regularly to church in Giffnock, "Tom had explained. "She took us and we went to Sunday School. Funnily enough, it was Q who reneged first. He went back to please Abi, refound his faith and the rest, as they say, is history. Olly and I lasted longer. Olly did a stint in Ireland and saw too many deaths caused by religion for him to remain a believer. He's a bitter atheist although he did let Pat take Laura and Rose to church with her when they were younger as he wants them to make up their own minds and he felt that they couldn't do that without experience of church. Moving about as much as they do, Pat let her church – going slip too and the girls don't go now either, Me, I go occasionally…suppose I'm an agnostic and Susan goes faithfully every week. Helen and Sarah love the Girls' Brigade and go to church quite happily."

"He said, Sir, that the funeral will at The Linn Crematorium on Wednesday afternoon at 2pm. He's asked Neil, Arthur Cunningham's assistant manager, to say a few words but apart from that there will be just music and a humanist, named by his father, will lead the whole thing. Apparently, his father left an envelope in a safe at the bank with instructions to Neil Kerr to open it on his death. The lawyer is a Mr…"

"…Blackwell, "said Salma, coming into the room. She grimaced.

"I've just spent over an hour on the phone to find that out. Grace Hawken and Jo Lambert are his nieces. Luckily, I got on to Grace first as she lives in England, in Chalfont St Peter's. She's a widow with no children. Jo lives in Australia with her mother, Nell, who is Arthur Cunningham's sister. Naturally, I had to explain why I was ringing and Grace asked a lot of questions then spent some time telling me why none of them had kept in touch with Arthur. Apparently, when his mother died, Arthur did the dirty on his sister, Nell, and emptied the house of everything valuable before she could get home from Australia. I rang Jo in Australia. She told me name of the family lawyer. Grace had forgotten it. Blackwell was the third name in the address book."

"Sorry, Salma," said Penny.

"Not your fault, Pen. Jo and her mother have never been back in UK. They don't even have a passport."

"Sir," said Penny. "I asked Tom if he'd made any 'phone calls that lunchtime and he said he couldn't remember either making or receiving calls that day but he'd been really engrossed in his writing round about then so it might have slipped his mind. He said he believed that we had ways of finding out things like phone calls. Surely, he'd have made sure that he had an alibi if he intended to murder his father, Sir?"

Fraser was frowning and his boss asked what was troubling him.

"Well, Sir unless all or some of the family are lying, they hadn't seen their father for ages so how would they know about his appointment at the Dental Hospital?"

It was Davenport's turn to frown.

"If that is the case, then the field is considerably narrowed down…."

"…to the dentist?" queried Penny, sounding sceptical.

"Or to someone on the bus or at the hospital who killed without premeditation…"

"…who happened to be diabetic." Davenport finished off Salma's statement.

He looked at the white board

"Let me sum up. If we take off those with alibis, we're left with Tom Cunningham, the sacked female from the bank…"

"…Jenny Flynn's her name, Sir," Frank's voice came from the door.

"Thanks, Selby. Come and join us. Right let me reiterate. Tom Cunningham, unless Selby you found out anything relevant about Susan?"

"I did, Sir. I showed the photo to the serving staff at M&S tearoom and one of them said she remembered Susan and her friends, as one of them, a Miss Peacock, had been assistant head in the school she'd gone to. She had been going to go over and introduce herself but things got busy and when she looked over there was just one woman sitting at the table, sipping a coffee and doing a crossword. She recognised Susan from the photo I showed her. I asked her if she had any idea what the time might have been and she said she was just going off for her break and it was about 2pm."

"So Susan Cunningham's catered for," Davenport groaned

"Sir, I think you can forget the two Australian women too. I asked if they'd been over to the UK recently and the reply was, not at all. Neither even has a passport," Salma reminded him.

"So at the risk of repeating myself, let's look at who we have left."

Davenport turned once again to the white board. He rubbed out, added in and then stood back.

"Right, we have:

Tom Cunningham

Oliver Cunningham

Pat Cunningham

Grace Hawken

Jenny Flynn

Woman who had engagement ring

"Selby, any luck at the Dental Hospital?"

"No Sir. I showed the photo of Arthur Cunningham and the only person to recognise him was a receptionist on Level 6 who described him as rude. Nothing new there! I went down to the department which dealt with Mr Cunningham and neither the surgeon nor the anaesthetist could remember seeing anyone suspicious. Sir, they were both dressed in green gowns so the murderer could have dressed in one of those and blended in."

"Yes, Frank that's probably what happened. Right folks, I'm going home for lunch again. I'll drop in to see Oliver and Pat Cunningham on my way. I've not met them yet. If they can remember any of the other people at the pub that lunchtime that will be another two off the list."

Frank had had a snack in town so he stayed upstairs to write up his report while the other three went down to the canteen for lunch. Fraser spotted a friend from his former unit at the station and went across to have lunch with him, leaving Penny and Salma to have a much longed for chat about Penny's wedding and how Salma could get to know Dr Ahmed better. On Sunday, they hoped for at least the afternoon off as Davenport was fond of saying that all work and no play made his team stale and he had agreed to it the preceding week. They arranged there and then to meet at Penny's, on the proviso that Salma's older brother or sister could look after her two younger siblings.

Chapter 25

When Charles got home, his house was quite full. Pippa had invited her friends, a motley selection of friends past and present. Fiona appreciating how good the youngster had been, had offered to let her have four friends for a pizza meal.

"Damn, Fiona, I'd forgotten about the invasion! Still, I suppose you'll be glad to have me home on time for once."

Fiona, sitting at the kitchen table with baby Kathleen in her arms, smiled up at him.

"Yes, my Love. I'd be grateful if you would ask what kind pf pizzas I should order shortly. They started out in the lounge but they're now in Pippa's' bedroom. I'll order two pizzas so get their two favourite ones."

"Who did she invite eventually?"

"Oh, Hazel and Kerry; Hazel's dad brought both of them, Kathy from down the road…she was made up with the fact that this little one is called Kathleen…and Ronald!"

"Ronald? I didn't know that she still saw him. Should she be having males in her bedroom now?"

"Oh, Charles, don't be stuffy. I'm sure Pippa just sees him as one of the gang and even if he did have 'designs' on your daughter, there are two chaperones in the room with them."

Fiona laughed then her face changed.

"Oh Charles, the hospital rang and we can have Kenny home for one overnight stay. They will give us everything we need or might need in an emergency. The only stipulation is that the room is cleaned thoroughly and that only you and I go in."

"When?"

"Sunday. We can collect him in the morning and take him back on Monday morning. I think they do this at a weekend so that both parents can be there. Is it possible for you to be here all day?"

"I'll make it possible, Fiona. I'll ask the team to come in for the morning only: they need some time off. When I go back after lunch, today, I can assign duties for the morning. I think we need to ask Pippa to have an overnight stay with one of the crew upstairs…*not* Ronald…as that will lessen the chance of any germs around Kenny. We can both go to the hospital and one of us can hold Kathleen and one Kenny."

"I think perhaps we have to keep Kathleen out of the way too, Charles. So one of us can collect Kenny. I imagine that they will put him in a kind of incubator thing which can be strapped into the passenger seat...oh gosh maybe not…"

…" why don't you ask Caroline to look after Kathleen until we've settled Kenny in then I can take her home. She can't bring her wee one but I'm sure her husband could babysit for a short time or I could ask my sister Linda."

Fiona had befriended a widow whose husband's murder they had solved a few years ago. Caroline had remarried and Ron and she had had a baby boy recently. Fiona had seen a lot of Caroline after she too became pregnant.

"Yes, I'll ask Caroline. Ron's a great hands-on dad so no problem there. I'll give her a ring now while you see to the choice of pizzas."

When Charles came downstairs to request a pepperoni and a cheese and pineapple pizza, Fiona met him with the news that Caroline would be delighted to come. She would drive herself over and back.

"So all we need to do now is a complete clean out of the bedroom. Kathleen will have to come in with us. I'll get that done tonight..."

"...we'll both get that done tonight, Charles, once Kathleen is settled down for the night," said Fiona, firmly.

Charles did not have a hard physical job but she knew only too well how stressful a murder case was.

"Has Pippa chosen where her sleepover is to be?"

"She got three offers. That young lad had the sense not to offer," said Charles, sternly. "She chose to stay with Hazel and I'm sure she will tell us why before they leave."

Charles telephoned the pizza order and it arrived just before he left to go back to work.

He took it upstairs with cans of coke and a kitchen roll and his daughter solemnly explained that she was going to stay with Hazel as she didn't have much time to see her at school.

"Hazel has rung her dad and he is going to take them both down to Newlands when he picks up Hazel and Kerry later this afternoon," Charles informed his wife before kissing her and his little daughter.

Later that evening he brought Fiona up to date on the murder enquiry. She had been there at the very start and wanted to know every detail.

"The three sons sound nice, normal young men, Charles. They haven't got any reason for suddenly wanting their father out of the way, have they?"

"I know, love but why would anyone at the dentist's want rid of him either?"

"Could it have been someone at the Dental Hospital?"

"That's as possible as anything else but it all seems unlikely…a student dentist wanting rid of him? Why?"

"Well you've had no failures yet, Charles so let's just trust that some clue will turn up. Let's get to bed."

CHAPTER 26

When Penny came in on Wednesday morning, she found Fraser engrossed in reading something on his desk. She went across the room and looked down. It was a newspaper page.

"Is that the paper we found among Arthur Cunningham's things?" she asked her colleague. "Salma wanted us to work on that but we did other things instead."

"Yes, I couldn't get to sleep last night and I remembered that I'd thought that it might be an Ayrshire paper and there might be something in it to do with that girl from the bank that Arthur Cunningham flirted with, according to that other bank girl, Jean Something…"

"…Jenny Flynn was the girl he flirted with," provided Frank. "Where's Salma? Not like her to be even near late and it's 8.55."

"Here I am. Didn't have time this morning to get breakfast as the two pests wouldn't get up and by the time they got ready and ate and I ran them to school…well…here I am."

"Where's the boss?" asked Frank.

"Bob told me that he'd rung in to say that he was taking the DS into the hospital to visit their wee baby boy. He would then take Kathleen to his sister's," said Penny.

Davenport had told his team the reason for their Sunday afternoon off and they all looked sombre now. Salma took off her jacket and hat, showing her shining, raven black hair. She went to her desk and booted up her computer. She was soon engrossed in a page on humanist funerals which she had never heard of till it was mentioned on Saturday that this was the kind of funeral that Arthur Cunningham wanted. If her boss asked her to attend, she wanted to be prepared.

Frank went to his own desk to write up his investigation into Susan Cunningham's visit to Marks and Spencer's to meet her friends. Penny stayed looking over Fraser's shoulder at the newspaper page spread out there. Together they read the four items it contained

Four were pertaining to deaths: one was of an elderly man who'd been a schoolteacher in Troon Primary School in the 60s: one was the death in his fifties of a bank manager in Maybole ; the third was of a young woman after a short illness and the last of a man whose death was the result of a long illness.

"Could he have kept it because of the death of the bank manager…a friend of his perhaps?" ventured Penny.

"Well, 'friend' and 'Arthur Cunningham' don't seem to go together," said Fraser. "From what we've heard he's hardly likely to have kept an intimation of that sort."

"Yes, why keep the notice of a colleague's death?" demanded Penny. "What else is there?"

Fraser read out two birth announcements:

"To Mark and Margaret O'Brian, a son, Peter James, a brother for Alice. Mother and baby both well"

"To Olivia Flynn a daughter, Lisa. Granddaughter for Josephine and Robert. Mother and baby well."

"No father for Lisa," mused Fraser." I wonder..." His thoughts were interrupted by the arrival of their boss.

"Just had word that Arthur Cunningham's will is to be read after the funeral. One of you can go to the funeral and one to the will reading. I'll let you know tomorrow."

"Sir," said Fraser. "I've been looking again at the newspaper page we found in Arthur Cunningham's house. The only possible things relevant to him are, I think, the death of a bank manage and the birth of a baby with no father's name. We don't think that Arthur would have kept the death announcement of a colleague, though it's possible. Could it be that he fathered a child? The woman who left the bank was Jenny Flynn. This mother was Olivia Flynn. Could this baby be a relation of hers? Her sister's perhaps? Why would that interest Arthur Cunningham so much that he kept the paper?" He handed his boss the newspaper page.

"Well thought out, lad," said Davenport, having read the relevant parts of the paper. "Get on to Neil Kerr at the bank and ask about the bank manager and get Jenny Flynn's address. We've been so busy thinking the murderer was family that we've let this side slip."

"Maybe the baby died, Sir and this Olivia Flynn wanted revenge."

"All these years later, Pen. Hardly likely," said Fraser.

"Funnier things have happened, Son. Let's humour Penny and look through the next few years 'Hatches, Matches and Dispatches" for the same paper. Do we know the paper by the way?"

"No, Sir, I'd say it was a local paper as one of the main ones would have had more deaths and births in it, I think. Jenny Flynn lived somewhere in Ayrshire so should I try the local papers there first?"

"Good idea. I'll leave you to it."

"Sir, Erin and I went to The White Cart yesterday evening with the photo of Oliver and Pat Cunningham. Anne, the manageress, says she'll show it to the two groups who come in regularly on Tuesday lunchtimes."

"Thanks, lad."

Penny rang the bank and reported back to Fraser that there had been no manager that Neil Kerr was aware of dying, unless perhaps it was the manager of another bank, the TSB or the Clydesdale. She had got Jenny Flynn's last known address.

"But we're back to wondering how Arthur Cunningham knew this fictitious person so well that he kept the paper page," said Fraser. "It just doesn't seem like a thing he'd do."

Fraser was busy googling local Ayrshire papers of which there were plenty as every little village seemed to have its own daily or weekly paper.

Penny called Frank over from his desk where he was struggling to get his notes up to date and suggested that they both help Fraser. Salma seemed engrossed in her researching of humanist funerals.

Silence reigned.

Charles Davenport's, "Gosh, I thought you'd all gone home early," brought a laugh from his team. His, "Even Penny silent. Wonders will never cease," brought an even louder laugh from Fraser and Salma and a derogatory, "Some miracles take a bit longer," from Frank.

Nothing was found.

 Sir, is it worth one of us going to the village this paper, The Carrick Gazette, came from, Maybole, and seeing if we can find out who this woman was?"

"Well there's nothing much else needing done immediately. We'll maybe have more to look into after the funeral and the reading of the will tomorrow. Go tomorrow and take someone with you in case there are church records to read through, Fraser, and go to that address we got for Jenny Flynn.

Fraser, knowing that Penny would be up to date with her notes, chose to take her with him the following day.

There was an air of excitement. Would they find anything relevant to their murder case in the backwoods of Ayrshire?

CHAPTER 27

As Salma had expected, she was asked to attend the funeral on Thursday.

"As second in charge of the department, I'm delegating this one to you, Salma," Charles had told her. "I saw you yesterday beefing up on humanist funerals and I came close to being at my wee son's funeral last week and I don't think I'm in the right frame of mind."

Salma had assured him that she did not mind and had, in fact, as he said, read up about this type of event so she knew what to expect. She went to the washroom to tidy her hair

She arrived at 11.50 and had to park on the winding path leading up to the crematorium. This probably meant that the ongoing service was fully attended and that there would be space in the car park when it finished but Salma did not want to risk going all the way up only to find that there was no space there. Luckily there was always a folding umbrella in the glove compartment of the police car as the day was grey and drizzling.

She walked up the hill and, sure enough, the car park was emptying and streams of people were coming out of the crematorium. She stood behind the part of the building which housed the toilets and small waiting room. This gave her shelter from the wind and rain. No one joined her. She watched as the hearse and two large limousines came slowly toward the building. These vehicles were followed by only two private cars. As the limousines emptied of passengers, Salma recognised Tom Cunningham whom she had seen before and guessed at the others as there were three men and three women in the front two rows at the right-hand side by the time she went inside, Salma knew from a previous visit, that these were the rows for immediate family. In between the couple whom she thought were Tom and his wife in the front row was an older woman. Salma could only see their backs and in the second row there were three young girls whom Salma guessed might be the eldest of Arthur's grandchildren. They were seated between the other two sons with two women at the ends of the row. Arthur Cunningham's other sons and their wives she assumed. She had no time to look at the other people present though perhaps unsurprisingly there were few other mourners.

As strains of "My Way" reached her ears she realised that she was not at all surprised at his choice of music. From what she knew of the deceased, this was exactly what Arthur Cunningham would have chosen. She thought he would probably have always done things *his* way with scant interest in anyone else's opinion. Tom had told Penny that Neil Kerr, now acting manager of the bank, would be speaking and a man seated behind the family, rose and went to the lectern. He managed to paint a very neutral picture of Arthur Cunningham, saying he had been an astute bank manager. His speech was short.

A middle-aged man rose from an empty row at the front on the left-hand side and made his way to the lectern. It was obvious that he did not know Arthur Cunningham very well, if at all, as what he said were generalisations and had more to do with his belief in humanism than with an individual. One of the men in the second row was fidgeting a bit and Salma wondered if this was Quentin Cunningham, the minister son who would no doubt be hating this service as it would go against all his beliefs.

The speaker stopped and asked them all to stand while he intoned, "Ashes to ashes, dust to dust," before presumably pressing the button to lower the coffin as down it went, slowly, into the bowels of the building.

There were no hymns and no music as the speaker walked out of the chapel, motioning to the family to follow him.

Salma stood in her place at the left-hand side and watched as the family filed out. In the row in front of Salma, stood a man and a woman who waited as Salma did till the others had left before filing out behind her. In the foyer, the three sons, Salma guessed, waited to speak to the mourners. She noticed that the man and woman preceding her, those she assumed were the assistant bank manager and his wife shook their hands while the other couple passed behind them and left quickly. Feeling that she could hardly race off after the two who had left, Salma waited to shake hands with the three sons, realising that she was no further forward in finding out who the older family member was either. She felt very conspicuous in her uniform but was greeted with three smiles when she went down the line.

"Sergeant Din," Tom explained to his brothers. "I expected a police presence at father's funeral. Is it not true that the murderer often turns up at the victim's funeral, Sergeant?" he joked. "'Fraid you haven't got much choice, unless you suspect Neil Kerr or his wife. We didn't know them but they've just introduced themselves. He was my father's assistant manager at the bank."

"There were two more people on the other side of the crematorium, Sir," volunteered Salma, "but they didn't wait to introduce themselves. "Can I ask who the older lady was with you and were the three young ones, Mr Cunningham's oldest granddaughters?"

"Yes to both questions. You *can* ask and the older lady is my mother. The kids are my eldest daughter, Helen , Olly's daughter Laura and Q's daughter Becky. This is Olly, Oliver, the middle brother of the family."

Olly stepped forward and shook Salma's hand then Quentin was introduced and shook hands too.

"We thought that Helen, Laura and Becky who are the eldest should be allowed to attend today. They didn't know their grandfather so it was a chance to show them what a funeral is like without them being too upset," said Quentin. Noticing his ministerial collar, Salma realised that it had indeed been he who had fidgeted throughout the brief ceremony.

"My eldest is only nine but she'd have been indignant at being left out, being the elder of our two, "added Quentin.

Tom coming forward again, asked if Salma would come to the Busby Hotel for refreshments and she agreed to go, hoping to have a chance to speak to Arthur Cunningham's wife. It seemed unlikely that the two strangers would attend. They had been in front of her so she had only caught a glimpse of their backs and they had hurried out while she waited to speak to the sons and she had only seen the backs of their heads then and inside the crematorium. She did not even know if they had come together.

She looked down the path towards the crematorium gates and saw a small black car passing the only other car, her police car. There was no one walking down so she felt sure that the mysterious twosome had come and gone together. She was too far away to read a number plate but thought that the car might be a Volkswagon, Polo or Golf.

Back at the hotel, a cup of tea in her hand, she asked Tom if he knew the identity of the two guests but he had not even seen them. Quentin and Oliver had not seen them either.

"You don't glance round under these circumstances," Quentin said, apologetically.

He put his hand under Salma's elbow and steered her across the small room to where the older woman was standing with her three granddaughters.

"Mum, this is Sergeant Din, one of the police officers in charge of the case. Come on you three, let's get you a coke each."

With that, he escorted his daughter and two nieces to the table on which drinks and sandwiches were arrayed.

"Hello, Sergeant. I'm Carol Paterson, Arthur's wife though it's funny to call myself that after being apart for so many years. We didn't get divorced. I just wanted to get away without any long winded legal business. I reverted to my maiden name a few years ago."

She laughed.

"I stayed on longer than I wanted to but Arthur wasn't cruel, just unpleasant and I wanted to see my sons settled. I saw them all married. Arthur only attended two weddings, that of Tom and Susan and Olly and Pat. He hated the fact that Q went into the church so he wouldn't go to his wedding. Poor Q… he must have hated that abomination of a funeral today!"

"Did you see your grandchildren, Mrs Cunningham…before today, I mean?" Salma asked the elegant, grey-haired woman."

"Just Helen and Laura at their christenings, two of the three girls who were present at the funeral today but the three families came out once to Canada a few years ago and I saw them all then. I only came across yesterday," she added.

Salma spoke to Neil and Anne Kerr and then left, having gleaned from Neil what she already suspected, namely that Arthur Cunningham was not an easy man to work with.

"I gave the staff the opportunity to come today but no one wanted to," he said.

Anne told her that Arthur had been quite generous at her charity functions but that she suspected that this was more for show than out of kindness.

Nobody had seen, let alone recognised the two strangers who had made a hasty exit after the funeral.

"Gran, you've to come back with Dad and me," Salma heard one of the youngsters say.

"OK, Becky," she heard the woman reply.

"How on earth can she tell them apart?" Salma marvelled. They looked remarkably alike to her. All fair-haired and petite.

She went over to a small group consisting of two granddaughters and, she imagined one of their mothers.

"Hello I'm Sergeant Din. Thanks for inviting me back."

"Girls, get your things together. We'll be leaving shortly," said the woman. The girls went off and the woman turned to Salma with a smile.

"I'm Olly's wife, Pat. Can I help you at all, Sergeant?"

"No, just wanted to say thanks for the refreshments and tell you that one of my colleagues will be present at the reading of the will...this afternoon I think."

"Yes, at about 2 pm at the manse, Quentin's house. I expect you will have all our addresses."

Salma went across the room to speak again to the only two other people who had attended the 'wake', Neil Kerr and his wife Anne.

"How could we have known that his toothache was going to result in his murder," said Anne.

"How did you know about his toothache?" asked Salma.

"He had it at one of my fun events just after Christmas. Neil heard him gasp and asked what the matter was."

"Did you by any chance see the other two, non-family members at The Linn?" Salma asked.

"Yes they were in the row across from us. They stood out because there was no one else except yourself," said Neil, "but I didn't know them. She had snowy white hair yet didn't look old enough for that."

"Were they a couple do you think?"

"I couldn't say. He looked quite a lot younger but then her hair aged her so I can't be sure," Anne agreed.

Back at the station, she told the others what had transpired at the funeral: the lack of mourners, the fact that Mrs Cunningham senior had been there, the fact that two unknown people had attended but sped off immediately afterwards and the fact that both Neil Kerr and his wife knew of Arthur's toothache.

"The only wee thing I noticed was that the grandmother of the three wee girls there seemed able to tell them apart very easily for someone who only saw them at two of their christenings, at least that's what she told me, apart from the time the three sons went to Canada with their families a few years ago. Kids change a lot in a few years and I thought the three I saw were remarkably alike. I also felt that Pat Cunningham made sure I didn't talk to the youngsters but that might have been in case meeting a policewoman was scary or she didn't want them to dwell on the fact that their grandfather was murdered…if of course the kids have been told that."

"Frank. See if you can find that out this afternoon when you go to hear the will being read," Davenport told the constable.

Frank duly went along to the large manse, home to Quentin and Abigail Cunningham. He was ushered into the lounge where a suited, bespectacled middle-aged man was sitting at a table, presumably brought into the room for the purpose of the will reading. Frank sat down on a dining room chair and looked round. There were no children present.

The lawyer shuffled some papers in front of him and gave a dry cough. There was immediately silence in the room.

"Good afternoon. My name is Morris Blackwell and I am the lawyer in charge of the affairs of the late Arthur Cunningham. Let's get straight down to business.

The lawyer went on to read out all the preamble necessary and Frank, bored, looked round the room. As they were seated in a semi-circle in front of the table, he had a good view of everyone except the two on his right whom a quick glance told him were two women.

"….I leave my house to my son Thomas who as a penniless writer will probably need it most. I leave the rest of my estate to my son Oliver. I leave nothing to my youngest son, Quentin as he being a man of the cloth will want nothing to do with worldly goods."

Frank saw the man wearing the dog collar glance across at one of the women on his right. He had a rueful smile on his face.

"Don't worry, Love. I didn't want any of his money anyway," the woman said.

"I know you don't, Abigail," said Tom whom Frank recognised from his visit with Penny to Arthur Cunningham's house, "but I don't want his house. It'll be sold and the proceeds divided equally among the three of us and Mum."
"Penniless writer...huh!" said the other woman on Frank's right. "When was this will written? You've written two successful novels…and yes, I agree with Tom, we don't want his house and I'm happy to share the proceeds."
"It's kind, Tom and Susan, but. we have to respect the old man's wishes," said Quentin.
"Rubbish!" said the other man, Oliver, Frank now knew. "Likewise with the rest of the estate. It will be divided among us all. OK with that, Pat?" he turned to ask his wife who sat next to him.
"Of course, Olly. It goes without saying that we divide everything four ways. We have two children each so we're equal in every way and your Mum must have her share."
The older woman sitting on Frank's left, had been trying to speak and now had her chance. "Nothing at all for me, boys, though it's very kind of you. I am planning to remarry out in Canada and Jason has more than enough for us both." This obviously was not news to her family as there were no gasps of surprise.

"She must have told them this already. Wonder if her husband knew. Not that it matters as he wasn't leaving her anything anyway," Frank told his boss later.

"She could have fought that will as his wife,"
mused Davenport. "Arthur Cunningham was as
nasty in death as he was in life. He could have
set his sons against each other and his wife
against his sons. And as for leaving nothing to
his youngest son and saying what he did about
him not wanting material things, was a low blow."
"Yes, and saying that Tom was a penniless
writer, showed how little he knew about his
eldest son," said Frank, indignantly.
"Did you find out if the kids knew about the
murder, Frank?" asked his boss.
"Yes, Sir. They had told them all except the
youngest one. Said they didn't want any one of
them finding out at school."
"Did you think to ask the lawyer the date of this
will?" asked Davenport.
Frank flushed.
"No, Sir, sorry I didn't. It's no excuse I know but
I've never been to a will reading before and I got
caught up watching all the reactions."
"Not your fault, Selby. I should have reminded
you to ask that. I forgot that you hadn't attended
a will-reading before. I'll get along to my room
and ring the lawyer."
He left but was soon back with the interesting
news:
"The will was dated three days before Arthur
Cunningham died!"

CHAPTER 28

Fraser chose to take Penny with him to Ayrshire, to Maybole. They left with Salma. At first the journey was quick on the M77 but once off that at the Dutch House roundabout, the roads were narrower though more scenic.

"How come you know these roads so well, Brainbox?" asked Penny, making use of Frank's nickname for her colleague.

"I brought my aunt here a couple of times to see Jan de Vries."

"Who's he?"

"He's dead now I think but he used alternative medicines and my aunt had ME and her doctor was at a loss about what to give her. She felt her didn't recognise ME as an illness and she'd read Mr de Vries column in Then Sunday Post…"

"…do people actually read that paper?" laughed Penny. "I used to like it when I was younger. My Gran bought it and I read The Broons and Oor Wullie. She loved the bit that was in diary form with wee stories for each day. My dad said he was embarrassed having to buy it for her!"

"Yes, my grandma bought it too and my aunt lived with her. De Vries's medicines were very expensive but my aunt gave them a try for about six months. Didn't help her and she suffered for about another year before the ME mysteriously went. Oh drat! I've come the wrong way. I was thinking of Troon and we're going to Maybole." Fraser managed a three-point turn and they went back to the Dutch House roundabout.

"Look out for signs to Maybole after we've passed the outskirts of Ayr, Penny," he said. They passed a sign for St Quivox which Penny said made her think of Cornwall where she and her parents had gone a couple of times. She got our her mobile phone and using Google Maps, located Maybole.

"Not far now. I love watching that wee blue circle on the screen move as we move," she told her companion. "What did you think of Arthur Cunningham not knowing that Tom has had books published? If I'd been Tom I'd have sent him copies!" said Penny.

"Me too. Tom must be a nicer person than we are."

"Yet he's the only member of the family who had the opportunity to kill his dad!"

By now they were approaching the village of Minishant, a picturesque little place with chalet-like houses lining the street.

"Hey, I'm moving down this way soon, "Penny said. "Look out for any good pubs for Gordon."

There were no pubs to be seen and as they went into Maybole, no churches either.

"Penny spotted a steeple but when they got up closer it was the ruin of an old church and further on what could have been a church was the town hall. They drove on up the narrow street. They came to Carrick Academy and as the road was about to lead them out of Maybole, Fraser turned the car and Penny wound down the window and asked a passer-by if there was a church nearby.

"The nearest one, my dear, is the Baptist church, across the road and down to the right then there's the Catholic one up to the left and sitting up high on the road. You can't miss it; it's got large statue of the Virgin Mary outside."

Penny also asked her where Market Street was and it was before the turn off to the church so they decided to go first to Jenny Flynn's last known address. When they got there, the name McDonald was on the door. Fraser knocked on the door and when it was opened by a young woman with a toddler at her side, he asked if she could tell him where the last owner, a Jenny Flynn, had moved to. She had no idea but suggested that they try the woman next door who, she said, smiling, knew everything about everybody.

"Afraid I've tried to avoid her since we moved in about a month ago. All I know is that wasn't the name of the folk who lived here before us."

Fraser and Penny went next door and the elderly lady invited them in. Realising that she was probably lonely, they accepted her invitation and once she had made them a cup of tea, she sat across from them and told them about Jenny Flynn.

"Poor lassie. I don't know why she stopped going to work so soon into her pregnancy but she did. Her mother and uncle visited her but no one else. She had a wee baby girl, a bonny wee thing and she seemed happy enough but tragically she took her own life. She left a letter asking her mother to look after the wee one who was by this time a toddler."

Penny asked if she knew where Jenny's mother lived but she did not have that information.

Thanking her for her hospitality and managing not to give her any information that she was obviously very keen to have, they left.

"So Jenny Flynn and Olivia Flynn both had babies round about the same time," said Fraser. They drove up to the church.

They both got out, walked up to the massive wooden door with large brass handles and on finding the door open, walked in.

It was dark and gloomy inside. Fraser called out, "Anybody here?"

There was no reply so as their eyes grew accustomed to the gloom, they walked towards the altar. There were more than halfway there when they heard a door open and a light came on over the chancel. They saw a little old lady carrying a vase of flowers and trying not to scare her, Fraser coughed loudly and they both moved into the light.

"What a fright you gave me, young man! Why are you here in the church?

Unexpectedly the woman who was wearing a purply,heather-coloured tweed skirt, sounded English, not Scottish.

Fraser and Penny approached her, holding up their warrant cards.

"I'm Constable Fraser Hewitt and this is Constable Penny Price. We're from Glasgow and we'd hoped to see the minister to ask if he had a register of hatch...births, marriages and deaths. It's in connection with a murder in Glasgow."

The woman had retraced her steps and put on more lights. She came back towards them and in the light, they saw that she had a twinkle in her eyes.

"I may be old but I also say,' Hatches , matches and dispatches"

Penny saw that Fraser's face was red. Obviously, like herself, he flushed when embarrassed.

"I'll get the minister for you on one condition, Constable Hewitt."

"What's that Mrs…"

"Miss or should I say these days Mizzz Hobart, spinster of the parish you might call me. I'd like you to say, 'There's been a murder' the way Taggart said it," she said, rolling her rs.

Fraser laughed and complied and Penny giggled.

"Thank you. I'll now get the minister for you." With that, the little lady went out the door through which she had come in.

"I love these old churches," said Penny. "If it wasn't for the fact that I want to be married in my own church, I would choose somewhere like this. What about you, Fraser, are you going to marry Erin?"

"Oh yes but we want to save first. Erin's only just been made permanent at her school and it will probably be about three years before I reach that dizzy height, if I'm lucky enough to get a permanent post."

"I thought you'd soon be getting promotion in the police force. Why on earth change jobs at this time? I wouldn't change jobs for anything!"

"I've enjoyed being with you lot but before that, the department I was in was so boring and I don't think teaching will ever be boring from what Erin tells me and I love reading books and poetry."

"I think you'll make a good teacher 'cos you've got what I've heard is the crucial thing… a sense of humour but it'll mean putting off your wedding, won't it?"

"Yes, but it'll be worth the wait and we might move in together while we save for a wedding. Neither of us is religious like you, Penny and neither are our parents so they won't object, especially if they're saved the expense of a wedding!"

At that moment, a tall figure wearing denims and a tee-shirt came through the door, followed by Miss Hobart.

"Hello. I'm George Mackay, minister here. How can I help you?"

Penny, blunt as ever, blurted out," You don't look like a minister!"

"In denims, no dog collar and with long, curly hair! Yes, it took my congregation a while to get used to me, didn't it, Mattie?"

The little lady grinned.

"I loved you from the start, George dear. Now excuse me while I get the flowers sorted for tonight's service. We have a wee communion during the week, once a month. One of the minister's innovations."

She suited her actions to her words and left them.

"Right folks. What can I do for the Glasgow polis?"

"We'd like to look at your register of births and deaths. Mr Mackay. I'm assuming that you have one."

"Please call me George. Yes, we do have, not just one but umpteen. They're in the vestry. Follow me."

Once in the small room, he delved into a cupboard, turning his curly mane to ask what year they were interested in.

"We're not entirely sure," said Penny.

"This one goes back about twenty years. He hauled a book out of the cupboard and laid it on a rickety table which, had it been human, would have groaned with the weight. "There are loads more. 'Fraid I can't help you unless it's something recent. I've only been here about six months."

"It's further back than that, "said Penny, ruefully. "It was too much to hope that you'd be old and doddery and lived here for years."

Fraser and George laughed.

"Penny always tells it as it is," said Fraser and Penny blushed.

"We're going back about five to ten years," he added.

"Well, as there's only one relevant register needed and two of you, I'll leave you to it. Just leave the thing on the table when you leave. Good luck."

Calling out, "Cheerio, Hattie. See you tonight," he departed.

Fraser opened the register.

"Once I've read the first page, Penny we can take a page each. You do the right side and I'll do the left. We're looking for the name Flynn...Olivia Flynn. Her baby was Lisa Flynn. Silence reigned.

When Hattie came down from the chancel, Penny asked her how many churches there were in Maybole.

"Just us and the Catholic church. I call it the 'church on the hill'."

It was well past lunchtime before they had finished reading and they had found no Flynns in the closely - written pages. They decided to make their way towards the town and stop at a convenient place for a late lunch. This turned out to be a Costa shop and they lost little time in eating a toasted teacake accompanied by a latte each.

Back on the road, it took them about five minutes to find their next church

"I think we might be lucky here, Penny," said Fraser. "Flynn sounds like an Irish name so Olivia was probably Catholic."

They walked up to the door which again was open. Father Dunn, whom they found in the sanctuary, took them into the church office and brought out the relevant register. He was quite taciturn and obviously had his mind on other things as he asked no questions.

About an hour later, Penny found the name Flynn.

"Here, Fraser, Olivia Jennifer Flynn, died in October ..six years ago."

"Jenny Flynn!" exclaimed Fraser. "The name of the girl who left the bank under a cloud. The one who committed suicide. Worth coming here, Penny. Jenny Flynn is the same Olivia Flynn mentioned in the newspaper cutting."

"Should we check to see if the baby died?" However more searching did not reveal the death of a Lisa Flynn.

Father O'Brien who had given them the records, saw them out. Penny stopped at the door.

"Father, do you remember an Olivia or Jenny Flynn who died about 6 years ago?"

His prim lips tightened.

"I remember the funeral…yes but more than that I am not prepared to say."

He walked off.

By now it was almost six o'clock but at least their hard work had determined something. Olivia-Jenny Flynn had had a baby and committed suicide when the baby was a toddler.

"It's obvious that they *are* the same person as the priest was obviously not pleased that he'd had to bury her. Suicides shouldn't be buried in sanctified ground, "said Fraser. "I wonder who persuaded him."

CHAPTER 29

It was 9 am the following day and the team had congregated in The Incident Room.

"Right. Let me sum up," said Davenport. "As Frank and I know, the will was written only three days before Arthur Cunningham was killed.

There were gasps of surprise from the other three.

"Frank heard yesterday that two sons, Oliver and Tom, inherited but were going to share with the one left out. They wanted to include their mother too but she announced, to no one's surprise apparently, that she was about to remarry and her husband was well off. From what I've heard about Arthur Cunningham, I'm surprised he didn't disinherit them all!"

"Could the one, Quentin, who got nothing, have been in an older will if there was such a thing and tried to kill his father before the new will could be written or signed?" asked Frank.

"I don't think Quentin is short of money. He lives in a lovely big, old house," said Salma.

"Yes, but it's not *his* house, Salma," said Fraser. "It belongs to the church and when he retires, he has to find somewhere to live.

"Do you know *everything*?" asked Frank disgustedly.

"I knew that Frank and I'm not a brainbox," chipped in Penny. "His wife doesn't work so they can't be that well off with two kids and a house to save for. She hesitated then went on, "But I can't see him committing a murder…he's too nice."

"So were some of the other murderers we've unmasked over the years we've worked together," said Davenport.

"It's more likely to have been Carol, Arthur's ex…sorry not ex…Arthur's wife. Maybe he refused to divorce her and she has this new man whom she wants to marry," said Fraser.

"Look, Team," said Davenport, rubbing his ear. "Before Salma tells you two about the funeral and you two, probably Penny, tell us about your trip to Ayrshire yesterday, I think we should refresh what we know about the possible suspects even the few we've previously discounted.

He turned to the board where the names of the family were written.

"Right, Tom Cunningham. Any motive?"

"Hated his father from early childhood…." began Fraser.

"…made worse by his father ridiculing his writing ability. I think he told us Arthur called it his 'scribbling'.

This from Penny.

"Why wait till now to commit murder?" said Davenport.

"Been nursing his wrath to keep it warm, as Burn's put it in, 'Tam O' Shanter', said Fraser, earning a glower from Frank who hated it when his colleague quoted from literature he had never heard of or even had heard of.

Davenport wrote, 'hatred and belittlement' beside Tom's name.

"Alibi?" he asked.

"None," they chorused.

"Susan Cunningham?"

"Hated Arthur for belittling her husband. Had worked in hospital before marriage so could have knowledge of insulin," said Frank.

"Alibi?"

"Lunch with friends, "Penny volunteered.

Needing to write nothing across for Susan's name, Davenport went on to mention Oliver and Pat.

"I went to visit them yesterday and they did share a joke at the White Cart. I didn't need to lead them into that bit of information because when I asked if they'd seen anyone else there, Pat said that one man had looked over at them when Pat had burst out laughing at a joke Oliver had told her. She couldn't describe the man or any of his friends but Oliver added that there was another small group there too so that seems to give them both an alibi, albeit a weakfish one. Oliver probably hated his father as much as Tom. Quentin and Abigail both have alibis though Quentin had his father's mockery of his chosen career as a motive and perhaps he knew that he was in an earlier will so we've narrowed it down to only Tom from those six. What about Arthur's wife, Carol Cunningham?"

He rubbed out Oliver, Pat, Quentin and Abigail and added Carol's name.

"She'd a bit of a journey to come from Canada," said Frank, sarcastically. "Surely she'd have had to have had prior knowledge of the Dental Hospital visit."

Salma had been sitting quietly but she spoke out now.

"I've told you, Sir, what was bothering me from the funeral. Will I repeat that?"

"Right Salma, let me summarise what you told me and then we can go on to what's been bothering you. According to Salma, there were two mystery mourners at the funeral and they along with Neil Kerr and his wife were the only non-family members at the crematorium. Mr Kerr asked the staff at the bank and no one wanted to attend. Now, Salma, on to what has been bothering you."

"Well, Sir, as I said to you yesterday, after the funeral Carol Cunningham seemed to be able to tell her granddaughters apart and they are all petite blondes."

"Nothing special about that. I knew a couple of twin boys who were identical but our teacher could tell which was which," said Frank.

"Yes, but your teacher saw them five days a week. Carol hadn't seen hers for a couple of years and in that time children can change a lot. Also, I had the feeling that the parents were keeping the children away from me."

"Nothing strange there either, "said Frank "Big bad policewoman...keep kids away from anything unpleasant maybe?"

"What is the point you're trying to make, Salma?" asked Davenport. "You've mentioned this twice now."

"Maybe Carol Cunningham has been over more recently. Maybe she asked Arthur for a divorce and he refused her and she killed him to get her freedom."

"Sir, that's the best motive so far, "said Penny excitedly. "They'd keep the kids away in case they mentioned this in Salma's presence."

Davenport smiled and turning to the board, he added, 'possible motive' beside Carol's name on his now very short list.

"Well done, Salma."

Davenport continued:

"I haven't met all the family so I propose to call all the sons in today. Which of you has seen them all?"

It transpired that it was only himself who hadn't seen them.

"Right, Selby. We'll do the interviewing. That works out well as Fraser and Penny will need to get their reports typed up. By the look of young Penny's face this morning, you two found out something relevant on your trip to Ayrshire yesterday afternoon. OK Penny, you'll probably burst if you don't get to tell us all and I think Fraser will let you do the talking."

"Penny bursting all over the room would be messy, Sir," chipped in Frank then reddened as he realised that he had interrupted his boss.

Davenport laughed.

"Right Penny. The floor is all yours."

"We found out from a neighbour..."

Penny paused for effect.

"...that Jenny Flynn committed suicide when her daughter was a toddler.

Then Sir, we hit it lucky at the second church. Stupidly we didn't think with the name Flynn that the record would be in a Catholic church so we wasted some time at a Baptist Church.

However, we found the name Olivia *Jennifer* Flynn in the death records..."

"…Jenny Flynn!" interrupted Frank, receiving a glare from Penny.

"Well done Sherlock," she retorted." Yes, Olivia Flynn and Jenny Flynn are the same person."

"The priest obviously knew something he wasn't prepared to tell us. Don't priests have to keep quiet about things…"

"…Yes, they can't tell what they hear in the confessional box," said Frank.

"But we didn't ask about that," stated Fraser. "He just said he remembered the funeral but more than that he wasn't prepared to tell us."

"Maybe he thought you were going to ask about her confessions and pre-empted you," said Davenport. He turned to the board and wiped off Jenny Flynn's name.

Frank had been looking thoughtful.

"Some older priests might still not want to bury a suicide in holy church ground," he said.

Fraser had also been thinking.

"Sorry, Frank, to bring up Shakespeare again but wasn't Ophelia in 'Hamlet', to be buried outside the church grounds because she committed suicide. Maybe Father O'Brien was persuaded to bury Jenny Flynn against his better judgement. I wish we could have found something out about the baby, Lisa Flynn. Maybe she died and Jenny got depression and killed herself."

"It's likely that Jenny was an unmarried mother," said Davenport. "Does the Catholic Church see such mothers as sinners perhaps?"

They all turned to Frank.

"Some priests still take a hard line but not all," was his verdict.

Davenport had started writing on the board.

WHO KNEW THAT THE WILL WAS BEING
CHANGED?
WHAT WAS IN AN OLDER WILL?
WHEN DID CAROL CUNNINGHAM COME
ACROSS FROM CANADA?
WHO WERE THE TWO MYSTERY GUESTS AT
THE FUNERAL?
WAS LISA FLYNN ARTHUR'S CHILD?
WHY DID JENNY FLYN COMMIT SUICIDE?

"Right, Selby. Get on the phone to the three
sons. Give them interview times. I think they are
all flexible. Quentin's a minister so can plan his
own timetable: Tom's a writer so works at home
and Oliver is, I think I was told, on leave from the
army. We'll interview them all on the same day if
possible, so leave time in between. Salma, get
on to the lawyer and ask about an earlier will. If
he tries to hide behind a cloak of confidentiality,
remind him that his client is dead and this is a
murder case. If there *was* a will, ask him what
was in it."
He paused.
"Penny, get on to Neil Kerr at the bank and see if
anyone there knows anything about a baby and
Jenny Flynn."
"Sir, the woman who worked there…Frank was
looking at his notes…Jean Anderson, said that
no one kept up with Jenny after she left."

"Ok but Penny just check. Maybe Jean Anderson didn't know everything that was going on. Then you and Fraser get your notes about yesterday up to date.

Before you do that Fraser, go and visit any of the sons…your choice…or wait…Salma, do you know which family grandma was staying with?"

Salma said that she did not know but that that one called Becky had asked her grandmother to come with her

"Whose daughter is Becky?"

No one knew so Penny went out to get her notes. She ran back into the room with the information that Becky was Quentin's oldest.

"Would have chosen him anyway, Sir. He's got the biggest house," said Fraser, earning himself another glower form Frank.

"Find out if you can, when granny arrived. I'd like to have that information before I meet them."

"Right slackers, enough chat. Off you go. We'll meet back here after lunch."

CHAPTER 30

Fraser arrived with the news that granny was indeed staying at the manse and had arrived two days before the funeral

Tom Cunningham was interviewed, Frank having decided to call them in in order of age.

He sat looking relaxed in his chair.

"I'm not so nervous now having been here before, "he laughed. "How can I help you?"

"I'm afraid it's not a laughing matter, Mr Cunningham, as of your brothers and the three wives, you are the only one of the family without an alibi for the time of the murder."

Tom looked serious now.

"You've told my colleagues that you hated your father. Maybe that hatred and the knowledge that you would inherit in his will, made you decide to kill him."

"Yes, I did hate him but why should I wait till now? I didn't know that I would inherit anything in his will, in fact we were all surprised that he left any of us anything. I don't need money how."

"Who or what else could have benefitted by an earlier will?" Frank asked.

Tom thought for a few seconds.

"I've no idea. He never showed any interest in his grandchildren and to my knowledge he didn't support any causes. Anyway, none of our daughters could have murdered him!"

"Was it not odd that he left your mother who was still legally his wife, out of the will?" asked Davenport.

"Maybe he thought...oh I don't know," said Tom. "Maybe he thought she might marry again, as I believe she is going to," continued Davenport.

"But he wouldn't have known that."

"Why are you so sure of that? She might have written to him or phoned him to ask for a divorce and surely you would have known that as you all keep in touch with your mother. Would she not have told you all first?"

Tom said it had been a surprise to all of them when she announced it at the will reading. Davenport mentioned that his constable had not seen any signs of surprise on hearing about the marriage but Tom merely said that his mother was an attractive woman so it was not a shock that she had found someone else.

"That's probably why we didn't gasp out loud. Just surprised it hadn't happened sooner," he added. and, realising that he was going to get no further, Davenport switched off the tape.

Fortified by a coffee made on Davenport's own coffee maker, he and Frank were back in the interview room half an hour later.

They challenged Oliver Cunningham in the same way as they had challenged Tom, only this time saying that although he had an alibi, he might have aided and abetted Tom in the planning of their fathers' murder.

"A bit of a coincidence that you should be on leave when your father is killed, surely?" he suggested.

"Why would we want to get rid of my father now? Why not years ago?" retorted Oliver.

"His will was changed not long before his death. Maybe you found out that he intended to change it and thought you would be disinherited in the new will."

"So I got leave…some weeks ago because I knew that my father was about to change his will. I don't think that holds water, Sir. Why would any of us know that the will would be changed and anyway we didn't expect to be in any will! So the will was changed recently, Sir?"

"Yes, three days before the murder."

"What about your mother?" asked Frank. "Why was she left out of it?"

"I've no idea. I don' think she expected to be in his will either. After all they've been apart for some years."

"So he didn't know that she was planning to marry again, then?"

"Well we didn't know till recently and we're closer to her than he was."

Once again Davenport ended the interview. When Oliver had gone upstairs, Charles decried the mobile phone.

"I think Tom phoned him and prepared him for the question about his mother's plans to remarry and so no doubt will Quentin be prepared too." Some minutes later, facing Quentin Cunningham, it did appear that he had been forewarned though he looked more uncomfortable than his brothers as he assured his questioners that his mother had not rung or written to them telling of her plans to remarry.

"And I'm sure that she hadn't got in touch with my father either," he added.

"How did you feel being left out of the will, Sir?" asked Frank.

"I never thought I'd be in one in the first place."

"I put it to you that you and Oliver abetted your brother Tom in the planning of the murder of your father," said Davenport.

"Would Tom not have prepared an alibi if this had been preplanned?" asked Quentin.

"So you've discussed alibis, Sir?" said Frank.

"Of course we have. Tom told us he was writing and had no one to back that up, not even Susan.

"We might have been very suspicious if you all had gilt-edged alibis, Sir," countered Davenport.

"Well, all I can say is that none of us believed we'd inherit from my father and that hatred of him...well as a Christian I can't say it was as strong as hatred on my part...dislike of him...didn't fester for years and then just erupt. Anyway, how would we know that he was going to be at the Dental Hospital that day?"

For a third time, Davenport switched off the tape recording machine and escorted Quentin upstairs.

"Thank you, Sir. Would you please ask your mother not to go home to Canada just yet. Get her to ring the station and fix an appointment for herself to be questioned."

Back in his room at the top of the corridor Davenport said to Frank.

"It will be interesting to see what Mrs Cunningham senior has to say. My money's on her and Tom committing this murder though I'm not yet sure of their motive."

"I thought Oliver looked a bit worried when you said the will had been changed only three days before the murder. I wonder why, Sir?"

"Make a note of that Frank when you're transcribing the interviews."

Davenport looked despondent.

"Trouble is what Quentin pointed put, how would they know about the dental appointment?"

CHAPTER 31

Penny ended up going to Salma's on Sunday afternoon as neither of that young lady's siblings had time to spare to look after their young brother and sister. Salma had bought them two DVDs so they were happily ensconced in front of the TV in the lounge, clutching a bag of crisps each. The two young women went into Salma's bedroom and, taking two pillows from the bed, sat on the floor with the pillows at their backs. First, they discussed Penny's forthcoming wedding, deciding that as soon as the current case was solved, they would go into town together, probably to Debenham's to choose their dresses.

"Gordon's going to wear a kilt. Have you seen those bridal dresses which have tartan in the box pleats?

"Oh no, Penny. You'd have to find out what tartan he was wearing without giving away what you were going to do and anyway would that go with a veil...you must have a veil and a long train for me to hold up."

Salma sat entranced by the picture she had formed in her mind.

"Salma, I don't want a fancy dress, well not a meringue one..."

"" I wasn't thinking of a flouncy thing with masses of lace and things, more an elegant dress with a plain train....I'm a poet and I don't know it," she giggled.

"Well, we're on the same wavelength then as I want something elegant."

She laughed.

"Gordon won't recognise me: he's never seen me elegant, just once in a dress. What colour of dress do you want, Salma?"

"That's your choice, Pen. Not mine. Will you be having any flower girls?"

"No. I've got no young relatives and Gordon has none and anyway we both agreed that we didn't want any kids at the wedding. You won't be offended if I don't ask any of your family, Salma, will you?"

"Of course not. You hardly know them. Are you paying for the wedding yourselves?"

"Yes though Mum and Jack want to pay for our honeymoon which is super of them. They've offered us £2000. Isn't that great of them? We were going to go to Tarbert but might go to Bali now."."

"So if you don't mind me asking, how much can you spend on the wedding?"

"Well if we ask thirty people at £30 a head that's nearly a thousand pounds plus flowers and cars. The best bit of news that I haven't managed to tell you yet is that there's a flat over the vet's and Gordon's pal is married and needs something larger so he's offered it to us and we're going to rent it from him and we've got about four thousand saved between us which should well and truly cover the wedding."

"Where do you plan to have the reception?"

"Oh Salma, we went to The Busby Hotel on Friday evening and they'd just had a cancellation for Saturday June 21st so we grabbed it. Gordon can choose any date as he's almost self-employed but I have to choose a weekend for you and Frank and Fraser and the boss and the DS and for Mum and Jack too although Mum said she'd get any day off as I'm her daughter. I just hope that we haven't got a big murder case on then. However, Mum was keen for us to have a venue with nice surroundings and she suggested the Manor Park in Skelmorley, near Largs and I love it as we went there quite a lot when I was younger, for afternoon tea, so we rang The Busby and cancelled it and got in touch with Manor Park and they can have us on that date so we've booked there."

Penny was almost breathless as she finished this explanation. Salma laughed and, going into the kitchen, brought them both a glass of lemonade.

"I was going to apologise for it being a soft drink but you can't drink anyway with driving," she told her friend.

"Right, let's say we go into town the first Saturday we have off. I think Mum and Jack will babysit your two if Shazia or Shahid aren't available."

Penny put her glass down on the table next to Salma's bed and Salma did the same.

"Right my friend, spill the beans about the doctor," said Penny grinning.

"Not many beans to spill, Pen. I saw him that one time on my own and I think he liked me. He complimented me on my hair and told me about his wife dying and about his daughter but I just felt…you know…something between us. I've never met anyone who's made me feel like that. Kind of breathless and my heart started racing too."

"Very Mills and Boon, Miss Din," said Penny. Salma aimed a punch at her friend's arm.

"Trouble is, how on earth can I meet him again?"

"Well, you could call him into the station to sign a statement about Arthur's medication."

"But I've written that already."

"He doesn't know that does he? We could do it at some time when the DCI is away."

"Then what?"

"Well you said his daughter was about ages with Farah. Is there something you could invite her to?"

Salma looked excited.

"It's her birthday a week on Monday. I could invite some of her classmates and tell him it would give him some time to himself if Serena…that's his daughter's name, came along…"

"…and he might offer to come along and help," laughed Penny, "and even if he doesn't, he'll have to drop her off and pick her up and he might suggest he repay you for that invite and invite Farah to his house."

Penny as usual was getting carried away on a wave of excitement. Salma laughed.

"You're a genius Constable Price."

In Erin's house, Fraser was discussing with his girlfriend, his chances of getting accepted for teacher training.

"I don't think they'll be taking anyone on now…it's usually around September I think," said Erin. "I've forgotten that part but you could ring the college and try and if not it just means you waiting a bit longer and at least you have a job to tide you over. I think you'd make a great teacher. You've got the first criterion…a good sense of humour."

"Thank you kindly, Madam. The biggest snag I can see is that I won't be getting paid for a year and I might not get a permanent job at the end of it. You were lucky to get one after your probationary year. It might put our engagement and wedding off for longer, Erin. How do you feel about that?"

Erin looked serious.

"We could get engaged and plan to marry when you got settled."

"Would you be prepared to wait?" asked Fraser.

"You know I would. We could always move in together. That's not frowned on these days is it and neither of us is really religious, neither are our parents so I don't think they would disapprove."

Fraser enveloped her in a bear hug.

A similar conversation was taking place in a café in Shawlands. Frank had just proposed to Sue. Unlike Gordon, he had no ring and had just blurted it out. Sue looked worried.

"I know my folks like you, Frank but how would yours take it, especially your dad?"

Frank frowned.

"He won't like it one little bit, Sue. Oh, he likes you well enough but not I think as a daughter-in-law. If only I'd saved a bit more, I could buy a flat and then it wouldn't matter so much but with still staying at home, it could make life difficult. I certainly couldn't ask you to move in with me there! If only I could get promotion. Will you marry me?"

"Yes, Frank, I will but I don't think we can get married right now. I haven't saved much either and I would never move in with you, not if it was going to cause trouble between you and your parents. My parents wouldn't approve of you moving in with me either. Besides if we did marry soon, what if we had kids and one set of grandparents wouldn't have anything to do with them…and I'm sorry, I won't convert to being a Catholic as I like my own church and it's been a big part of my life."

"I wouldn't ask you to, Sue so what do we do?"

They decided to just go on as they had been doing but save hard and hope that Frank's parent would get used to the idea of their son having a Protestant girlfriend.

In Newton Mearns, Charles and Fiona were finding that having their little son home was a mixed blessing. He had slept on the car journey from the hospital but had woken when the car movement stopped. They had been told not to pick him up too often and to keep him in the incubator the hospital had lent them. He did not cry but they could see his face turn towards them when they spoke, however softly. They had brought two kitchen chairs into the bedroom that had been Kathleen's for a short time. They were wooden and had been scrubbed clean. They were not comfortable but they could not leave their baby son.

They would sit with him through a long night.

CHAPTER 32

Charles, alone in his room, made himself a coffee. He rang Fiona to find out how she was, promising to be home in good time that night. His wife laughed and told him that she of all people, knew that he couldn't make promises like that and she was proved right as Charles was just about to ascend to 'heaven' to talk to Solomon Goodchild about the case when his phone rang. It was Solomon himself with the news that there had been another sudden death on Charles' patch. He asked his DCI to come upstairs and they could discuss the first death and he could give Charles the little he knew about the second.

Riding up in the elevator, Charles felt his spirits rise at the fact that Solomon was in charge of him right now and not Grant Knox who always set his teeth on edge with his constant desire to inform the press that everything was on the point of being solved. Solomon did not call him 'man' and make him feel like a naughty schoolboy visiting his headmaster.

Seated in Solomon's office, with a cup of tea this time and a digestive biscuit which he had to stop himself 'dunking' in his tea, he informed his superior that they had ruled out five of the immediate family members. He praised Salma for her ideas about the grandmother, telling Solomon his sergeant's gut feeling that the woman had been over from Canada before the visit for the funeral.

"I've read the details of the case that you gave me yesterday, Charles but take me over the names still on the list of suspects."

Charles had printed off the names still to be discounted and handed Solomon the list which now read:

Tom Cunningham

Carol Cunningham

Grace Hawken

Woman who got the engagement ring.

"Tom's a likeable man...I know that doesn't rule him out, Sir. If Carol did indeed come over to ask for a divorce and was denied it, she would be a strong suspect especially as she and her sons haven't 'come clean 'about the visit, if indeed she made one. Grace Hawken is a niece. We haven't got around to her yet, I'm afraid but she would seem a rank outsider in the murder stakes. We haven't found out who the mysterious ring person is yet but it could be Jenny Flynn who was sacked from the bank and if it is, then Jenny is dead. She committed suicide."

Charles sat back in his chair and Solomon handed him back the short list.

"Right, this new death is probably not connected to the murder of Arthur Cunningham but I'm always suspicious of two sudden deaths close together so humour me on this one, Charles and look into it. If indeed the murder is linked to Jenny Flynn, then this man lived quite near her, well, in Ayrshire."

He handed Charles a sheet of paper with instructions to read it once back in his own department, saying that he was confident that both cases would be solved in good time and saying that he would handle the press if need be. Charles apologised for not being further on with the case. He was mindful that Grant Knox would be harassing Solomon for results.

"As I said, Charles, I have every confidence in you and your team. Grant Knox is away for a while so he isn't here to worry about the press." When Charles went back down to his own department, only Salma and Frank were there. He told them that there had been another murder but that he had not as yet read up on what Solomon Fairchild had given him about this.

"I'll do that over lunch and when the others come back, I'll discuss it with you all."

Salma had gone to the lawyer's office as he had asked her to come in rather than him tell her things over the phone.

"Do you want me to tell you about the old will, Sir, or wait till the others come back?"

"Wait I think. Frank and I still have Arthur Cunningham's widow to interview, probably this afternoon so better wait, rather than us having to repeat ourselves. Write up what happened. Selby, get the tapes and make transcripts of our three interviews. Have lunch when you are both ready. I'm going home as usual."

Bumping into Penny on the way out, he repeated his instruction to wait till after lunch, asking her to write up what, if anything, had happened at the bank.

"Tell Fraser to do the same about his visit to Mrs Cunningham senior even though she'll be coming in for an interview. I'll apologise to him myself for what might have been a wasted journey though it did help to know how long she'd been here before I spoke to the sons."

Penny had just greeted Frank and Salma when Bob at the desk came in to tell Salma that there was a call for her. She came back, grinning. As Frank chose that moment to leave the room, Penny asked her what was so funny.

"Do you remember that I'd thought about inviting Javed Ahmed's daughter Serena, to Farah's tenth birthday party, well he's just invited Farah to *her* birthday on Saturday afternoon!"

Her face fell.

"What if we haven't solved this murder and I have to work on Saturday?"

As they went to the canteen, Penny tried to reassure her friend that the case *would* be solved, telling her that their boss had told Frank that he was sure that the murderer was Tom Cunningham, perhaps egged on by his mother.

At home, over lunch. Charles read the information he had been given. A man had been found dead in his house in Maybole in Ayrshire. There was a contusion and a large lump on the man's head. Martin Jamieson was out at the scene and would get back to Charles s soon as possible.

"Were these deaths connected, Fiona? I wouldn't have thought so had it not been for the Maybole connection. It would knock on the head my idea of one of the sons being involved in the murder of his father."

"Just have to keep an open mind, Love. Investigate all angles."

"Well at least I don't have God breathing down my neck but I didn't ask Solomon when he was due back."

CHAPTER 33

After lunch, the team met in The Incident Room. Davenport took his place at the white board with the rest sitting in front of him.

"Right folks, me first. There's been a murder in a house just outside Maybole in a wee place called Whitefaulds. It's quite an isolated spot. The man lived alone. There was a contusion and a lump on the back of the man's head. Martin Jamieson is on the case and I'm waiting for his report. Meanwhile I'll let Frank sum up our three interviews and I'll just say that we have Arthur Cunningham's widow coming in later today, hopefully. Over to you, Selby."

Frank stood up.

"Only one son doesn't have an alibi but as Quentin Cunningham and Oliver Cunningham both pointed out, would Tom not have made sure of an alibi had he been the murderer..."

"... not if it was unpremeditated," chipped in Penny.

"Yes but that would mean Tom having insulin on his person..."

"...did we check that none of the family is diabetic?" asked Davenport.

"Sorry, Sir that was my fault. We didn't," said Salma apologetically. "I think I assumed that they'd have mentioned it when we asked about their father having the condition but of course they wouldn't if they'd injected him with the stuff. I'm so sorry."

"Not just your fault, Sergeant. I didn't think about it when I took over from you. I'll ask Carol Cunningham if any of her sons has the disease. Carry on Selby."

"Oliver got leave before his father's will was changed therefore he couldn't have planned the leave in order to commit a murder

However, the main thing that came across...I think you'll agree, Sir, was that none of the men thought they would be in *any* will of their father's. They all agreed that they hated or disliked him but why wait till now to get rid of him?

"Yes, and they didn't know it was a new will until when?" asked Salma.

"Well I mentioned to Oliver but it didn't come up in Tom's interview, did it Frank?" asked Davenport.

"No Sir, nor in Quentin's."

"I told Frank that I would put my money on the widow if she found out that the will was to be changed. Ok I know she said she didn't need the money but that's easily said. I've called her in and will ask her outright if she was in the country at the time of the murder. She might have come across to persuade Arthur to divorce her and he refused and told her she would be disinherited now. I think that's all that came out of our interviews. Penny, what if anything, did you find out at the bank?"

"Just that Jenny was friendly and then just stopped being friendly She started to keep herself to herself about six months before she was sacked for pilfering. No one kept up with her after that as she had discouraged friendship latterly. I went to the bank, Sir, 'cos I thought that it would be better to talk to all the women there but there were only three and one was a lot older, almost at retiral age."

"Thanks, Penny. What's your gut feeling about the bank thing, folks?"

Salma said that she thought that Jenny was having an affair with Arthur and Fraser agreed, saying that Jenny could have been the shy girl in the jeweller's shop. Penny added her two pence worth, saying that Jenny might have held out for an engagement before letting Arthur have sex with her. Frank wondered if she might have got pregnant so Arthur engineered the sacking to get rid of her. Davenport reminded them that Jenny had died before the murder so could not be the murderer.

Next it was Fraser's turn to tell of his visit to Carol Cunningham at the manse.

"I realise that you are now calling her in for interview, Sir…"

"Sorry Hewitt, I should have apologised earlier for that but go on, son, what did transpire when you met her?"

"She said she came across when Quentin rang her to tell her of Arthur's death. When I asked how she came to know her granddaughters so well, she said she got lots of photographs from each family. When I asked her about her upcoming marriage, she said that she had been going to ask Arthur for a divorce but he had died before she could do that. Incidentally, Sir she seems to have just found out about the cruel way her husband had treated her sons. She said they had protected her from that knowledge. She wished they hadn't as she would have left Arthur earlier and taken them with her. He had been unkind to her but not bullying."

"Right, Salma, your turn. What about a previous will. I take it there was one?"

"Yes, Sir there was an earlier will, written before Mrs Cunningham left him."

"In that one he left his estate, in its entirety, to his wife so that must mean, Sir, that she had asked him for a divorce recently….or…?

"…He intended to remarry," said Penny.

"Surely Neil Kerr at the bank would have known if that were the case," said Frank. "Hard to believe that a pompous, self-centred man like Arthur Cunningham wouldn't have wanted to tell folk that he had found another woman."

"And anyway if that were the case the will would have left everything to the new woman," said Frank looking pleased that he had worked that out before Penny who looked embarrassed at making such a silly comment.

"What did the sons say about their mother remarrying, "asked Salma.

"I asked Tom and Oliver and they said they were surprised to hear this at the will-reading."
"No they weren't "said Salma. "None of them showed any surprise."
At that opportune moment, Bob came in to say that a Mrs Cunningham had come to see DCI Davenport.

CHAPTER 34

Carol Cunningham must have been in her late fifties but she looked about ten years younger. Dressed in a pair of cream trousers with a sweater in matching cream and black underneath an unbuttoned black jacket, she looked very elegant and totally composed as she sat at the basic interview room table.

Davenport had Salma with him this time. He switched on the tape recording machine and said, "1.56pm on Monday 18th March. Charles Davenport and Salma Din in attendance, interviewing Carol Cunningham."

He sat back and nodded to Salma who smiled at Carol before asking her what her relationship had been with her late husband.

"As I said at the funeral tea, Sergeant Din, Arthur was unkind and unpleasant but not cruel. I've only now found out that he was cruel to my three sons though in my defence I stayed until they were grown up. I've no idea why they didn't tell me but they claim that they thought that everybody's fathers were like that!"

"Thanks, Mrs Cunningham…."

"…call me Carol please. I'd rather not be known as Mrs Cunningham. I've gone back to using my maiden name of Paterson and as you know, I'll be changing that name soon."

"Carol, I noticed at the funeral that you seemed to be able to tell your granddaughters apart and they are so similar. Oh I know that you saw them all a couple of years ago but kids change so much in their early years."

"Grannies are expert at these things, Sergeant," smiled Carol. "And I've seen photos in the intervening years."

Davenport leaned forward. He said severely: "I put it to you, Carol that the reason that you could tell the girls apart and the reason why the children were prevented from speaking to Sergeant Din after the funeral, is because you connived with one or all of your sons to murder Arthur. I put it to you that you did not arrive here in Glasgow after the murder but before it. You didn't want the girls to let that particular cat out of the bag, did you?"

Carol Cunningham had gone pale. The hands lying on top of the table were gripping each other so tightly that the knuckles were white.

"Surely I would have kept out of the children's way in that case, stayed at an hotel?"

"Well if, as you said, you only arrived here for the funeral, then I have to tell you that your eldest son, Thomas Cunningham is the one suspected of the murder of his father. He has no alibi for the time of death."

It seemed to Salma that the woman went even paler. He lipsticked lips stood out starkly against her alabaster white skin. Suddenly she looked every year of what they believed her age to be.

"Ok, I won't sit here and have my son blamed for something he couldn't and didn't do. I did come across before the murder. It will be easy for you to find this out. I came over on 19th February. I came to ask Arthur for a divorce. He refused to give me one…"

"..so with or without Thomas's help you killed your husband," said Davenport, sternly.

"I didn't kill him. I don't need a divorce. Peter and I have been living together for nearly a year now. We would like to be legally married but it wasn't crucial."

"So why, Carol," asked Salma, "did your husband change his will a few days after refusing you the divorce?"

"I don't know what was in his earlier will."

"He left his entire estate to you!" said Salma.

"So you think I killed him in the hope that he wouldn't be able to make a new will, is that it? I don't need his money. You heard me say that at the reading of the will, Sergeant. I repeat that I didn't know what was in an earlier will. He could have changed it many times for all I knew and I didn't expect anything. Neither I am sure, did my sons."

"I think you killed him because of a combination of three things, "said Davenport. "You thought he might be about to disinherit all the family, you wanted to be free to marry again and you had just found out how cruelly he had treated your sons. The only thing I'm not sure of is whether or not Thomas helped you."

"I can give Tom an alibi, Inspector," said Carol, defiantly. "We were together when Arthur met his death."

"Tom said he was writing."

"That was when we were trying to hide the fact that I was here at the time."

"Not a great alibi if you both committed the murder. Very well. You may leave now but I am instructing you to stay in this country. I would like you to hand in your passport."

The woman went into her handbag and pulled out her passport.

"All I can say is that neither I nor my sons, killed Arthur."

"One more thing, Carol. Are any of your sons or yourself, diabetic?"

"No."

"Says a lot that the sons didn't want to be known as Mr Cunningham and his wife didn't want to be associated with the name either!"

This from Salma as she and her boss left Carol at the top of the stairs.

"I know I said we suspected the murder to be a family thing but how on earth did any of them know that he was going to be at the Dental Hospital that day?" said Davenport.

" Yes, Sir, the only people who knew about anything connected to Arthur Cunningham's teeth, that we know about, were Neil Kerr and his wife. Maybe Arthur told Neil why he'd be off that day but why on earth would they want him dead?"

"I don't want to take Mr Kerr away from the bank unnecessarily so perhaps you would go to the bank, Salma and ask if he knew about the dental appointment."

Davenport went back up to his room and Salma went to get her hat.

She returned about an hour later with the news that Arthur had told his deputy that he would be away that Tuesday but had given no reason.

"Neil Kerr said that it would have been totally unlike his boss to give any reason for his absence."

"So, team," said Davenport when they had gathered in the Incident Room, "we are back to square one. No one in the bank knew and it's unlikely that the family knew."

He pointed at the names left on the white board:

TOM CUNNINGHAM
CAROL CUNNINGHAM
WOMAN AT JEWELLER'S
Across for the last name he wrote; IF NOT
JENNY FLYNN
A N OTHER who knew about the appointment at the Dental Hospital.
GRACE HAWKEN

"We haven't interviewed Grace Hawken yet although it would seem to be a remote chance that a niece whom he probably hasn't seen for years would have the need to get rid of him unless she was in cahoots with the family and did it for them so that they could all have alibis. That would make her a kind of hired killer...very crime novel stuff and not really likely. Any other ideas folks?"

Penny spoke up;

"What about someone at the dentist's? Would the receptionist know about Arthur's appointment?"

Frank laughed.

"That's about as likely as the niece doing it, Pen. I would say even more unlikely."

At that moment, the phone in Davenport's office rang. He left them but was soon back to tell them that Martin Jamieson had found out that the dead man discovered in Ayrshire had been killed by a blunt instrument. There had been a vase found by the body and it had hair and blood on it.

"So, we have another murder. Is it connected with the murder of Arthur Cunningham?"

Davenport looked at his watch.

"It's late now, folks so get along home. Tomorrow, in the absence of any other ideas, Penny, you get along to the dentist's. See who would know about Arthur Cunningham's appointment at the Dental Hospital. Frank, you visit Grace Hawken and see how friendly she is with the family and when she last saw Arthur. I figure as she didn't come to the funeral, they either didn't think to tell her or she just didn't come.

Fraser and Salma, I'd like you to interview neighbours of…"

He looked down at the sheet of paper he had brought from his room.

"…John Dalrymple . He lived in quite an isolated spot but there might be a neighbour near enough. If not, try any pubs in the surrounding area. If he lived alone then he might have ventured out for companionship."

He handed Salma the sheet in his hand.

"The address in written on this. Fraser, you should be au fait with the area now."

With those instructions, they left.

Charles sat for a bit longer in his room then he too left for home.

CHAPTER 35

When Charles got home, he found his wife looking excited. She poured him a whisky and lemonade, told him that dinner would be ready in ten minutes and led him into the lounge where she picked up the paper she had been reading.

"First, Love, I've seen what might be the perfect house for us in Troon."

"Ayrshire where there's been a suicide and a murder!" he laughed. "I wanted somewhere quiet and peaceful!"

"Whose murder?"

"Today Martin Jamieson confirmed that a death was indeed a murder unless the dead man knocked himself unconscious."

"Don't be sarky! The suicide, was that of the girl from the bank?"

Charles had kept his wife abreast of the investigation so far.

"Yes."

Fiona handed him the paper.

"I'll say nothing and see if you can pick out the house I mean. There are quite a few in Troon."

Silence reigned while Fiona checked on the dinner and Charles read. He walked through to the kitchen.

"Is it this one with four bedrooms and a partially floored attic, overlooking the sea?"

"It is. Oh Charles, it would be perfect…a room for Pippa, one for us and one each for our babies. We could make the attic into a living area for Pippa or a guest bedroom …and…"

"Whoa. Let's think about it a bit. When's the closing date for offers?"

"That's the thing, Charles. The closing date is Friday so I imagine that they've had offers. It was only today that I've found time to read the 'Houses' part of the paper."

"Right then we'll think about it tonight after dinner. Now, you said, 'First'. What's the second thing you've got for me?"

"Oh Charles, maybe this should have been the first thing. We can have Kenneth home for two days over the weekend."

"Oh help! I'm delighted that he's well enough to come home but I can't take Saturday and Sunday off at this stage of the current investigation. I could take one afternoon off and let the others cope, I suppose and let each of them have half a day off if they want it. What about Kathleen and Pippa?"

"The hospital is going to give us a tent thing for over his cot with an oxygen supply. I asked about infection but as they said, we have to have as normal a family life with him home as possible so we can't farm Pippa and Kathleen out for ever. We should just keep them out of the room this weekend. Kathleen's cot can come into our room. It's sensible Charles, as you and I might be carrying infection too and we'll be in his room."

"Where is Pippa?"

"Where do you think? In Kathleen's room. I think she's reading her a story. Oh I know she's too young to listen to a story but having said that, I haven't heard a peep out of her for ages. That's why I had time to read the paper!"

At that moment Pippa came into the kitchen.

"What's for tea, Fiona. I'm starving! "

"Is Kathleen asleep?" asked her father.

"Yes, she went off almost as soon as I started reading to her, Dad. I want her to like books so I thought I'd start right away." Pippa said earnestly.

"We're getting Kenneth home for the whole weekend, pet. Isn't that great news?"

Pippa's face fell.

"Does that mean that I've got to stay over at someone's house for the whole weekend?"

"No, love," said Fiona. "The hospital people think we should try and be as normal as possible but we'll ask you to keep out of his room and we'll take Kathleen's cot in with us."

"She could come in with me," exclaimed Pippa.

"Not yet," said Fiona, "but when I start bottle-feeding her, I'll take you up on that kind offer. Now, dinner. Sit down you two and Pippa can tell you about school and you can tell us both about work."

Pippa told them about the new play they were doing, based on a book called 'The Demon Headmaster'.

"Mr Snedden said as we did Shakespeare before Christmas we should have a modern play this time. It's about a headmaster who has hypnised…"

"…hypnotised," said her Dad.
"Hypnotised the school except for a few pupils, I'm one of the ones not hyp...notised."
"Do you like English, Pippa?" asked Fiona coming to the table with steaming plates of casserole stew.
"I love it, Fiona. Much better than horrible maths!"
As she started tucking into her dinner, Fiona asked Charles how the investigation was going. He told her they'd come down now to Tom Cunningham, the eldest son, with or without the help of his mother or vice versa with Tom helping her or one of those two on their own.
"Frank's going tomorrow to see a cousin but I think that's a bit of a wild, goose chase."
"What's a wild goose chase, Dad? "And what's for dessert, Fiona?"
"Jelly and fruit."
"You can't catch a wild goose because it just flies away so if someone goes on a wild goose chase it means it won't come to anything. Penny's going to the dentist in Shawlands to find out who knew about the dead man's hospital appointment and Salma and Fraser are going to a wee village whose name I've forgotten, to see any neighbours or friends or acquaintances of the murdered man."
"They're a good team, aren't they, Charles? I miss them."
"Yes and I'll miss them too if we move."
"Move Dad. Where to?"

"Fiona and I have been thinking that we'll have to move to a bigger house as the babies will have to have a room each and as I'd like to have a less hectic life to be able to help with Kenneth, we might move to a quieter place. Would you be very upset to leave your school, love?"

"Oh, Dad. I love my school. Can you not get a bigger house here?"

"It has to be what's best for us all, Pippa, and Fiona and I would like a fresh start in a place where no one has known us before and I would dearly love to have a quieter job. Would you not like to have me home more?"

"That's not fair, Dad. You know I'd like you here more but I'd have to start all over again making new friends."

"We thought about getting a house with a large attic space to make into a living room cum bedroom with ensuite for you and twin beds so that a friend could come and stay. Your dad might have had to move in his job anyway and better that you move school after first year than after you'd chosen your subjects at the end of second," said Fiona. "You'll probably have different teachers next year in your present school and you always make friends don't you and you can have your old ones to stay."

Pippa mulled this over as Fiona brought over her jelly and fruit.

"Well, I'd prefer to stay here but I know I'm too young to make these decisions so I'll do my best if we do move."

With this statement showing that she had an old head on her young shoulders, Pippa finished her meal, asked to be excused and went off to her room to get her homework done.

CHAPTER 36

Taking advantage of a school day and the fact that three-year-old Lizzie was upstairs having her afternoon nap, the Cunningham family had once more convened in the lounge of Quentin's manse. The mood was sombre this time, Carol having told them of her visit to the police station and the fact that they thought that she or Tom or she and Tom together, had killed Arthur.

"It didn't help that we'd lied, me verbally and the rest of you by omission, about my earlier visit to Glasgow. We were stupid to do that as they guessed through my being able to tell the girls apart after some years and us keeping them from talking to the sergeant at the funeral. All they needed to do was accuse Tom and I told them the truth, that I was here and so could have committed the murder. I said I could give you an alibi and then they said we could have planned it together, Tom."

"That was a silly lie, Mum. We weren't together."

"I know. Anyway, they could have got the information from flight lists. They've taken my passport. Jason's getting worried and I'd to dissuade him from coming over immediately.

"I'd like to meet him, Mum. Surely he knows that he has to ask my permission to have your hand in marriage!" quipped Tom.

"Tom, this isn't a time for Jokes," said his wife sternly. "Are you sure that you didn't make any phone calls that lunchtime?"

"Not totally sure, love but I was so engrossed in my writing that you were home before I even thought of lunch!"

"Mum, where were you at that time?" asked Oliver. "I know that Pat and I invited you to come out for lunch with us but you said you'd planned something…"

"…to help me murder father. Sorry folks."

Tom held up his hands in surrender as they all glared at him.

"I went to the shopping centre in East Kilbride to see if I could find a dress suitable for my wedding. Oh, I know, your father wasn't going to give me a divorce but we'd have had simple blessing at Jason's church. We'd looked into that possibility and although the minister couldn't actually marry us, he could give us a wee blessing."

"Quentin looked worried as he responded to this. "I don't think I could have found my way to blessing a union which would make you a bigamist, Mum."

"Don't be a drama queen, Q," said Oliver. "Where would this have happened, Mum? Not in a church, I imagine."

"No of course not. In Jason's house with just a few guests and all of you of course if you could have come over. No Quentin, darling, I wouldn't have asked a minister to do anything wrong in the eyes of the church but Mark, the minister is a young man and I think things are more liberal nowadays. He's blessed a few gay couples recently. However, it doesn't matter as I'm free to marry now. Someone did us all a favour by murdering your father."

"So no alibi for you either, Carol, unless something unusual or memorable happened in any of the shops round lunchtime," said Pat.

"I'm afraid not. I went into Debenham's and M&S but didn't see anything I liked so no assistant will remember me trying something on and the wee place I had a bowl of soup in was packed so I don't think that I would be remembered there."

"Didn't your last novel have a death by insulin in it, Tom?" said Susan, looking anxious.

"Yes, it did and you've all read it so it's not just me who knew about that kind of death."

"What if the police read your book and realise that you knew that insulin injected into someone without diabetes is fatal?"

"I don't imagine that they have time right now for reading novels, Susan," said her husband.

He sounded a bit less cheerful.

"I take it that you, my love and all the rest of you, do know that I'm not a murderer?"

Five raised voices assured him of this.

"But, Tom," said Quentin, into the silence that followed, we know you but the police don't know you, nor do they know Mum who has the best motive for killing father."

On this serious note, Abigail got up to go and collect Becky from school, asking her husband to see to Lizzie if she woke up and Tom, Susan, Oliver and Pat also prepared to leave.

"We've put our two into Care Club at their school every day for this week. They love it and we thought it would give us a free rein through this awfulness," said Pat.

"We're lucky that Helen brings Sarah home now that she's almost at secondary school age, "said Susan. "I wish now that they came home for lunch. That would have given Tom an alibi."

CHAPTER 37

This time it was Fraser and Salma who were on their way to Ayrshire, to a small village called Whitefaulds just outside of Maybole. Salma had never been to Ayrshire and Fraser regaled her with snatches of poems from Robert Burns.

"A good one for this case would be one about toothache which he called the hell of all diseases," Fraser laughed. He went on to quote some of 'Tam O' Shanter', the tale of a drunken Tam galloping his horse away from witches who caught up with him on the bridge at Alloway and how Tam got away but he left behind his horse's tail: "Left poor Maggie scarce a stump," said Fraser in ghoulish tones.

"Erin and another teacher at her school run the Burn's club and last year they took two winners in the Burn's competition to Alloway. They were hard bitten young guys, one who had a father in the Bar L...."

"...in the what?" asked Salma.

"Sergeant Din, don't you know the name of the prison the likes of us get folk sent to?" laughed Fraser. "Its real name is Barlinnie. Well these two boys stood on tiptoe to look into the shell of the church mentioned in the poem and one said excitedly, 'This is where the witches were dancing' and once they were on the bridge one asked Erin exactly whereabouts the mare's tail had come off! She hadn't the heart to tell them it was all make believe."

They were approaching Maybole so he pointed out the church where he and Penny had found out about Jenny Flynn's death and soon they were entering Whitefaulds. It was a small place and the house they were looking for was one of two, side by side with fields all round. Both houses had a garage.

"Well, if a neighbour as close as this doesn't know anything about whatshisname…"

"…John Dalrymple," supplied Salma. "Yes, it would be hard to live so near and not know anything," she agreed.

They parked the car in a rutted lane in front of both houses and got out. They figured that the dead man's house was the one with all the windows closed so walked up to the door of the other house. As they expected, the inhabitant knew John well and invited them in, having closely inspected their warrant cards.

Fraser preceded Salma inside and was shown into what he later described as a small parlour. It was full of furniture: settee, two armchairs, a piano and bureau. Every surface was covered in ornaments and a cairn terrier and cat had taken up residence on the two armchairs. The woman lifted the dog off one chair and, introducing herself as Edith Gray, invited the two visitors to sit on the settee, warning them that they might have dog and cat hairs on their uniform trousers when they left. Fraser sat down and Salma perched on the arm of the settee.

They had hardly sat down when Edith rose and went into the kitchen, taking the terrier with her. She popped her head out of the kitchen door to say that she was making a pot of tea and had some newly baked scones to go with it.

Fraser rubbed his hands together and settled back more comfortably into the chair while Salma tried to look comfortable on her perch. Mrs Gray returned with a tray, sat down and dispensed their tea from a large teapot.

"I've put Terry outside as he'd just try to wheedle your scone from you."

Their mouths full of scone, Fraser and Salma were delighted when, without any prompting, the old lady started to talk about her late neighbour.

"John was a lovely, young lad, about your age, son but thinner and shorter than you," she smiled at Fraser. "He probably weighed 9 stone soaking wet. He was a good neighbour. He helped me out at times and came in occasionally for a game of scrabble but he didn't make a nuisance of himself by coming in too often and I did likewise."

"How long did you know him, Mrs Gray?" Salma asked.

"He came here not long after Lachie, my husband, died....in 2010. We had a few too many malts one night and I cried over him about Lachie and he told me about the death of his young wife in childbirth. I was so happy for him when he met a new woman a few years ago but she stopped coming round after only a few months and when I asked him about it, he clammed up. After that he was very morose and to tell you the truth I wouldn't have been surprised if he'd killed himself. It was me that found him. Horrible it was. Could he have done it himself?"

Fraser looked at Salma who nodded at him.

"Well, Mrs Gray, the police have discovered that John was murdered, hit over the head."

"Oh, my God, whoever would want to kill John?"

"Did you see anyone that day, around his house or anything strange?" asked Salma.

"Well I heard a car arriving but it drove off almost immediately. I suppose that was strange as John didn't have visitors after the young woman I mentioned stopped coming."

"That's what we want to find out," said Salma. "Did you ever see the new woman? You said she stopped coming around so did you meet her?"

"Only once when she arrived, just as I was going out and I think she must have had a child as there was a child's seat in the back of her car."

"Can you describe her? Do you know her name?" asked Fraser.

"She was dark haired, slim like John but he never told me her name and I didn't want to be a nosy neighbour, so I didn't ask."

Fraser asked if she had a key for next door and when she produced it from behind a vase on the mantelpiece, he asked her to accompany them next door.

"We hope to find the name of a relation. I don't suppose you know of one, Mrs Gray?" asked Salma.

"No dear, I don't think he had a family. He only ever mentioned the wife who died in childbirth. The baby must have died too. If there had been a grandparent looking after his child, he'd surely have had photos in the house He never talked of parents of brothers or sisters but as I said, apart from one drunken night we didn't talk about personal matters."

By now they were in John's house, a two-bedroomed cottage, twin of the one next door. The parlour was uncluttered but also had a bureau which Salma went towards, asking Mrs Gray to witness what she did. Fraser went into the bedroom which was furnished, the other being a storage space littered with odds and ends such as suitcases and boxes, a guitar and lots of books scattered over the floor. There was still the chalk diagram of where the body had lain.

Salma found an address book, old and dog-eared and a file with bank statements in it. The drawers held memorabilia, photographs of a young woman in various stages of pregnancy, pictures of a registry office wedding, programmes from school shows. None of a baby. Salma asked Mrs Gray to look through the photographs to see if she recognised anyone and the old lady sifted through them while Salma looked through the address book. To Fraser who came out of the bedroom, she said that it seemed as if it was a female relative's address book as there was a name 'Elsie Dalrymple' on the inside cover. "Too old a book to be his wife's," she told him. "Probably his mother's which must mean that she's dead as she wouldn't have handed over her address book while still alive."

Salma turned to Mrs Gray.

"Any luck with the photographs?" she asked.

"Just one."

She held out a coloured photo of a thin, young man holding a toddler, aged about 18 months "This is John but I don't know who the youngster is. Could it have been his child? Surely not. He'd have had more pictures!"

Salma and Fraser looked at the photograph. The child was female.

"Are you thinking what I'm thinking?" asked Salma after they'd handed the key back to Mrs Gray, promised to let her know the funeral arrangements which might take some time if no next of kin could be found and were in the car driving back to Glasgow.

"You're thinking that the young woman could have been Jenny Flynn and the child her daughter," said Fraser. "But who would want to kill John Dalrymple so long after Jenny Flynn committed suicide?"

As Salma had no idea at all, they drove home in comparative silence.

CHAPTER 38

Penny lived very near the dentist so had a lie in which she enjoyed. At 9.30 she walked along Coustonholm Road and with not having a car to park under the railway bridge, she avoided the ubiquitous pigeons

There was a woman with a toddler at the desk but it was only minutes until they were seen to and Penny found herself facing a pleasantly smiling woman in her fifties or sixties. Her hair was white but she had a young-looking face.

"Hello, how can I help you"

Penny held up her warrant card.

"My name's Penny Price. My colleagues and I are investigating the death of Arthur Cunningham who was a patient here."

"That was a terrible thing to happen," the woman said. "As I told your colleague, Mr Cunningham was not a pleasant man but for someone to murder him…."

Her voice tailed off.

"Why I'm here is to find out who would know that he was going to be at the dental hospital on that day at that particular time," said Penny.

"Well the Dental Hospital sends an appointment card to the patient of course and also lets the practice know. I get that information and I tell the dentist concerned and one or other of us puts the information into the practice computer. I suppose it's possible for any of the other dentists to see Mr Cunningham's file but it's very unlikely that any of them would be interested in Kirsty's patient. Is it not possible that he told a workmate or a friend?"

A young girl came in at that moment and the receptionist's face lit up.

"Here's my lovely granddaughter. Come on round behind the desk, pet," she said, adding to Penny. "She's been having a brace fitted. I've got time off to take her to school now."

Penny smiled at them both and left.

Penny repeated her conversation with the receptionist to her colleagues, back at the station, adding that they knew that Arthur Cunningham had not informed his deputy where he was going so would hardly be likely to tell an underling at the bank and now there were few at the dentist's who would know.

"He didn't seem to be a man with friends, Sir," she added.

"What about the neighbour who gave him a lift for the bus?" asked Frank who had come in just after Penny.

"Sounds farfetched to think of the man hearing that Arthur was enroute to the dental hospital. Arthur was hardly likely to tell him that as he seemed to be a very private man. However, if he did, the neighbour drives there, parks, lies in wait for Arthur, and follows him to the department…no follows him to the *wrong* department, then to the correct one, finds a uniform and happens to be diabetic," said Davenport. "I don't think so but it's possible I suppose. We'll have to see if the man has an alibi for lunchtime on February 26th. Penny, would you pop round there on your way home today, in fact go now after we've heard what Frank has to say."

Penny nodded.

"It all hinges on someone with insulin either on their person or who had specifically taken insulin that day for the purpose of murdering Arthur Cunningham," Davenport said.

"We know that none of the sons is diabetic. What about Carol? No point in wondering about the wives as they all have alibis."

No one had thought to ask Carol Cunningham/Paterson if she was diabetic.

"I know we asked her if her husband was but she isn't likely to volunteer that she is, is she?" said Penny. "Would you like me to ring her, Sir. I don't imagine she would lie about it as she would know that we could contact her doctor in Canada. Or we could have her tested for it."

"Ring her and ask for the phone number of her doctor in Canada."

Penny left the Incident Room. She came back about twenty minutes later to say that Carol was not diabetic. She had given Penny the required phone number and as the time over there was appropriate Penny had rung and got the same news from the GP.

"So, team, we have Carol and or Tom Cunningham procuring insulin specifically for the purpose of killing Arthur or Grace Hawken, the niece, doing likewise unless she was diabetic. Frank, put us out of our misery: tell us that Arthur's niece is a Type 1 diabetic who was in Glasgow city centre that day with no alibi !!"

They all laughed.

Frank told them that Grace, like Jo Larbert in Australia, had no love for her uncle and had not seen him for years. He had not attended her husband's funeral ten years ago and she had stopped even sending him a Christmas card about five years ago as he had never sent her one. She knew he had died but saw no reason to attend the funeral.

"I remembered to ask if she was diabetic, Sir and I'm afraid she isn't. She has an alibi for that day as she lectures in English at Stirling University and was standing in front of about fifty students, talking about....'The Mayor of Casterbridge,'" Frank read from his notes

"I read that for school," said Penny making a face. "I think it was about a man selling his wife at a market. We could ask Fraser who..."

"...probably has the whole set of Hardy books at home, "finished Frank.

"Well, as it's not relevant to the case don't bother asking him," said his boss.

"All we've narrowed the killer list down to is Tom Cunningham and or Carol Cunningham who, having procured insulin from somewhere and by some chance having found out that Arthur was going to be at the Dental Hospital that day at lunchtime went into town, robed up and injected him with the insulin or A N Other who hated Arthur enough to kill him, is diabetic and knew of his appointment.

"Let's meet up after lunch and hopefully by them Salma and Fraser will be home from Ayrshire with some information about our second murder. If Mr Fairchild's hunch is correct, the two murders are linked and we might get somewhere from this second murder. If they are indeed linked, then maybe we'll find some important common denominator."

They left the Incident Room. Frank to write up his interview with Grace Hawken, Davenport to ring home and Penny to go to Arthur's neighbour.

CHAPTER 39

Penny and Frank went to the canteen when Penny returned, as Salma and Fraser were not yet back from Ayrshire. Frank told Penny about the boss helping him to fill in an application form for promotion and she talked a bit about her wedding preparations. Then Frank told her that he had proposed to Sue and not exactly been turned down but been asked to wait a while. Fraser and Salma joined them at this point but needing nothing to eat after having grabbed a sandwich from Tesco on the way home, they simply slotted into the conversation. Fraser told them that he and Erin were now unofficially engaged and were going to move in together. The wedding would be after Fraser had completed his teacher training and hopefully got a job.

"Gosh," said Penny. "I'm leaving around July, maybe June if I can get a sideways move down in Ayrshire. The wedding's on the 21st of June. Fraser will be leaving when college starts. Frank, you'll probably get promotion and be at another station and Salma…"

She hesitated and Frank rounded on Salma.

"What about you, Salma?"

"Well my brother has been hounding me about getting married and I think he might have a point," said that young woman, sending Penny a warning glance which her friend took to mean that she did not want anyone to know how she felt about Javed Ahmed.

"That would mean the boss having to start again with a whole new team," said Fraser.

Charles Davenport coming into the canteen at that moment and hearing Fraser's words, had to be told about their future plans. He looked a bit startled then told them that he and Fiona were planning on a move, possibly to Troon where he might have an easier workload and could help with the two babies, especially Kenneth. He left them to get a sandwich.

When he returned to the table, Penny said, excitedly," If you get a post in Troon, maybe I could get a job there too Sir!"

Frank guffawed, loudly.

"The poor man's probably leaving to get away from all of us, Pen. You'll be wanting me to get promotion to the same station next. What about Salma? Has she to persuade Mr Mohammed Right to move down there as well."

Knowing that Frank would never now be knowingly racist towards Salma, the rest all took this as the joke it was meant to be.

"And have I to get a school in Ayrshire so that I can teach all your children?" asked Fraser.

As Penny and Frank had finished their lunch, Davenport, suggested he make them all a decent coffee upstairs and they all trooped out, laughing. Once in the Incident Room with their coffees, Davenport took his usual stance in front of what were now two white boards.

"Don't know what we're all finding so funny when this damned case is going nowhere. Heaven help us if Grant Knox comes back and hears us!"

The team sat down, now looking serious.
Davenport turned to one white board on which
he had written 6 questions.

"Right. No one knew that the will was being
changed or no one is admitting to knowing it and
the only person worse off after the second will is
Carol Cunningham who claims, and I believe her
for what that's worth, that she will be well off with
her new man in Canada. The older will left
everything to her so the sons might have hoped
that a new will would include them if they'd
known about the new will which they claim they
didn't."

Davenport pointed to the third question.

"We now know that Carol Cunningham/Paterson
did come across from Canada to ask for a
divorce which she wasn't granted but she claims
that she wasn't much bothered about whether or
not she could marry her new man as they've
been living together anyway.

"I'll leave the fourth question just now. We don't
know but we suspect that Lisa Flynn, the baby
mentioned in the cut-out newspaper, was Arthur
and Jenny Flynn's daughter. Jenny committed
suicide and we don't know what happened to the
child."

He noticed Fraser and Salma looking at each
other.

"When I've finished summing up, we'll get your news, Salma: hopefully good news. Finally, we don't know why Jenny Flynn committed suicide but it doesn't take too much of a leap to think she might have felt the stigma of being an unmarried mother or perhaps couldn't cope with no job to bring in money. No matter why she left the bank, I don't see Arthur Cunningham giving her a good reference. Last question."

He pointed at the fourth line on the board.

"Who were the mystery guests at Arthur Cunningham's funeral?"

"Sir, the more I think of it the more I am sure that they came together, "said Salma. There was only the one car driving away from the crematorium. The woman had light-coloured hair and the man was dark. Maybe it was the hair but I got the impression that she was older than him."

"Right, Salma what did you and Fraser find out this morning in Ayrshire?"

Salma stood up.

The man who died, John Dalrymple, had a woman friend, dark –haired…"

"…like Jenny Flynn," said Penny.

"Yes, like Jenny Flynn, Penny and John's neighbour thought that the woman had a child as there was a child's seat in the back of her car We found a photograph which the neighbour identified as being of John, with a toddler, a girl. It doesn't help us with what happened to Jenny Flynn's daughter but it's possible that this was her, Sir."

Salma handed her boss the photograph

"But who would want to kill John Dalrymple?" asked Frank.

"Maybe he knew who killed Arthur Cunningham and was blackmailing them," stated Fraser.

"Could John Dalrymple be the other guest at the crematorium?" Davenport asked, looking at the photograph.

"I think the man at the funeral was darker than John looks in the photo though I might think that because the woman's hair was so light."

Davenport turned to the second white board.

He rubbed out 'Grace Hawken' and under A N Other he wrote,

WHITE-HAIRED WOMAN
DARK-HAIRED MAN.

So that leaves us with two unknowns plus Tom Cunningham and his mother, Carol.

"I was wondering, Sir, why Oliver Cunningham looked worried at his interview," said Frank.

"Yes, son you said that before but I think it might just be that he knew that his mother had been in Glasgow although it might be worry that his brother Tom might be guilty."

Should we call him in again, Sir?" asked Salma.

"Yes, why not. I'll leave you to arrange that Sergeant. Ask him to bring in copies of his brother's novels. You and your sidekick, Penny can interview him tomorrow."

CHAPTER 40

As soon as she came in on Wednesday, Salma rang Oliver Cunningham and asked if he would come in to the station later that morning. Fraser had volunteered to write up their notes of the visit to John Dalrymple's neighbour. Davenport had been called up to see Solomon Fairchild. Frank was reading a letter which had come that day stating that he had been put on the next list for promotions in Strathclyde. Penny was proof-reading Frank's chat to Grace Hawken as Frank's written work was prone to have mistakes.

Charles was invited to sit down and offered tea or coffee. Once settled with his drink, he told Fairchild of their recent findings.

"We think, Sir that you were right to think the two murders were connected. We are surmising that John Dalrymple had struck up a friendship with Jenny Flynn as we found a photograph of him with a toddler who could well be Jenny's daughter. We are pretty sure that the daughter belonged to Jenny and Arthur Cunningham. Why else would he keep the notice of her death?

We've ruled out all the family for Arthur Cunningham's murder, except for Tom Cunningham the eldest son who has no alibi and Carol, the dead man's wife who likewise has no alibi. Not much motive for either to have committed the murder. Carol had come across to ask for a divorce which wasn't granted but she's been living with her partner in Canada for some time so marriage wasn't crucial. I think she just wanted to tidy things up, Sir. Tom, like all the sons, didn't like his father but there was no recent event to spur him on to murder. He writes murder mysteries. I mean to get hold of them. We've dismissed Arthur's two nieces. One hasn't left Australia, hasn't even got a passport and the other lost touch with her uncle years ago. Neither benefits from either the old or the new will.

There are two unknown people who attended the funeral and didn't wait afterwards. Sergeant Din didn't get a good look at either one."

"So you've narrowed it down to either of them, Tom Cunningham or Carol…Paterson I think I read her name is now."

"Yes, Sir but I've also added in a shadowy person who perhaps murdered again. Constable Hewitt suggested that perhaps John Dalrymple was blackmailing the murderer so had to be murdered too. That's not so incredible I suppose. I feel that the Jenny Flynn angle needs more thought. I liked both Tom Cunningham and his mother although I know that nice people can be murderers."

"What's happening next, Charles?" asked Fairchild.

"Penny saw Arthur Cunningham's neighbour, the one who gave him a lift to the bus stop but he had an alibi for the time of the murder. Mr Spencer works from home and his son comes home for lunch from school every day. It was clutching at straws to think of him hearing that Arthur was off to the Dental Hospital and going there after him, complete with insulin but I had hoped that they'd had a running battle over a leylandii hedge!"

Solomon laughed.

"We've called in Oliver Cunningham to ask why he looked worried after finding out that there was a very recent new will. I rang him before I came up to see you to ask him to bring a copy of his brother's two novels with him. Penny went to the dentist's yesterday and found out that anyone there could have found out about the Dental Hospital appointment so I suppose we need to ask them all where they were on the day of the murder. Anything else, Sir?"

"No Charles, I think you've got all angles covered. Grant's away till Monday so you've got five days to get it all solved."

He laughed but Charles, hearing that news, felt under pressure for the first time. Solomon kept him a few minutes longer asking about his staff, especially Frank as he had read that young man's promotion application form.

"You think highly of him now, Charles, don't you?"

"Yes, Sir."

"Well that's enough for me. I'll endorse his application."

Salma and Penny interviewed Oliver Cunningham and he admitted to worrying for a second that someone in the family had heard of the new will to be read and worried that his father had disinherited the family.
"But I realised right away that none of us sons knew what was in the first will. When I later wondered about my mother, I guessed that she wouldn't have known either though might have suspected that she'd been left out of a new will if she was indeed in the first one."
Oliver handed over the copies of Tom's novels, looking worried again.
"I might as well tell you that the second book deals with a murder by insulin," he said. "But surely Tom wouldn't be daft enough to use the same modus operandum even if he was murderer material which he isn't. None of us has any motive for suddenly killing our father. Yes, we loathed him but we'd erased him from our lives and we had no reason to think we'd gain from an old will even had we known there was going to be a new one."

"He's right you know" said Davenport, when they were once again settled in the Incident Room. My gut feeling is to pursue the Ayrshire angle. "What are your feelings, Salma?"

"Well I'd like to know who the mysterious couple at the crematorium were, Sir, and I think we should question the folk who work at the dentist's as they seem to be the only ones who knew that Arthur Cunningham would be at the Dental Hospital that day."

"Ok. After lunch you get off to the dentist's. Take Penny and have a wee break before you come back. I imagine you've not had much girl time recently and will want some with Penny's wedding coming up. Ask their whereabouts on the date of the second murder, March 15th. Fraser, you're the quickest reader. Skim read Tom's second novel. Oliver told me that one dealt with an insulin murder and I'd like to see how similar his fictitious one is to ours.

Off they all went, Frank feeling relieved that his boss had not given him the other book to read.

CHAPTER 41

Penny and Salma decided to go for their coffee before going to the dentist's. They discussed going into town to look at wedding dresses for Penny at the weekend but thought it would be better to wait until the case was closed. Salma told her friend that she had given up hope of taking her sister to Dr Ahmed's daughter's party on Saturday.

"If I'm meant to get to know him, something else will turn up," she said philosophically.

The receptionist at the dentist was pleasant. She looked younger having had her hair restyled. Penny was complimenting her on how much younger she looked when Kirsty, Arthur Cunningham's dentist, came into the reception area.

Salma introduced herself.

"See you noticed Jo's new hair," Kirsty laughed. "We didn't recognise her at first. Think I might copy her as I'm beginning to look like my granny."

"My young brother had been on and on at me to have it done. Said I looked like our mother," the woman said, sounding husky. "Excuse my Talullah voice but I've got a bad cold. I'm only in today replacing Lorna who's also got a bad cold."

Salma asked if she could speak to anyone who would have known about Arthur Cunningham's appointment at the Dental Hospital in February.

"That would be myself, Jo, Lorna the other receptionist and my boss, Ian, I imagine, if he checks over these things," said Kirsty. "I'm free right now as there's been a cancellation so come along to my room."

Kirsty had a full diary of appointments for Friday March 15th. She told them that she only worked three days at the practice but went into help with students at the Dental Hospital on Mondays and Tuesdays. She laughed when Salma told her that Arthur Cunningham had been murdered there on a Tuesday in February.

"Well I would certainly be there and I didn't like him but I had no reason to murder him. I'm very involved with students on those days and I always go to the canteen at lunchtimes with some colleagues. When exactly was the murder committed?"

"Lunch time." Penny smiled to rob her next words of any threat. "We'll need to check up with your colleagues."

"I'm in here on Fridays."

Kirsty went down the corridor and asked the receptionist to go to her room. The woman looked nervous when asked about the dates of the two murders.

"My days off are Tuesdays and Thursdays unfortunately and I was off last Friday with this dratted cold. I pick my granddaughter up at school for lunch on those days and on other days she has school dinners and she comes here after school on my work days. But why would I kill Mr Cunningham? He wasn't nice but that's not a reason for murder," she laughed nervously.

As they walked back down the corridor behind the receptionist Penny said, glumly, "Everyone disliked him. Probably wouldn't have rescued him from a burning building but no one seems to have an overwhelming hatred for him!"

The boss, Ian, met them at the desk. He'd been forewarned by Kirsty and had the computer set up for his appointments in February/March. Salma stepped round the desk and checked the appropriate dates.

"I never met the man," said Ian.

"What age is Lorna?" asked Penny.

"She's just 18. It's her first job," said Kirsty. "She only came to us in September so I doubt she's had any runs-in with the dearly departed."

They were just getting into the car and trying to avoid the pigeons when Salma stopped. Telling Penny that she wouldn't be long, she went back into the dentist's.

Jo, the receptionist, was talking to a young girl who had just gone in ahead of Salma. She introduced her as her granddaughter. Kirsty was offering her a sweet from the jar on the reception desk.

"Thanks Kirsty but I'm not allowed sweeties," said the child.

"Well done, Jo. She'll grow up with good teeth. Think it's a silly idea of Ian's to have sweets on show but maybe he's trying to make sure we have new patients," she laughed.

"Does your brace feel better now, Elizabeth." The youngster nodded.

Salma asked for Jo's full name and address and home phone number and that of Kirsty the dentist and asked Jo if anyone from the practice had gone to the funeral.

Back in the car, Salma apologised for her hasty exit.

"Sorry, Pen. Just wanted to ask if any of them went to the funeral. We've still got a woman and man unaccounted for and two of those women we've just seen are or were white-haired. However, they just laughed and said they hadn't liked him enough to go. I got their names and addresses and phone numbers.

She looked down at the slip of paper and read out: "Jo Jones and Kirsty Stephen"

She sighed.

"Pity one hadn't been Flynn."

They arrived back at the station to find that Fraser had read the relevant parts of Tom's novel.

"It's an elderly man who is murdered," he told them all. "He's killed by his daughter whom he's been molesting for years. She, like her mother is diabetic and she injects him while he is sleeping. In the denouement, it's explained by the police doctor that insulin will kill a non-user if given in a large enough dose."

"Surely, Tom Cunningham wouldn't be so stupid as to copy his own plot" said Penny.

"No, but his mother might have read the book and copied it," said Davenport.

"Salma, you're looking very thoughtful. What do you think?"

"About what, Sir?"

"Do…you…think…it's…more…likely…that Arthur Cunningham…was killed by… his wife…rather…than by… his… son, Tom?" Davenport said slowly and sarcastically.

Salma felt her cheeks getting hot as she realised that she hadn't been paying attention.

"I don't think it's Tom and I don't think Mrs Cunningham had any real reason for killing her husband, Sir. I think as you said earlier, that it's linked in some way with the second murder in Ayrshire. However, should we not check everyone in the family has an alibi for Friday?"

"That's what I was going to ask you to do, ladies and gentlemen. Salma, you and Penny go and see Quentin and his wife Abigail. Hopefully Carol will be there too as it's nearly evening meal time. Fraser, you and Frank visit Tom and Susan and then Oliver and Patricia. We're lucky that none of them works office hours."

Driving to Tom's flat, Penny asked Salma why she had not been listening to their boss back at the station.

"It's so unlike you, Salma. You're always the good pupil," she laughed.

"Something's niggling at the back of my mind, Pen."

"What?"

"If I knew that it wouldn't be niggling, would it, you silly clot?" said her friend.

Tom had been seeing his publisher on the Friday and had taken Susan with him into town. They had stayed in town for lunch, having first put their daughters into Care Club at 3.30 so they did not have to rush home and had treated themselves to a movie.

Oliver and Patricia had stayed at home painting their living room. They had had to stop on the arrival of two army colleagues of Oliver's. The two men had stayed till about three thirty then Oliver and his wife had gone to school to pick up Laura and Rose.

Quentin had once again been parish visiting. His wife had been at home with their younger daughter Lizzie and had hosted an early birthday party for the wee girl, meaning to have another party on the actual day for her cousins. Carol had helped her.

"As we know that the murder was probably at or around lunchtime, thanks to John Dalrymple's neighbour, "said Davenport back at the station. "That would seem to let those three couples out. I imagine," he said, despondently," that Quentin's parishioners will again give him an alibi."

It being about six o'clock, he sent them all off home with a request for them to come in promptly at 9 the next day for a brainstorming session.

CHAPTER 42

Friday saw the team in The Incident Room prepared for the brainstorming session that their boss had promised them. He came in shortly after they had seated themselves.

"Sorry I'm a bit late but before we start I've got some news for you. We put in a bid for a new house and Fiona has just rung to say we've been successful in our bid."

"Where is it, Sir?" asked Penny, never one to stand on ceremony with anyone.

"It's in Troon and…"

"…. Gordon and I might live there too…. sorry, Sir," Penny blushed.

"That should put the house prices in Troon down a bit," Davenport laughed.

He went out, calling over his shoulder for someone to help him carry down cups of coffee from his coffee machine.

Once they were all back in the room, Salma asked about how Pippa was feeling about change of school.

"She's only just moved up to secondary school and made new friends, Sir"

"She wasn't too happy but we've sweetened the pill by telling her that she can have her own attic suite of rooms and have her friends to stay. We plan to convert the huge attic for her: large bedroom with twin beds, toilet and wash basin and wee alcove for kettle and such like. I'm sorry for her but I have to do what's best for all of us and I want to be in a smaller station with hopefully less erratic hours. A quieter place will be better for Fiona to take two wee ones out and about. There are four bedrooms so we can have one kitted out for Kenneth, a separate one for Kathleen when she leaves our bedroom, one for visitors and a large bedroom with en suite for Fiona and me."

"Gosh," said Fraser. "There's not going to be much of our team left here. I'm hopefully off to teacher training college in October and Penny's off to Ayrshire. Just Frank and Salma left here!"

"Well, while we *are* all here, "said Davenport drily, "There's the small matter of two murders still unsolved and Mr Knox gets back in four days. Perhaps we should get on with our jobs. Let's see who we have left on the suspect list." He turned to the white boards and rubbed out Tom Cunningham, Carol Cunningham and Grace Hawken, leaving:

White- haired woman
Dark- haired younger man
Woman who got the engagement ring (Jenny Flynn?)

Under this he wrote:

Jenny Flynn: suicide because no husband and no job?

Had she any family?

Was she friendly with second deceased, John Dalrymple?

"Right folks, what other questions do we want answered?"
Having filled up his two white boards, he turned to a flip chart and held his hand poised over a fresh, white sheet of paper.
"Who were the two strangers at the funeral?" said Salma. "Or is that the same thing as your white-haired woman and dark haired man, Sir?"
"Probably, Salma."
"Who had access to insulin?" said Fraser.
"Is there anyone at all connected with either case who has no alibi? "said Frank. "Sir, it could have been two separate murderers."
Davenport groaned, "Yes lad, you've put my fear into words. Two different murderers either connected or not connected. Penny, what about you?"
"Could Tom and Susan both be lying about where they were on the day of John Dalrymple's death? I hope not. I like them both but it's possible."

"I think, as I've already said, that we can rule out the family. None of them could have been at all sure that they were in the old will even if they did know a new one was being considered and there is no apparent reason why any of them should suddenly hate Arthur enough to kill him *now.* We've checked the dental hospital records and none of them were patients there that day and had the sudden urge to remove Arthur from the planet, all supposing they happened to have insulin on them.

No the scenario is absurd and also they had no motive except Carol being refused a divorce and as she's been living with the man in Canada, not being allowed to be officially married is hardly a murdering matter."

"Sir, would it have to be a strong man who killed John Dalrymple?"

"He looked quite puny and small in the photos we saw," said Salma. "Anyone could have hit him over the head. Were there fingerprints on the vase?" she asked hopefully.

"Not one so the murderer either wore gloves or wiped it clean afterwards," replied her boss.

"Sir, the person must either have driven there or got a taxi," said Salma. "Will I check the taxi firms round that area?"

Davenport nodded his assent and Salma left the room.

"Salma and I think that the young woman whom the neighbour said came round a few times, might have been Jenny Flynn. The child with her was a young girl," Davenport said.

There was silence while the rest digested this idea.

"So, let me think," he continued. "Jenny kills herself, leaving her daughter…"

"…she must have known someone would care for her daughter, Sir," said Penny.

"John Dalrymple takes on the wee girl. He is so angry with the man who didn't help Jenny or the baby…Arthur Cunningham who got engaged to Jenny then got her sacked when she became pregnant…that he kills him. Maybe he's diabetic…and someone who liked Arthur…" Frank's voice tailed off as he realised from the incredulity on his colleagues' faces that there was no one who even half liked Arthur and certainly no one who liked him enough to avenge his death.

On his other point, Mrs Gray would have seen John with the toddler surely, deduced Fraser.

Salma came into the room at that point.

"Only two taxi firms in that area, Sir and no one took anybody out to those two houses that day. Of course, the murderer might have taken a fare from Glasgow but checking up on that would be a huge job."

"Not so huge if we ask the main firms to put out a radio call," said Davenport.

"Look up all the taxi firms in the yellow pages. We might just strike it lucky. All of you get onto that now.

CHAPTER 43

They were all hard at work with their desk phones when Salma's mobile phone rang. She picked it up and went quickly out of the room. When she returned Penny saw that her friend was looking happier than she had for some time. She mouthed over Fraser's head, "What's happened?"

"Tell you later," Salma mouthed back.

They finished their calls and Salma went up the corridor to tell their boss.

"Right then. Get up to date with all your paperwork and we'll see what comes of this idea."

Penny went across to again help Frank decipher his notes which were usually a shambles. She liked paperwork and already had all her notes up to date.

Fraser asked Salma what, if anything, she could remember about the two unknown cremation attenders.

"The blonde-haired woman and the dark-haired man, "said Salma.

"That sounds just what my lecturer said when we were doing Shakespeare's sonnets at university. Apparently, Shakespeare wrote one dedicated to a dark-haired woman and a fair-haired man," said Fraser.

"Eh?" said Frank, earwigging from across the room. "Was Shakespeare a poof? I knew that there was a reason why I didn't like him apart from the fact that the guy couldn't write in sensible English."

"Frank Selby! How many prejudices have we got to get you out of?" said Penny angrily. "You've met my flatmate and he's a homosexual and you like him."

"I know, Pen. Sorry but I've had my prejudices as you call them for so long now that it's hard to realise that I offend someone. I wouldn't say 'poof' in front of anyone I knew was gay…honest."

Penny looked a bit mollified by this.

"To answer your first question, Fraser," said Salma, "All I can remember was that the woman was older than the man. I know what you're going to ask, was the young man John Dalrymple. I don't think so as this man was quite burly, smaller than the woman in height but broader than her."

"Who could they have been? No other family member's been mentioned. It wasn't anyone else from the bank as Neil told us no one wanted to go. The boss has always said that murderers often turn up at funerals. He was right in a few instances, wasn't he?"

"It would explain why they didn't wait to shake hands with Arthur's sons, certainly," said Salma. "Anything else? What about their car or cars?"

"As I told you all before with the silly arrangement at The Linn, you arrive to find cars parked all up the driveway so you park behind them. Then you get up to the crematorium to find the car park empty. When the previous cremation's finished, the mourners walk to their cars on the driveway and when you come out, your car is on its own. As the family came in funeral cars and Neil and his wife must have got into the carpark, I assume, there was only my car and one other on the driveway. It was a black or dark blue car, small, maybe a Corsa or a Polo of Golf. The two strangers went down the hill to that car."

Penny came across to them.

"Was that true, Fraser, about Shakespeare? What brought that up?"

"Salma mentioning a fair-haired woman and dark-haired man. Shakespeare wrote one of his sonnets to a fair haired young man."

"Poetry! I thought that Shakespeare only wrote plays…boring ones at that except Macbeth. I liked that one."

About to walk over to her own desk, Penny stopped.

"Salma didn't you say the first time that the woman was white-haired, not fair-haired?"

"Yes, Pen, you're right I did. Some detective I'd make," Salma laughed.

The laugh reminded Penny that she wanted to know what good news her friend's phone call had provided and she beckoned Salma away from Fraser's desk to her own.

"OK, what did the phone call say?"

"It was Dr Ahmed. His wee girl has measles so her birthday party has been postponed. I'm sorry for her but glad for me. Surely the case will be solved by the time the party is rescheduled! I was just about to resort to getting him to sign a statement of our interview with him!"

Penny linked her arm through her friend's and walked her to the door, calling over her shoulder for the two men to join them for their canteen lunch.

CHAPTER 44

It wasn't until halfway through the afternoon that Fraser took a call from one of the taxi firms he had contacted. One of the drivers remembered taking a fare out to Whitefaulds. Fraser asked that the driver come to the station when he had finished his shift and was told that business was light at the moment so he would be with them shortly.

Matt Thomson, the taxi driver, appeared thrilled to be in an interview room at the station or the 'nick' as he called it. Unlike many of the rooms previous occupants, he was completely at ease and stretched his long legs under the table.

"Right Mr Thomson," said Fraser who had been allocated this interview. "What can you tell me about the person you took to Whitefaulds last Friday?"

"Aren't you going to caution me, tell me to tell the truth and record the interview?" asked the man, looking disappointed.

"No that's only for suspects, Sir," said Fraser.

"Well I'm not surprised at you wanting to know about this character. I'm going to say to say 'he' but it could have been a reasonably well-built woman. He jumped into the cab as soon as I pulled up. I was aware of a long black coat and that's all as I was pulling on the handbrake. Needn't have bothered as I was straight off again. Glad to get a fare for that distance as business has been slack recently. You wouldn't believe the short journeys I get!"

"Ok Mr Thomson. Did you get any further impression of your passenger on the journey to Ayrshire?"

"Not really. I tried to chat to him…or her…but got only monosyllabic answers so I gave up. I looked in the rear-view mirror from time to time but he or she was always looking down and I all I could see was a black, woolly hat!"

"And when he or she got out?"

"Must have read the meter. He got out, handed me the correct amount plus a good tip and turned his back on me. To tell you the truth I'd half expected him to dive off without paying…he was so secretive. Had my fill of those jerkers. Do you know I once drove a guy in a turban? Looked in the mirror and he'd collapsed. I was passing a police station and I dived in and told them I thought I had a stiff in the car and when we got out to the cab, he'd legged it. Policeman told me it had happened before."

"You've said, 'he', a few times, Sir. Did you get the impression it was a man?"

"Well the person was the height of a tall woman or a smallish man and he or she seemed quite well built, though the long, quite bulky coat could have made me think that."

Fraser offered the man a cup of tea of coffee and was not surprised when he accepted with alacrity. Fraser guessed that the man would regale his mates in the local that night with his spell at the 'polis station'.

"So, Sir, no further forward except that the visitor to John Dalrymple was possibly quite well built," Fraser reported to his boss in his room at the far end of the corridor.

"Right! Assemble the others in The Incident Room, lad. I'll be down shortly."

Ten minutes later, Davenport turned over to another fresh sheet on his flip chart.

"Right we heard Selby's scenario...ok it turned out to be unlikely but we need some inventiveness, some instinctive feelings in the absence of hard evidence. I'll give you a few moments to think then just give me your thoughts. I'll start with mine.

"Jenny Flynn killed herself and her brother wanted revenge...ok don't know if she had a brother. He was diabetic. He was attending the dentist's in Coustonholm Road and overheard the receptionist telling the dentist that an appointment had come in for Arthur Cunningham at the Dental Hospital. While he sat there, the receptionist left the desk and he went round it and read the date. He decided that fate had played into his hands, so armed with a syringe he went to the hospital on the correct date, waited for Arthur to arrive, followed him to the two different floors, grabbed a white coat and took his chance before the dentist arrived to do the operation.

This unknown brother suspected John Dalrymple of toying with Jenny's affections and having committed one murder saw no reason not to commit another."

"Ok Sir, my turn," said Penny." My gut feeling is still, though I like them, with Tom and Susan Cunningham. Tom had been to see his father to ask for a loan. He was left alone in the kitchen and there on the table was the appointment for the dental hospital. He went home and told Susan that his father had refused to help him. He felt mortified and rejected. Susan who had been a hospital receptionist and had read Tom's novel thought she could get insulin from a doctor friend whom she'd helped out once, saying that her daughter was diabetic and had run out of insulin....it would be on a Sunday so she couldn't go to the pharmacist. Tom committed the murder...he has no alibi except one given by his mother who might be in on the act. On the Friday, Susan and Tom said they'd been together but one of them, probably Susan so that they'd both be equally guilty...."

"...Whoa young Penny. That'll do. Thank you."

"Penny, you should write books. What an imagination," said Frank in admiration.

"Sir I've given you my scenario. I can't think of another one even though it was obviously ridiculous."

"Ok Selby, you're excused. Fraser?"

"Jenny Flynn left a letter asking her family to avenge her suicide. Her brother...like you Sir I don't know if she had a brother is diabetic. He went to see Arthur to tell him about Jenny's death to give him the chance to do the right thing by his baby daughter and pay for her upkeep. He refused.

Arthur was called to the phone and left him in the kitchen where he read the letter giving Arthur the appointment for the dental hospital …sorry Penny to be copying your idea. He or another member of the family went to the dental hospital and injected Arthur with the lethal dose of insulin. One of them went out to Whitefaulds and killed John Dalrymple…"

"Yes but why does this person or these people want John Dalrymple dead?" said Davenport, his frustration showing in his voice." Never mind, let's get Salma's take on it before we come to that part again. Salma?"

"Like you all, except Penny, I'm sure that the murder is connected to Jenny Flynn and I agree that someone close to her avenged her death. I'm sure it was the two who attended the funeral. You always say, Sir that murderers often attend the funeral of the person they killed, to get closure perhaps. The fair haired…sorry Penny, the white-haired woman, looked big enough to fit the taxi man's description. John had to know them, Sir. You don't kill someone you don't know unless you're a hitman.

What reason would this person have for turning up at John's house at all? Sorry, Sir I'm asking more questions rather than giving possible answers. There's still something niggling at the back of my mind and I keep hoping if I don't try to think about it it will come forward."

"Maybe Jenny Flynn had introduced someone in her family to John," said Frank.

Davenport had been scribbling notes on the flip chart. Now he sat down on the edge of a desk.

"Right folks, let's look at all our scenarios. Mine first."

"At the risk of sounding a crawler, Sir, I like your scenario best, "said Fraser. "In my opinion, it has to start at the dentist's where the appointment for the Dental Hospital could be seen or heard about. It couldn't have been a causal reference because no one is likely to have said, "That awful man Arthur Cunningham is having a tooth out at the Dental Hospital at 12.00 on Tuesday February 26."

"No, more likely to have just been, that awful man Arthur Cunningham is having a tooth out at The Dental Hospital. Hope it chokes him," said Penny.

They all laughed.

"No offence Penny but I can't see that any doctor would supply a friend with insulin. I tried once to get an antibiotic from a doctor friend at a weekend and it was no go," said Fraser.

"Maybe Susan was blackmailing this friend into supplying it. Maybe she knew that her friend was having an affair and…"

The laughter from the others put an end to her reasoning and good natured as always, she laughed too.

"What if it was mentioned and someone casually asked when or stole a look at the letter as you and Fraser both suggested," said Davenport. "I think we've hit on the scenario but there are a lot of loose ends, the main ones being WHO knew or got to know of the appointment and HOW did they get the insulin. Sleep on it and we'll resume this discussion in the morning. Sorry to bring you all in on Saturday again."

CHAPTER 45

On Saturday morning they assembled once again in The Incident Room. Davenport looked quite anxious. He was obviously thinking of Grant Knox's imminent return. It had been nearly 4 weeks since the first murder. Luckily Solomon Fairchild was more adept at dealing with the press so the coverage of the second murder had not been linked with the first one but all it needed was a quiet news' day for someone to bring up Arthur Cunningham's murder having not been solved and if this happened after Knox was back in harness, Charles would be in big trouble.
"What can he do to you anyway, Love," Fiona had said before he set out that morning. "There will always be unsolved cases and you'll be getting away from him soon, hopefully. Will you be able to take the afternoon off to go with me to collect wee Kenneth?"
"If I can't take time off, who can?" he retorted.
Frank had an interview the following week. The letter had been waiting for him when he got home the day before. He too looked anxious. He was hoping that his boss might take him through some interview techniques but knew that the non - solving of the present cases might make time for this difficult, if not impossible.
Penny and Fraser were their usual sunny selves and when Davenport arrived in the room, they were in the middle of a discussion about the pros and cons of living together as opposed to marriage.

"I'd love to get married to Erin but we don't want to cause our parents a huge expense and with me opting out of the police force, I won't have money for some time so we can't foot the bill ourselves. We want to be together so sharing a small flat is the answer in the short term."

"I'm lucky that Gordon has a well-paid job and I can work too until any children come along. I wouldn't have felt right living with him but that's my church upbringing," said Penny.

Frank who had overheard this, put his oar in.

"You're a lucky dog, Fraser! My parents and Sue's would be horrified, both being churchy folk if we moved in together, unmarried. I just hope I get promotion soon then I can start to save in earnest. Like me, Sue wasn't expecting to want to marry soon so she hasn't saved much either."

At this point, Davenport came to the front of the room.

"Any further thoughts, anyone?"

Silence reigned as they looked at each other, glumly.

Fraser broke the silence.

"I know it's obvious, Sir but the first murder had to be done by someone linked to the dentist's in Shawlands. No one else could have known about the appointment unless Arthur Cunningham had a new woman or told his cleaning lady."

"If Arthur had a woman he would maybe have given Carol the divorce she wanted," said Salma. "He surely wouldn't have done something so uncharacteristic as tell a casual female acquaintance about a dental appointment.

"Can't see him telling a prostitute either!" said Frank. "Thanks for the sex, here's your money and on by the way I'm having a tooth out at the dental hospital on Tuesday!"

That made them all laugh and the tension that had been almost like the proverbial elephant in the room, dispersed.

"Right, let's look at the dental practice workers. We know that Kirsty knew as she put in for the appointment and the receptionist would tell her when the date came through..."

"...and so the receptionist had to know," said Penny.

"Right. Kirsty has a cast iron alibi. Although she was at the Dental Hospital that day she was in the canteen at lunchtime and no doubt lots of folk could back her up. It would be a silly lie as we could check that up...and we might have to if all else fails," said Davenport.

The receptionist, Mrs...does anyone know her name?" he asked.

"Jo Something," Salma said. "Hang on a minute I wrote it down the other day. She riffled through her notebook.

"It's Jones."

"Mrs Jones is off work on Tuesdays and she is also off on Thursdays which was the day of the funeral. She said she was off last Friday with a heavy cold so she had the freedom to commit the first murder, attend the funeral and kill John Dalrymple but what on earth would her motive be?" said Salma.

"Salma, you said her hair was fair then you changed it to white. She's recently had it dyed a light brown so she could have been the unknown woman at the funeral," said Penny excitedly."

"Yes but what is her motive?" said her boss, echoing Salma.

"She admitted that she didn't like Arthur Cunningham but if that was all the motive needed there would be a long queue of possible suspects," said Fraser.

"A long queue of suspects! Surely not."

Davenport grinned and the rest turned round to see their ex detective sergeant coming into the room, wheeling a pram.

"I thought it was time that you all saw our daughter and I've brought cream cakes to stimulate your brains."

They gathered round the pram and Fiona handed Charles a box of cakes.

Knowing that they did not have time to waste right now, Fiona took herself and her daughter up the corridor, telling them that she would feed Kathleen and help herself to coffee after making coffee for all of them to have with their cakes.

"Well, where were we?" asked her husband.

"Looking for a motive for the receptionist," said Fraser.

"Who also has to have access to insulin, don't forget," said Davenport.

"Glad I don't have diabetes," said Penny, licking her fingers. "How awful to not be able to have such gorgeous cakes or chocolates!"

Salma stiffened.

"Sir, that's what was niggling at the back of my mind. Chocolates. Sweets of any kind. The receptionist's granddaughter refused a sweet after her treatment that day Penny and I went down. Kirsty praised her for looking after her teeth but what normal child would refuse a sweetie after a visit to the dentist. What did she say again, Penny?"

"I wasn't there. I was in the car. You went back for some reason."

"That's right, to ask if any of them had been to the funeral. The receptionist said she didn't like him enough to go to the funeral. The wee girl said "I'm not allowed sweeties," said Salma. "Sir, could the girl be diabetic and if she is, could her granny be diabetic too?"

"Well done, Salma," said Davenport. "Just one problem now. Why, even if she killed Arthur Cunningham did she go on to kill John Dalrymple?"

"He knew she had committed murder and blackmailed her," said Frank.

"If they came to the funeral together then they were close so maybe they planned the first murder together and he lost his bottle and wanted to confess," Fraser chipped in.

"We have no contact details for the dentist folk. Will the practice be open this morning? Salma, get the Yellow Pages, find the number and try it."

"I've got the addresses and phone numbers for both Kirsty and Jo Jones," Salma replied. "I'll try Mrs Jones at home first."

Salma hurried off. On the way back, she almost literally bumped into Fiona with the pram in which Kathleen was sleeping soundly. Together they entered the Incident Room.

"No one at home but the practice is open, Sir, till midday. Private dentists take turns at being open at weekends and it's their turn to do Saturday morning."

"Some good luck at last. Salma and Fraser, get off there now. If Jo the receptionist is there bring her in for questioning and if she isn't there get go to her home later and bring her in. The rest of you, including me will grab lunch. Fiona, sorry I can't take time off for us to lunch together and I'm afraid I can't now take the afternoon off."

Fiona, declaring that she did not have time to have lunch out either, gave Charles a hug, saying she understood.

"If this is the case solved then you can have the whole day with your wee son tomorrow."

She departed. Fraser and Salma, stopping only to get their hats, raced off in her wake

It did not take long for Salma and Fraser to reach the dentist's in Shawlands. The receptionist, Jo, was on duty at the desk.

"Hello, Mrs Jones," said Salma. "Could we speak to the dentist present, please. I know it won't be Kirsty as she only deals with national health patients and won't be in today."

"Just call me Jo," said the woman, coming out from behind her desk. She walked up the corridor and came back with a man they had not seen before. He introduced himself as Harry Wilson.

"Hello, I'm second in charge here. Ian and I take it in turns to man the fort on Saturday mornings. How can I help you?"

Fraser took his arm and led him back up the corridor.

"Sir, you may have heard about the murder enquiry into the death of one of your patients at the dental Hospital."

"Indeed yes. Afraid I can' t help. I never met the man."

"No, it's not you we want to talk to, it's your receptionist. Can someone take over from her while we take her to the station?"

"Right now?"

"I'm afraid so."

"Well, no one's come in for an emergency appointment so I can do it myself. How on earth can Jo help you?"

"I can't tell you that, Sir. Sorry."

The two men walked back down the corridor. Fraser nodded to Salma who cautioned a scared-looking Jo and together they went out to the car.

It was Davenport and Salma who accompanied the receptionist to an interview room where Davenport went through the preliminaries.
"Your name, please, for the tape," he said.
"Josephine Jones," whispered the woman.
"Louder please," said Davenport firmly.
"Josephine Jones, "she repeated, squaring her shoulders and putting her hands, clasped together on the table top.
"Mrs Jones. Is your granddaughter diabetic?"
"She is"
"Are you diabetic?"
"Yes.
"Mrs Jones. Arthur Cunningham was killed by someone who had access to insulin."
There was a long silence.
"Why would I want to kill him?"
"You tell me."
"I also put it to you that you took a taxi out to John Dalrymple's house in Whitefaulds and killed him.
"Who's he?"

Salma intervened speaking softly," Mrs Jones, Jo, no one would blame you for killing Mr Cunningham if you are in some way related to a woman called Jenny Flynn who is we suspect the mother of your granddaughter. We think he got her pregnant then refused to help her when the baby arrived. She killed herself leaving you to bring up the little girl."

The woman started to sob, "Jenny was my daughter."

"You heard that Arthur Cunningham was to have an operation at the Dental Hospital, you were off work that day so you went in…"

"I didn't kill anyone," the woman said.

"So the fingerprints on the vase in John Dalrymple's parlour will prove not to be yours," Davenport said.

"I wiped the …."

The woman realised what she had done and slumped over the desk.

"Bring her a cup of tea, Sergeant," said Davenport.

By the time Salma returned Jo Jones was sitting up. She was staring down at the table.

"Mrs Jones, why did you go to the funeral?" asked Salma

"I wanted to make sure that the bastard was really dead," said the woman.

"My husband said it was a bad idea to go but he went with me."

"But you knew that he was dead as you injected him with insulin at the Dental Hospital," said Davenport.

"Insulin that you had for yourself or your granddaughter," put in Salma.

The woman's face crumple again.

"I advise you to be completely honest with us now. It might help you in court. Do you want a lawyer?"

Refusing the offer of a lawyer, Jo talked while Salma and Davenport listened intently.

It was if a dam had burst.

"I think she was almost relieved to be found out, Sir," said Salma as, having given Jo Jones into custody, they made their way upstairs.

"Yes, your kind approach helped I think."

Davenport echoed this statement when they were in The Incident Room with the others. He told them the pitiful story.

As they had suspected, Arthur Cunningham had become engaged to Jenny Flynn but when she fell pregnant, he had masterminded her removal from the bank by accusing her of theft. He had promised not to press charges if she chose to leave of her own accord which the poor girl did. Jenny's mother had paid Arthur Cunningham a visit at the bank, begging him to marry her daughter, a well-brought up Catholic girl who was horrified at the state she had found herself in. He had refused, nastily, just as he also refused to pay towards the child's upkeep, suggesting that Jenny have an abortion and casting doubt on the fact that he was the father.

Jenny had given birth to a daughter whom she named Elizabeth, Lisa as she was to be called. She had put the birth announcement in her local paper, cut it out and sent it to Arthur Cunningham, hoping that he might change his mind about helping them.

"Fat chance!" said Frank. "I can't say that I'm sorry he's dead. It was what I said, he bought a cheap engagement ring to get her to have sex with him, then left her to fend for herself when she got pregnant. What a rat!"

At first, Jenny had stayed in Glasgow with her mum but had moved back to a tiny flat in Ayr where she had been brought up. Jenny had found a friend in John Dalrymple when she met him at a group counselling session. He had lost his wife and baby. Jo had met him a few times and she had revealed to him how much she hated Arthur Cunningham.

She had seen it as an omen when she read of Arthur Cunningham's appointment at the Dental hospital.

Wracked with guilt after the murder, she had agonised over the fact that John might suspect her and when he asked her to come and see him, she was almost certain. When she brought up the murder, he had said he wondered who else could have hated Arthur enough to kill him. That, coupled with the look he had given her, panicked her. She asked him for a cup of tea and when he turned away from her to go to the kitchen, she had picked up a vase and hit him over the head with it.

She had run away from the house. She had not taken a taxi home, thinking the train more anonymous even though it had been a long walk to the station. She had said as little as possible to the taxi driver on the way there and hadn't been sure why.

"I put it to her that it looked like a premeditated murder as she had taken a lot of trouble making sure that the taxi driver who took her out to Whitefaulds could not identify her and she broke down again," said Davenport.

Sobbing she had admitted that she had had thought of killing John.

"I'm afraid that a prosecutor will see both murders as premeditated. She went to the Dental Hospital with no other reason to be there and she had the insulin with her though she could argue that as a diabetic she always carried it."

"The insulin, Sir," asked Penny. "Who did it belong to?"

"Jo Jones was type 1 as was her daughter, Jenny and her granddaughter, Lisa," said Salma. "There was plenty of the stuff at home."

"When she read of Arthur's appointment at the Dental Hospital, she had noted the date and time. She got there well before he did and had sat in the waiting room on Level 3, an anonymous woman among all the people waiting for treatment. She had taken the white coat she wore at the desk at the dentist's, correctly surmising that no one would question anyone, no matter the colour of the coat. Telling, Arthur Cunningham that he would feel a little prick in the arm, she had injected him with a lethal dose of insulin and slipped away as he slid to the floor.

"I could have forgiven him for his rejection of Jenny and Lisa but I could not forgive him Jenny's suicide. I had a terrible job persuading the priest to give her a proper funeral and he refused her the full mass…my Jenny who had harmed no one…and *he* had a fancy funeral," she wept.

"If it had just been Arthur Cunningham she murdered then she might have got off comparatively lightly after a full confession but I doubt that the court will see the murder of John Dalrymple in the same light," Davenport said sombrely.

"I take it she had remarried," Fiona said. "If her name had been Flynn, you'd have got to the end much quicker.

They were sitting in the nursery watching their little son. It was Saturday evening.

"Yes, Jenny's father died, Jo said of a broken heart, weeks after Jenny killed herself.

Jo was struggling to make a life for herself with the wee girl had gladly married an old school friend."

There was a quiet tap at the bedroom door and Pippa's head came round it.

"She's asleep...Kathleen...just as I got to an exciting bit in the book I was reading to her. Dad, can I choose the colours for my new room? Fiona, can I touch Kenneth?

"Ok Miss Question Mark," said her Dad. "Yes to both questions.

POSTSCRIPT

It was a lovely, sunny day on June 21st when Penny came out of her church in Pollokshaws on the arm of her new husband. Salma's little sister, Farah, handed them a silver horseshoe and they stood smiling for a few photographs, not many as the church was now in the middle of a building site. The nearby multi storeys had come down and the foundations were being laid for low rise flats on either side of the church. The neighbouring pub had been demolished and the police station where Frank had spent a boring time when the team had been split up during his bosses' trip to Malaysia, was only operational one day a week.

Penny and Gordon, along with Penny's mum and husband, had chosen The Manor Park Hotel near Largs for the reception, Mr and Mrs Maclean being adamant about halving the cost. The hotel had lovely gardens and Penny and her mum had brought Penny's grandmother there on a number of occasions for afternoon tea. The old lady had died some years ago but both Penny and her mum had fond memories of the place. It was reputed to have a resident peacock but they had never seen it. It had been decided to have most of the photographs taken there. Penny and Gordon had planned transport for everyone, asking those with cars to take those without and, rather than pay for a wedding car from Glasgow to Largs, they had asked Frank to drive them in Gordon's car.

The few church photographs having been taken, Frank hurried to Gordon's car while Penny and Gordon followed more leisurely, Salma carrying the weight of the long train and veil. She had Penny had spent a whole afternoon choosing the dress which was dazzlingly white and had a bodice covered in little seed pearls.

Once inside the car, Gordon wound down the back window and threw out a handful of small coins to the delight of the small children standing round hopefully. It had been left to Fraser and the best man to make sure that everyone got to the correct cars and Salma made sure that her brother Shahid had Farah with him. Penny had been adamant that that there were to be no children at the reception with the exception of Pippa who could be expected to behave beautifully.

Frank made good time to Largs and Penny got a quick, "You look fabulous" from her new husband, before he and Frank started to talk about their respective football teams. The bridal pair had not long to wait for the car carrying Mr and Mrs Maclean and Salma to arrive, whereupon Penny had grabbed Salma with a plea to help her sort out her headdress and veil and Gordon and the others met with the manager to ensure that things were going well with the meal and spoke to the piper who was going to play everyone into the dining room.

Frank went out to the driveway to wait for his girlfriend Sue who was being driven by Javed Ahmed who had become a large part of Salma's life over the last few months. Fraser and his now partner, Erin, arrived first with Javed closely behind.

Gordon and Penny had kept the numbers down to thirty as they had promised themselves they would and Penny's mum had been ok with vague relations not being invited as had Gordon's parents.

Charles and Fiona Davenport had apologised for the fact that they would be a bit late as they had their baby daughter to take home first. She had been good as gold in the church. She was being looked after by Charles's sister Linda who was going to stay overnight. Charles, aware that the last few months had taken their toll of Fiona with constant visits to the hospital where their young son was still holding his own, interspersed with the occasional weekend at home for the wee lad, had surprised his wife with the fact that they and Pippa would be staying the night at the hotel. They had only recently moved into their new house which was not too far from Largs. Pippa was supervising the renovations to the attic which, as promised, was going to be her living and sleeping area. She had chosen shades of pink and lilac for the large room.

Penny who had always hated wedding speeches and thought they spoiled the meal for those who had to speak later, had arranged that their guests would gather round the cake with their drinks and Gordon and his best man would speak, keeping it short. After the cutting of the cake the guests could wander round the grounds while the photographs were taken. This would give her bosses the chance to arrive before the meal.

Gordon kept his speech short, welcoming everyone on behalf of "my wife and myself" which got the usual cheer. He told them that he had always known that Penny was special but now as Penny Black, she was Priceless. The two puns elicited groans from the assembled guests and Penny whispered to Salma that it was almost as bad as Frank's comment about there being a terrible Din in the room when Salma had first arrived at the station and Salma had quick wittedly retaliated about Frank being past his Selby date.

The best man was getting a bit long winded but Penny threw him a glare and he hastily wrapped up his speech. The photographs were taken, Penny asking for all the guests to be captured with their respective partners or family in the case of The Davenports who arrived in time to have their picture taken last. She also wanted one of the whole group and there was an unexpected bonus in the shape of the peacock which wandered into the frame and showed off his beautiful sea green plumage. Gordon picked up one feather from the grass and handed to Penny as a keepsake

The meal followed and then the dancing started. Penny and Gordon had practised their first waltz but Salma and Sam, Gordon's partner and best man had not had the chance to practise so were glad when Penny called out to everyone to join them on the floor.

Throughout the evening, Penny and Gordon who were also staying in the hotel overnight, went round the room talking to everyone and learned from Frank that he had heard the previous day that he had been promoted to a station in Giffnock.

"Didn't want to steal your thunder at your leaving 'do' yesterday, Pen, so I kept the news till today."

"That means that with Fraser going off to Strathclyde to do his teacher training, me off to my new station in Troon, the boss leaving for his new post in Kilmarnock, poor Salma will be the only one of the team left," she said sadly

"And I, with my great matchmaking skills, predict she won't be there for long if Javed has anything to say about it," laughed Frank

Looking across the room to where her friend was sitting listening intently to what the handsome doctor was saying to her, Penny had to agree with him. She knew from chats with Salma over the last few months that her interest in her promotion chances had vanished though she assured Penny that Javed had no problem with her working and even more importantly for her, had announced that he saw no reason why married Asian women had to wear the hijab.

As she watched them, Penny saw Salma wave her over and she grinned at Frank and left him to cross the room and tell Charles his news.

"Doesn't she look gorgeous in that ice blue colour?" Penny demanded of Javed.

"Penny, only you would say something like that on your day when you are the gorgeous one," said Salma.

"You're both beautiful," said Javed, tactfully. They both curtsied gracefully to him then Penny asked her friend to come upstairs to help her change. She loved her dress but she and Gordon were going to pretend to drive away then sneak back. She had bought a lime green short-skirted suit to be worn with a white blouse and with a green band in her dark curls she looked refreshingly attractive. They were flying to Bali the following day.

Penny and Gordon had a final word with Fraser and Erin. Penny had given Fraser both of Tom Cunningham's books as a leaving present.

"I think our real murder was more exciting than Tom's fictional one," he told her now.

"I felt sorry for Jo Jones but she had no chance of avoiding a long sentence with the second murder of an innocent man," Penny commented. "It was lucky that her husband was prepared to look after Lisa."

The last word was left to Charles Davenport.

"I want to propose a toast to Penny and Gordon and wish them a very happy marriage and to also propose a toast to Frank who's just been promoted. He raised his glass:

"To Penny, Gordon and Frank!"

There was a loud cheer.

"Finally, I want to raise my glass to my Team. I will miss them all.

To my Team!"

A rousing burst of applause followed.

Made in the USA
Columbia, SC
28 April 2018